"It isn't my usual course of action, but I feel everything is at risk. Including us. Except for tonight."

"I hate risk," she whispered. "I prefer a sure thing."

"Sorry, no promises. Except one. It'll be good."

Brit's breath caught, and she glanced down. She could feel the steady rise and fall of his chest. She'd never done anything like this with someone she knew so little. But she'd never known a man she'd been more attracted to, anyone she'd respected more. Anyone she'd wanted more.

"Brit . . . beautiful Brit . . ." His voice was low.

She raised her eyes and looked at his shadowed face. The angles and shaded slope of his jawline were outlined by the flickering light from the campfire. The man was mysterious in some ways, bold in others. She desired him more than she had desired any man. She wanted him, completely and thoroughly.

He gently lifted her face until their lips met. His tongue slid across her lower lip and she opened for his delicious invasion. The sensuous stroking of his tongue against hers sent tides of passion flowing fresh and new between them.

"Yes, Jake," she murmured breathlessly when he took his kisses to her cheeks.

"Hmmm?"

"Sometimes you have to go on intuition, and tonight mine says yes."

MARY TATE ENGELS

A Rare Breed

ZEBRA BOOKS
KENSINGTON PUBLISHING CORP.

ZEBRA BOOKS

are published by

Kensington Publishing Corp.
475 Park Avenue South
New York, NY 10016

First Printing: November, 1992

Printed in the United States of America

Prologue

Brit led the way, as usual. "Come on. The top brass will never know. They're tied up in a meeting at the lawyers' that's sure to last all afternoon." Juggling two paper bags from Deli Delite, she strode into the empty boardroom with a brashness that reflected a new confidence she'd never had before. Her two best friends followed, protesting mildly, but still willing to go with her.

"Brit Bailey, have you lost your mind?" Ana Evans stepped solemnly onto the thick carpet. "We shouldn't be bringing food in here." Her voice sounded small and hollow against the vast, windowless walls.

Kelly Carlson ambled the length of the room, dragging her fingers languidly along the sleek mahogany table designed to seat twenty. "Enter into the inner sanctum," she said in a wavering falsetto voice. "A place where men make the decisions and women take the minutes."

"And make the coffee," Ana added with a groan.

"There'll be no coffee-making today. This pleasure is all mine." Brit smiled mysteriously, her green eyes shining with devilment. They all knew that the room was off-limits for all but high-level management meetings. For the secretaries to bring in lunch was unthinkable. But that forbidden element made this little excursion all the more exciting as Brit began unloading the gourmet sandwiches she had ordered for the three of them. "I even got our favorite black walnut chocolate chip cookies for the occasion."

"What occasion?" Dark-haired Kelly returned slowly from the other end of the room. "Are you and Michael getting married?"

"Heavens no!" Brit objected quickly, tossing her blond curls. "Can't I buy you lunch once in a while without getting the third degree?"

"Sure," Kelly said. "But you never have any more extra cash than the rest of us. How did you suddenly get so flush? Rob a bank?"

Brit gestured at the food she had placed at one end of the table. "Please have a seat, ladies. I'll tell you in due time. This is a celebration! Let me do my thing."

Kelly took a seat and pushed an errant dark strand back from her forehead. "How long do we have to wait before you tell us?"

"Soon. Don't rush me." Brit grinned and proceeded with her plan. "Have you ever thought about what you'd do if you won the Lotto?"

"Have a blast!" Ana, who was busily unwrapping her sandwich, stopped and stared at Brit. "Did you win it?"

"No, no. Nothing like that." Brit folded her arms on the table and leaned forward, barely able to contain her news. "Indulge me for a minute. What would you do if you had the money for . . . oh, most anything you've always wanted?"

Ana didn't have to consider it very long. "If you want to fantasize, I'd go shopping. I'd buy myself a completely new wardrobe, strictly designer-everything. I'd get some of those comfy Italian shoes made of leather so soft they feel like hand-knitted slippers. I'd have matching accessories . . . no, wait! I'd buy really fine jewelry to add the finishing touch. Then, I'd march into Richard W. Brookbank's office, looking like a million bucks, and quit my job. That's my ultimate fantasy!"

"Yeah, new clothes would be great," Brit murmured. "What about you, Kelly?"

"If I had the bucks, I'd buy myself a brand-new car." Kelly's eyes narrowed and her lips thinned as she talked. "It would make me feel so . . . powerful to walk into a showroom and slap down the cash and drive away in *my* very own car. No negotiating, no monthly payments, nobody else's trade-in problems." She looked at Ana with a satisfied smile. "Then I'd quit my job."

Everyone laughed at Kelly's determination.

"What about you, Brit?" Ana asked, then before Brit could answer, continued. "Knowing you, you'd go for it all. Fabulous clothes. New hair style. French manicure. New sports car. Everything at once!"

Brit grinned. "Why not?" Then she twisted one

9

blond curl thoughtfully. "What if I said I'd like to go back to college and finish?"

"Why would you want to do that?" Kelly asked.

"Because I'm bored with my job, and I feel stuck. I'm ready for a change. And a challenge."

"You're quitting this rat race, aren't you, Brit?" Kelly asked seriously.

She shrugged. "I'm weighing my options, as they say."

"Okay, I'm dying to know," Ana demanded. "Tell us now what you're fishing around!"

Brit sighed. It almost sounded like a fairy tale when she said it aloud, but she couldn't contain her excitement any longer. Her friends deserved to know. "I've been notified that a production company in Hollywood wants to make a movie of my great-grandmother Bonnie's book. Since my parents divorced before Mom's car accident, my inheritance included the family's rights to the book. No one dreamed anything would ever come of that little book."

"A movie!" Ana squealed. "Oh, my God, a movie!"

"What little book?" Kelly asked.

Long Ago and Far Away. Brit pulled a thin worn book from her purse and shoved it across the table. "Gran Bonnie wrote an account of her life as a trader with the Navajo and Zuni Indians somewhere in Arizona or New Mexico. The book was published about fifty years ago, made a little revenue for her, then went out of print. Everyone forgot about it, especially me. No one was interested until *Dances with Wolves* was such a big hit movie. Then some producer started looking at this as a pioneer woman's adventure-love story. At least, that's what my agent says."

"Agent?" Kelly picked up the book and started curiously thumbing through it. "You have an agent? Neat."

"She negotiated reprint rights with a major publishing house, so the book will come out about the same time as the movie. The advance was quite nice." Brit dabbed the corners of her mouth with her napkin.

"Did they pay you for the movie?"

"They paid a nice chunk for an option to make the movie. Then, what we're asking is a fee plus percentage of profits and any videos, etcetera they might make in the future. But the best part is that they're willing to hire me as consultant on the movie. I'll be paid for doing something interesting for a change."

"And the opportunity to shop in those fancy shops on Rodeo Drive isn't a bad perk, huh?" Ana teased.

"You've got that right!" Brit said with a laugh.

"This is absolutely incredible! Almost unbelievable." Ana took the book and opened to a photograph in the front. "Is this her picture?"

"Yep. Great-grandmother Bonnie Gatlin."

"She's very pretty. Looks a little like you, Brit, with this blond hair."

"She was a remarkable lady. Her husband died after only a few years of marriage, leaving her with a young child and in charge of a trading post. She made friends with the Indians and eked out a living there instead of giving up and going back to Kentucky."

"Sounds like she was a good old-fashioned feminist," Kelly said.

"Hers is really a beautiful love story," Brit explained. "Bonnie fell in love again after her first husband died. I'm sure that's what the movie will concentrate on. Her other love."

"Listen to this," Ana said, reading from the book. *"Within a week after we buried John, I began receiving gifts of food on my doorstep. I was grateful to my anonymous benefactor, for it was mid-winter, and I had no way of getting anything on my own. One evening near dark, I heard a noise outside the cabin. I was determined to see who was out there. So I grabbed John's rifle and flung open the door. There stood a tall Indian with dark hair to his shoulders and dressed only in a breechcloth. He was certainly magnificent."*

Ana paused, and the other two urged in unison, "Go on!"

"We stared at each other for a moment, eyes meeting, surprise in both our faces. I remembered him as a man from the Zuni village. His name was KnifeWing. Even though I was still holding that rifle aimed at his middle, he calmly put a slain wild turkey on my doorstep and walked away. I knew immediately that he was a rare breed of a man." Ana looked up with a faint smile. "How romantic."

Brit took another bite of sandwich and tried to

act nonchalant. "Bonnie's other love was no ordinary man. He was a Zuni Indian."

"Well, I can tell you one thing," Kelly said, as she rose from her chair. "When this movie debuts, I'll be the first in line. It sounds like a wonderful love story. I'm very happy for you, Brit."

"Me, too. It couldn't have happened to a more deserving person. Don't forget your old friends when you make it big in Hollywood!" Ana joined Kelly to hug Brit warmly.

"I'll never, ever forget you!" Brit promised. The next day, she quit her job to pursue the challenge of her life.

Chapter One

Brit and Michael argued as they wove through the crowded Las Vegas Airport. They were an attractive couple, both blond and athletic, both in their late twenties. They looked like the ideal all-American couple, but they weren't.

Maybe it was a good thing that they were heading in different directions. It would give them time to think about their relationship. Michael was returning to San Diego where he managed a small electronics store. Brit was heading for Hollywood where she'd be special consultant on the movie of Great-grandmother Bonnie's life.

Coming here had been a bad idea, Brit now realized. Somehow Michael had convinced her that Las Vegas would do it for them, would make things better between them. They would have fun, see some shows, win some money, and forget their conflicts. But Michael had been wrong. The whole weekend had been a disaster. And that, she knew, had more to do with them than with gambling.

Still, Brit had learned some important things about herself. And about Michael. He had loved every moment of every wager. He had even stayed at the tables one entire night trying to win back what he had lost earlier. He could not bear losing. Why couldn't he understand that was the nature of betting? The odds favored the house. That was what she hated about it. She felt she didn't have a chance.

Brit tried to pretend that it didn't matter. But it did. She simply couldn't help it.

"Lighten up, Brit. It's just money."

"Just money?" She gritted her teeth. "How can you be so casual about it?"

"I'm not. I still think if I had a few more days, I could double my winnings. I could probably pay for the trip."

"Fat chance."

He halted and glared at her. "I'll pay you back, okay? I should have known that letting you pay for everything was a bad idea."

"Letting me? I don't recall too much objection on your part. Anyway, that's not the point." She shook her head for emphasis and the soft curls of her new hairstyle rearranged themselves around her face. "Flinging money into a bottomless pit is not my idea of fun, Michael. Now I know."

"You're too uptight about it." He turned and continued shouldering his way through the crowd, a suitcase in one hand, his airline ticket in the other.

Brit followed, lugging a hefty shoulder bag with

a Gucchi label. "It's my pesky middle-class values that keep getting in the way," she insisted. "Work hard. Save your money. Don't take risks."

"Sounds boring to me." He checked his ticket against the posted gate number and motioned. "This is it. Looks like they'll be boarding soon."

Brit sighed and lifted her face for the perfunctory airport kiss. Dutifully following her cue, Michael obliged. At his bland touch, the hope in her ever-optimistic heart dwindled, and she fluffed her blond hair self-consciously and looked down, as if embarrassed that others might be watching them.

"You know what? You've lost your sense of fun, Brit," he admonished, brushing her nose playfully with his finger. Then, before she could respond, he looked behind her, momentarily distracted, and whispered, "I'll be damned! There's Yolanda! I recognize her from TV!"

Brit turned just in time to see the recently popular comedian moving quickly through the crowd and disappearing behind a door. "Hmmm, so it is."

"See where your money gets you, Brit?" Michael asked as if this were proof of his claim. "It puts you in a position to see and do exciting things, in the company of famous people. Maybe next time we can try Tahoe. I believe I can really win big there."

"Well, we'll see," Brit murmured, thinking it would be a cold day in hell before she wanted to gamble again. There must be other, more exciting—and more satisfying—things to do with her money. "I think they're boarding your plane, Michael."

"Right. Don't have too much fun without me in La La land. See you in a few weeks. We'll celebrate your birthday in style. Call me tonight."

"As soon as I get there." Brit nodded, trying to pretend. But she was no actress. Maybe it was time to be honest . . . with Michael and with herself.

He headed for the ramp and, before he disappeared, turned to wave. Brit responded by raising one hand and wiggling her fingers. At that moment, she *knew*, knew beyond a doubt that she didn't love Michael. In a way, it was a relief to know, to finally admit it, if only to herself. More and more, they had been growing apart, their opinions increasingly distant. She wondered if her new lifestyle, and more specifically, her newly-acquired money had changed her. Or possibly, him. No, she refused to believe that. Their problem was love, or the lack of it.

Pondering the best way to end this relationship, Brit headed for her charter to L.A. This was another thing she couldn't get used to. When there was no room on any regular flights from Vegas to L.A., Michael had suggested that she charter a flight. So she had reserved a seat on a helicopter which made routine trips to and from L.A. Since she'd never flown in a helicopter, Brit was looking forward to the experience. Yes, she admitted privately, there were some advantages to having money, but they had nothing to do with the rich and famous, as Michael claimed.

"There'll be another couple on the flight, ma'am. I think you'll be thrilled when you see who it is," the ticket agent said when she approached the desk.

"Oh?" Brit dug out her credit card and tapped her fingernails impatiently on the counter. She did not feel particularly chatty after her encounter with Michael.

The agent grinned proudly. "It's Yolanda. I got her autograph."

Brit nodded politely. "How nice." When he finished with the paperwork, she followed him through a side door and was whisked across the tarmac in a little car to join a small group gathered beside a helicopter.

"Hi, I'm your pilot, Frank Scofeld, and this is Mr. and Mrs. Romero."

"I'm Brit Bailey." She shook hands with the pilot, then turned to the couple and recognized the comedian and TV star Michael had pointed out a few minutes ago in the airport.

"I'm Rudi." The big red-haired man nodded toward his wife. "And this, of course, is Yolanda."

Both Rudi and Yolanda were large people, both of them towering above Brit, who was not short at five feet five. Rudi's hair was curly, making his head look massive, and he sported a thick red mustache. Yolanda was nearly six feet tall and she wore her dark hair in a shoulder-length bob.

"Nice to meet you both." Brit smiled cheerfully

19

at the couple as the wind whipped their hair around. Wouldn't Michael get a kick knowing that she'd chartered a flight with Yolanda and her husband. Ana and Kelly would be fascinated with details of how Yolanda wore three sparkling diamond rings on one hand, and her husband wore a string of gold necklaces and gold bracelets.

"What time is it?" Rudi conspicuously checked his Rolex watch. "How long will this take?"

"About an hour and a half to two hours," Frank answered.

"We have to get to L.A. as soon as possible," Yolanda explained with an impatient sigh. "I want to have plenty of time to rest this evening. Tomorrow will begin early because we start shooting the show's new season. And, after all the cash we lost in Vegas, somebody's got to get to work."

"I know what you mean," Brit responded, thinking of her own losses at the gambling tables.

"Hon-ey, you couldn't possibly know the kinds of financial pressures I have in this business." Yolanda scoffed indignantly. "Sometimes I wonder if it's worth it."

"Yeah, babe, course it is," said Rudi, squeezing her shoulders in a quick hug with his huge arm. "Look at all the fun we're having. Every day it's something new and exciting."

"Yeah, yeah," she muttered. "This is fun? I'm hot. Can we get this show on the road?"

"I'm ready when you folks are," said Frank, rubbing his hands together.

The four of them boarded the chopper and,

within minutes, were whirling aloft. Brit sat in front with the pilot, leaving the Romeros to banter in the passenger section alone. The helicopter lifted, hovered briefly, then moved forward over the sprawl of Las Vegas beneath them. The city was much larger than Brit had thought, for there was more to it than the gambling strip.

Majestic music blared into the earphones and blocked the loud thrump-de-thrump of the helicopter's rotor blades whacking the air. Once they were moving in flight, Frank flipped the earphone switch so they could all communicate. "Folks, there's shrimp cocktail and champagne in the cooler. Any questions before we go back to music?"

"Got any beer?" Rudi asked.

"Yep. Help yourself."

"Oh, Frank!" Yolanda motioned to the desert floor beyond the city. "This poor San Antonio gal never had a chance to see the Grand Canyon. Are we going to fly over it?"

"No. The canyon's out of our way to the east."

"How far out of the way?"

"About a half hour, one way."

Rudi spoke up. "You want to see the canyon, babe? It's not too much trouble, is it, Frank?"

"It'll put us off schedule. I thought you folks were in a hurry."

"Not that much. What's an hour—right Brit? You don't mind, do you? Just a quick swing by the giant hole to show Yolanda?"

Brit shrugged. She had never seen the Grand

Canyon from this view. "Go ahead. I'm not in a great hurry."

"I knew you'd be a sport, Brit-babe. Can I get you a beer or something?"

"No, thanks," Brit muttered, wishing she could grab a nap on the flight to L.A. and knowing now that it would be delayed while they detoured by the canyon.

"Hey, Frank buddy, thanks a helluva lot. I'll make this worth your time and effort," Rudi promised.

"Never mind about that," Frank said. "Let me see if I can change my flight plan and get clearance for this." Frank began making contact with the ground and soon gave them all a thumbs-up as they proceeded eastward.

Brit didn't give the flight change a second thought. After all, how many times did anyone get a chance to view the Grand Canyon from a helicopter? This, too, would be one of those great experiences to tell Ana and Kelly.

Less than thirty minutes later, there it was beneath them. The Grand Canyon. "Magnificent" was a mere word that provided an inadequate description. The vision before her took Brit's breath.

Frank flipped the microphone on as he made a small circle over one corner of the huge abyss and his voice replaced the music. "This is a remote section of the canyon, folks, but you get the idea. That little silver ribbon down there is a tributary to the Colorado River, which is the main, big one through the canyon."

"Awesome," Yolanda murmured. "Look at that! Like a giant scoop out of Rocky Road ice cream!"

"Enjoy," Frank said and flipped the music back into their earphones.

Brit tried to memorize the beauty beneath her so she could tell her friends in San Diego about every detail. Suddenly she noticed Frank's quick, jerky hand motions as he fiddled with the instruments.

"What's wrong?" she asked spontaneously, then realized he couldn't hear her. Vivaldi's "La Primavera" continued to swell in the earphones as if nothing were happening. But something definitely was wrong. Brit just didn't know what it was. She watched helplessly as Frank struggled with several flashing red lights on the panel.

Brit tried to stay calm. But when the helicopter shuddered and began to dip and sway, her stomach made an abrupt flip-flop and fear knotted in her throat.

Frank switched on the microphone. "Okay, folks, we've got a little problem with the fuel line. Acts like it's stopped up. If I can land 'er, I think I can fix it. Make sure your seat belts are fastened. Hang on, we're going down!"

Both the Romeros jabbered excitedly at once. "Land? Where the hell are you landing? There's nothing out there! Are we going to crash? Oh, dear God, we're going down! I knew we shouldn't have—"

Frank switched them off, and glorious music

blared again. He pointed to a sandbar, indicating to Brit that he was aiming for it. The sides of the canyon slipped past as they headed down. For a minute or so, it appeared they would make it. But they were moving too fast—straight down—and Brit feared they were still too far from the tiny sandbar to land on it.

Then they were spinning out of control, tilting, dropping fast toward the canyon floor. A clump of tall cottonwood trees loomed straight ahead, seeming to charge closer and closer. The copter hit the trees with a bone-jolting crash, rotor blades biting like scythes. Leaves and twigs hurtled past the windows and thwacked the fuselage as the craft slammed between two branches with a wrenching screech of metal. Brit felt herself hurled sideways. The copter caught, teetered, caught again, and came to rest on its side, Brit's door down, motor grinding, swaying slightly like a suspended treehouse.

As soon as they stopped moving, Frank jerked off Brit's headphones and began pushing her toward the door. "Out, get out! Quick! Climb out of here and run! Get away from the craft so it doesn't fall on you!"

Pushing nervously on the door, finally kicking it open, Brit obeyed Frank. She could hear him yelling at the Romeros and their frantic, screaming responses.

As Brit climbed out of the chopper and began crawling along a branch, she was vaguely aware of the nearby sounds of rushing water. Closer, and much more frightening, were the cracking and popping of metal all around her. She inched along the flimsy limb until it dipped under her weight and dumped her into a shallow stream. With Frank's warning to move echoing in her head, she crawled and scrambled through the water as fast as she could. Seconds later, the main body of the helicopter crashed to the streambed.

Panting, Brit sprawled on the rocks near the shore and watched in horror as the helicopter began to break up and metal parts were washed away, rushing madly to God knows where. Brit lay there for a few minutes, trying to gather her senses and her breath. They had landed, no . . . they had crashed somewhere and now the helicopter was falling apart. Where was everyone? Were they safe? Was she all alone?

In a few moments, Brit's worst fears were dispelled. She heard voices and spotted her traveling companions lurching across the stream toward her. There was something about the poignant sight of all three splashing, stumbling, helping each other, drenched and bedraggled—but safe— that made Brit want to laugh hysterically or cry with relief.

As if drawn by the same magnet, they gathered in a tight little circle, all talking at once. Half an hour ago, they were strangers. Now survival had made them kin.

A loud popping noise turned their attention back to the crash scene. They watched helplessly as a large portion of the helicopter broke apart and floated away. At that moment, they knew their way out was gone.

"Can't we salvage anything?" Yolanda cried, suddenly aware that they were losing everything they had brought along with the chopper.

"Too dangerous to try." Frank's voice was dull with shock.

"Hey, bud, we have some valuable things in our luggage!" Rudi gasped, lunging forward. "I have to get them!"

Frank grabbed his arm. "Don't, please. I'm serious about it being too dangerous. The bird's falling apart. Anyway, I think we're too late."

Yolanda pointed. "Look!"

They all turned to watch their luggage plunge into the water, one bag after the other, as if they were on a conveyer belt that was supposed to dump them systematically into the river. They bobbed briefly, then disappeared.

Everyone was quiet for a few stunned minutes, observing a private, helpless vigil to their lost possessions.

"Gucci . . ." Brit murmured, silently recalling how much her new bags had cost. And now they were gone.

"You, at least, have your purse," Yolanda said bitterly. "Mine's feeding some damn fish right now!"

Brit looked down and, sure enough, her purse was still strapped across her shoulder. She had her cash, a book, and breath mints. And what good were any of those to her right now?

"There goes my camera!" Rudi yelled, cursing violently. "And my new leather jacket!"

"And my new diamonds!" Yolanda whined. "I put them in my bags! Thousands of dollars worth are being washed downstream to feed some big-mouth bass!" She clapped her hand over her mouth as if to quiet a scream.

Brit realized that her entire brand-new, expensive wardrobe that she'd bought with the first big check was floating down the river, too. She joined in the lament. "Oh no! My clothes! My Italian sandals! My Irish sweaters!"

"Only one consolation, folks," Frank said in an irritatingly calm tone. "We're safe."

"Do you know how much that camera plus all the attachments is worth?" Rudi demanded.

"Well no, but I'd guess you folks are insured," Frank reminded them.

"Insured? Who cares about that? Some things can't be replaced. How would you like a lawsuit the size of Montana?" Rudi threatened.

"Frank's right, Rudi," Brit agreed in a tone meant to soothe him. "At least, we're not injured. It could have been much worse. We could have been ki—"

"Yeah, Rudi," Yolanda interrupted sarcastically. "We can always buy more stuff. You'll like that. You're so good at it."

"I'm good at it? What about you?" Rudi snarled.

"My job is making the money, remember? That's why we were headed for L.A. Yours is spending it. Or gambling it away."

"You lost more at the roulette wheel than I did at everything combined!"

"Now, folks . . ." Frank admonished. "Bickering won't help things."

Brit was suddenly aware of water swirling around her ankles and began moving toward shore. "Where are we, anyway?"

"Somewhere in the bottom of the Grand Canyon." Frank followed her, glancing around with a bewildered expression. "Let's see now, we were flying over the far west corner."

"Oh, great," Rudi muttered, cursing again. He and Yolanda helped each other to shore. "The pilot needs a compass. Meantime I've lost thousands of dollars worth of jewelry, camera equipment, and clothes."

"Hey, what's that?" Frank pointed to an object bouncing in the river. He ran toward it, plunging into midstream without hesitation.

"What do you see?" Yolanda stood on tiptoe and stretched her neck. "Somebody's luggage? Mine, I hope!"

They watched with renewed optimism as Frank pulled something large from the water and hauled it toward them. "Look, folks! At least we still have the shrimp cocktail and champagne!" The bulky box proved to be the drink cooler, which Frank pulled to their sandy spot.

Something about the sight of Frank struggling to salvage that sturdy but cheap, in comparison to what they'd just lost, red and white cooler triggered Rudi's rage. Without warning, he leaped at Frank and wrestled him to the ground. The two of them rolled together, grunting, and grappling like slapstick comedians in an old movie.

Brit and Yolanda screamed at the two men to stop, but they continued wrestling ineptly.

"Damn fool—" Rudi muttered along with a barrage of curses.

"Crazy jackass—" Frank mumbled, trying to get the upper hand.

Finally Rudi, being much larger and stronger, rolled to the top and, straddling Frank, pulled back his arm to punch the hapless pilot. Brit yelled again and lunged forward, latching onto Rudi's giant arm, screaming for him to stop. She felt him try to shake her free, felt her whole body tremble as he used his roaring strength to loosen her grip and free himself from her.

She was whipped around like a rag doll and then—a different male voice bellowed, "Hey, stop! Stop that!" But there was no stopping. Rudi was a raging bull and continued trying to box poor Frank, who lay pressed to the ground. Brit held onto his arm, making the fight impossible and infuriating Rudi further. Suddenly, there was a loud smack, a low groan, and Rudi tumbled backward. Brit, still attached to his arm, went with him.

Briefly stunned by the impact, Brit finally managed to sit up and prop herself on Rudi's huge form, which lay still beside her. Yes, there he was. She hadn't imagined another man. There actually was someone who had interfered with the fight.

He had long dark hair and intense dark eyes and he hovered close to her face.

"You all right?" His voice rumbled low in his throat as his hands framed her shoulders and held her firmly for a moment.

"I'm fine," she lied. Brit thought she must be dreaming that a handsome stranger with dark hair to his shoulders appeared out of nowhere.

As soon as she claimed she was all right, he moved and she could hear him talking to Frank. Yolanda sat close, cradling her husband's massive head in her lap, murmuring, "Oh, Rudi-tudi baby, speak to me. Are you all right? Oh, come on, baby . . ." Gone was the quarrelsome attitude that had kept them bickering for the whole trip. Now she was full of smothering affection.

Brit pushed herself to her feet, trying to put things into perspective. Maybe she had fallen asleep on the flight and would wake up any minute and find herself safe and sound and nearing L.A.X.

"You sure you're all right, miss?" A hand touched her shoulder. "You look a little dazed."

Brit lifted her face and brushed her blond hair back. She stared at the most handsome man she could ever imagine in her wildest dream. "Who are you?"

"Jake Landry. I was working about half a mile from here when I heard the crash."

Yes, she thought. She was dreaming. Dreaming about her great-grandmother Bonnie's story. *There stood a tall Indian with dark hair to his shoulders and dressed only in a breechcloth. He was certainly magnificent.*

The difference was that this man named Jake wore a faded chambray shirt and frayed Levi's and looked quite contemporary. His shiny jet hair was short on the sides and slightly longer in back. He had the high cheekbones and chiseled features of a Native American. And he was absolutely magnificent.

"Did you say you work near here?" A flood of hope swept over Brit. Perhaps they were near some habitation, more people, and a way out. They could be rescued soon!

"I'm digging over there—" He gestured behind them.

"Digging? For gold?" Her eyes grew larger.

"Hardly." He chuckled and shook his head. The dark straight hair moved like silk tassels around his face. "Digging a ruin."

"A what?"

"It's an Indian ruin or cliff dwelling where Indians lived nearly a thousand years ago. There are several sites hidden in the canyon walls that are full of antique treasures. I'm documenting them."

"You mean like . . . archeology?" Brit's voice fell along with her hopes. This man wasn't here to rescue them. He had other interests.

"Exactly like archeology." His dark eyes gleamed when he mentioned eight-hundred-year-old pots and baskets no one had touched for hundreds of years.

Rudi groaned and the stranger named Jake

31

Landry started toward him. Brit quickly stepped forward. "Tell me, Jake. Are you . . . alone. Or is there a team of you down here working?"

"No team. I'm alone." He pulled a large handkerchief from his pocket and tucked it into her hand. "If there's any ice in that cooler, put a piece in here for that one." He nodded toward Frank. "He's going to have a doozie of a shiner."

Brit felt a surge of energy as the man's hand wrapped around hers. She recalled Bonnie's first reaction to her lover. *We stared, surprise in both our faces. Our eyes met . . .*

Jake quickly moved away, and Brit fumbled as she tucked the handkerchief around a handful of ice and went to Frank. His eye was already beginning to swell.

With a sideways glance, Brit watched as the tall stranger knelt beside a groaning, groggy Rudi. "Hey, you okay? I didn't hurt you, did I?"

Rudi mumbled something unintelligible, then seemed to wake fully and cursed a blue streak.

"Sorry, bud." Jake offered his hand and pulled Rudi to a sitting position.

"Sorry?" Yolanda was furious. "You jackass! You knocked my husband all the way over here! You could have hurt him badly. What the hell's wrong with you?"

"Look, lady," Jake said between thinned lips. "I don't know exactly what's going on here, but your husband was beating up that man over there. And he's bigger. I didn't see either of you women able to stop it. Somebody had to do something."

"It was a guy thing." Yolanda pouted defensively.

"No, it was a stupid fight, as most of them are. Now, why don't you get some ice for your husband, and we can talk about your situation."

Finally they gathered around the stranger, Brit and Frank on one side of him and Yolanda and Rudi on the other. As he spoke, Brit was reminded of Bonnie's description of her Indian lover. *I knew immediately that he was a rare breed of a man.* "Let's exchange names as a reasonable beginning. I'm Jake Landry, and I teach at Northern Arizona University in Flagstaff. I'm down here working on a research project."

"I'm Frank Scofeld, the pilot of this shipwreck. And these folks are my passengers." Frank held the iced handkerchief on his eye and gestured for the rest to introduce themselves.

"I'm Yolanda. And this man you knocked around is my husband, Rudi Romero."

Rudi spoke up. "She's the comedian on TV, Yolanda." Rubbing his jaw, he grumbled, "Damn, this hurts. You pack a wallop."

Jake shook their hands. "I don't watch much TV, but it's nice to meet you. Sorry about the punch, Rudi." He turned a curious expression to Brit.

"I'm Brit Bailey." She felt caught in the strange power of his dark gaze.

"Are you with them?" Jake asked.

"Me?" She shook her head vigorously. "Oh, no. I'm, uh, traveling alone. We just happened to charter the same flight to L.A."

"If you were heading for L.A., how did you get so far off track?"

Rudi stepped forward. "We were trying to show Yolanda the Grand Canyon."

"Yeah," Yolanda added scornfully. "And here it is!"

"Engine trouble," Frank inserted. "I was trying to land on this sandbar when we hit the trees."

"Probably a good thing." Jake shook his head and stuffed his hands in his pockets. "You're lucky to get out alive."

She smiled up at him. "And lucky you found us."

"But we're not lucky to have lost valuable luggage and clothes and jewels," Yolanda reminded everyone.

"My camp's not far away." Jake walked around and gave everyone a rudimentary inspection. "If you're ready for a little hike, there's some food left, maybe not enough for a feast, but enough to share."

"We have shrimp and champagne in the cooler," Frank offered.

Everyone was silent for a moment, balancing the incongruity of shrimp and champagne with their predicament.

Jake looked at Rudi, then at Frank. "Okay, guys, listen up. No more fighting, you hear? Whatever is going on between you two will have to stop. Agreed?"

After a moment's hesitation, and encouragement from Brit and Yolanda, both men nodded stubbornly.

"How the hell do we get out of here?" Yolanda asked.

Jake rubbed his chin. "I'm supposed to receive a food drop tomorrow. I'll notify the pilot that we need a rescue and he can go for help."

"What are you talking about?" Yolanda demanded, hands on hips. Her jumpsuit was torn and wet and she looked like she'd been in a fight, herself.

"Well," Jake explained slowly. "There's a pilot who flies over regularly and drops food once or twice a week."

"How long have you been down here?"

"Almost a month."

"Whoa!" Yolanda exclaimed, making a mug for the others. "I'll bet your wife loves this summer vacation."

"No wife. Just work," he said.

"That's it? No more contact with the outside world?"

Jake nodded, tight-lipped.

"What about a shortwave radio? Can't you just call someone?"

"A shortwave is too heavy. I didn't want to bother with it. Figured I wouldn't need it."

"Wrong! What if you got injured?"

"If I missed picking up my supply drop, they'd send someone to check on me."

"So you're saying that we have to spend the night down here?" By her expression, Yolanda was clearly amazed at the concept.

Jake swung the cooler to his shoulder. "Looks that way. Follow me."

"This is crazy," Yolanda objected. "I'm not camping. Just get me out of here, but I'm not sleeping on the ground."

Jake ignored her and, with no apparent alternative, Brit followed him. She admired his lean masculine form as he strode sure-footed and confident over the rocks. He wore thick-soled hiking boots that secured his tight-fitting jeans above the ankles. His hips were slim and his back, straight and sturdy. The pale blue shirt hung from broad, angular shoulders. Dark hair, needing a trim, barely brushed his slightly frayed shirt collar.

Brit stumbled and noticed for the first time that her expensive Italian shoes were ripped beyond salvation. They barely stayed on her feet. Then she saw that her dress, too, was virtually ruined. The exquisite silk with its tiny hand-painted flowers looked like something a shipwrecked character in a B-movie would wear, including an uneven tear that revealed a nice expanse of one thigh.

Yolanda didn't look much better. Of course, she still wore her diamonds, but both knees of her silver lame jumpsuit were ripped and one sleeve flopped beneath her armpit. Rudi still had his Rolex and gold chains, but his shirt had a couple of bloodstains and a large rip in back from the fight. Frank stumbled along, somewhat dazed, his shirt torn, also. The only one who was strong and sure

36

was Jake Landry, marching self-confidently ahead of them.

Brit concluded that she couldn't possibly dream up a more unusual — or potentially exciting situation. Jake Landry was better than a dream, actually. He was *real;* or, at least, she thought he was. To make sure she could relish him a little longer though, Brit decided to wait awhile before she pinched herself to see if she were awake.

Chapter Two

Jake sat on the cooler and propped his elbows on his widespread knees. This was their second rest stop in the last half hour, and he wondered if they'd make it to camp before dark. This group obviously was not in very good physical condition. He knew the terrain was rough to the uninitiated, but this bunch of prima donnas was getting to him.

"These things cost nearly two hundred dollars and aren't worth two cents!" Brit exclaimed unexpectedly, her voice shrill and echoing against the towering canyon walls. She flung the tattered shoes as hard as she could into the rocks. Sitting on a flat sandstone, she cradled one foot tenderly and massaged it.

Jake gazed at Brit for a long moment, thinking about taking matters into his own hands and massaging her feet himself. No, they needed to be on their way. And she would need those shoes. He drew on his rapidly dwindling patience and retrieved the flimsy items she had thrown, examining them as he made his way back to her. At first, he had thought she might be resilient and spunky enough to cope with the hardships of this wilderness. But apparently he had been wrong. With this latest outburst, she had fallen into line with the rest: complaining, miserable, and difficult.

"I'd hang onto these if I were you." He held them out to her. "They could come in handy."

She leveled her sparkling green eyes at his face. "Handy? For what? Knocking off lizards? They're torn and won't stay on. What good are they?"

"Well, the leather soles are still okay. It's only the straps that are broken."

"In case you haven't noticed, that's how I keep them on my feet." She tucked her legs up and hugged them to her chest as if resisting any further walking.

He knew he had to get her, and the others, going again. "Why, this one still works."

She gave him a doubtful glance.

Jake turned the battered sandals over in his large hands, showing her as he talked. "Put this on, and I'll rig up something for the other one until we get to camp. Then I can make you some shoes."

She looked at him incredulously. "Excuse me. You're going to make a pair of shoes?"

"Yep. Moccasins." He pulled a thin leather strip from his pocket, knelt before her, and patted his thigh for her to place her foot there.

A smile twitched at her lips. "Moccasins?"

He grinned slightly. "A skill my old grandmother taught me. Comes in handy from time to time." He reached for her foot and aligned it on the sinewed plane of his thigh. Then he began binding the tattered sole to her foot.

"Tell me you just happened to bring along that cord."

He pursed his lips and concentrated on his task. "You never know when you might have to tie something up."

"Yeah, right." Brit watched apprehensively as his hands slid over the silky top of her bare foot, inadvertently touching and caressing it as he worked. His fingers were long and bare and ringless and he worked with the skill of a surgeon.

Jake couldn't help but notice the slender shape of her ankle. He figured he had been partially right about her. She was spunky and had a sense of humor, but had probably been pushed to her limit by now, for she was pretty snippy. Well, what did he expect from a city gal? The mile-deep bottom of the Grand Canyon was not a beach in California. She had probably never been so isolated from society and the conveniences of modern life. He knew it wouldn't be easy to adjust.

Jake stood up and observed his work. "How's that? Think you can walk with it?"

Brit wiggled her foot, circling her ankle in the most exasperatingly sensuous way. Then she tested his handiwork with a couple of steps. "It'll do, I think."

Jake nodded, satisfied, then moved to where the group lay sprawled on large rocks. "I may as well tell all of you now that we don't leave any trash down here in the canyon. It's a pristine wilderness and, even though this part is remote, we have to take out everything that we bring in."

"Everything?" Yolanda made a funny face. "How can you possibly do that?"

"Just have to, that's all. Every bottle and can, every piece of paper, everything. I have large containers for trash, and we'll backpack it out."

"We?" she asked indignantly. "I'm not planning on backpacking anything out of here."

"Well, right." Jake shifted and looked away for a moment, close to losing his patience with Yolanda. He spoke deliberately to her. "When we leave, no matter how we do it, we'll take our trash. That includes you, too, I'm afraid, Yolanda. Okay, everyone, ready to go on? We aren't far from camp."

He hefted the cooler to his shoulder and the group trudged behind him, occasionally mumbling complaints to each other. Jake ignored them. The last thing he wanted to do was to baby-sit a bunch of spoiled brats used to the good life. He had work to do and couldn't afford to lose more time with them.

He despised the thought of catering to a celebrity who expected preferential treatment. He hated the animosity between the pilot and Yolanda's husband. And, dammit, he wouldn't let himself be distracted by an alluring woman like Brit who needed him to take care of her slender feet, whose smooth legs were long and shapely, and whose cat green eyes made him forget how to think straight. No, he couldn't, and he wouldn't. He repeated that pledge several times to himself as he climbed the rocks to his camp.

Hobbling along behind Jake, Brit felt as though she were moving through time as well as space. The red-rock amphitheater of the canyon walls rose up, enclosing the little group in a strange, different world. They climbed up to a small plateau above the riverbank where two tents, one fairly large and the other a small A-frame, formed Jake's camp. A box of pans sat next to a small one-burner stove on a flat log stretched between two rocks. Several leafy cotton-wood trees shaded the area and a sheer canyon wall formed a dramatic stone backdrop.

"This is it?" Rudi asked, voicing everyone's disappointment.

"What did you expect, the elegance and convenience of Caesars Palace?" snapped Yolanda. "This isn't Vegas. We're out here in the middle of nowhere. No running water, except in the river. No . . . nothing."

Rudi's gaze swept longingly at a distant edge where the sky met the canyon's magenta-colored rim. "How in the world are we gonna get outta here?"

"How are we supposed to sleep?" Brit pointed to the tents. "In there?"

"Sleep wherever you want." Jake swung the cooler easily to the ground and drew a semicircle in the air with a sweep of his arm. "Pick any spot."

"Out here?" Yolanda looked around. In the moment of silence that followed, she caught on. "Oh, no you don't! Not with the bugs and wild animals! I'm not sleeping out here!"

"My equipment is in the large one, where it's protected from the weather." Jake started toward that tent. "I've been sleeping in the pup, but you can have it."

"Thanks," Yolanda mumbled. "That's ever so generous of you."

Jake shrugged his angular shoulders. "The animals probably won't bother you. I can't guarantee about the bugs. It's actually nice out here under the stars. Now, you make yourselves at home, so to speak. I have some work to finish before dark." He disappeared inside the large tent.

Silence ensued as the four crash survivors looked bleakly at each other, then at their crude wilderness surroundings. It was obvious that Jake was not going to take care of them. He had his work. He had done his duty by rescuing them and now they were on their own.

"I'm not looking forward to sleeping outside like this," Brit ventured, feeling suddenly very insecure and small, trapped in a strange land with strangers. The wild animals Yolanda mentioned seemed real and threatening. Daylight had begun to diminish as the sun disappeared beyond the canyon walls. Night was rapidly approaching.

"What . . . kind of animals do they have down here?" Yolanda asked.

"Oh, probably bears, mountain lions, tigers." Frank chuckled devilishly as he rattled off the names of the fiercest creatures that came to mind.

"No, Frank." Brit folded her arms. "There are no tigers here. And probably none of the others, either."

"Don't forget the snakes," he added.

Both women gasped at the mention of snakes.

"All right, enough!" Rudi shouted, waving his arms at Frank. "Shut up, fool! We won't get a minute's sleep now. Besides, with no blankets, how are we going to keep warm tonight? It's already getting cool. I could use my leather jacket that's floating down the Colorado right now."

"We didn't crash into the Colorado River," Frank explained. "It's some small tributary. We're in a remote canyon far away from the usual tourist places."

"Where are we? Near anything?" Yolanda demanded.

"Beats the hell outta me. That's another thing we need to ask Jake." Frank walked around, careful not to get too close to Rudi. The hostility between them remained.

Brit glanced optimistically at the large tent where Jake had disappeared. "Maybe he has extra blankets in there."

44

"We'll probably all have to huddle together to keep warm tonight." Frank glanced mockingly at Rudi. "And hope you don't decide to attack anyone again."

"Hey, I said it's over, okay?" Rudi grumbled. "I . . . just lost it for a minute."

Frank rubbed his hands together and headed for the cooler. "I don't know about you folks, but I've worked up an appetite this evening. Hey, this shrimp looks mighty tasty. And how about a little champagne, too? We should celebrate. After all, we're still alive. I never thought I'd live if I went down in the canyon. Anybody else want some?"

They all gathered around with paper cups extended while Frank popped the cork and poured. Brit proposed a toast, hoping it would help to mollify the group. "To us. And to our safe rescue!" She lifted her cup with the others. The four survivors stood in an uneven circle, their disagreements forgotten for the moment, laughing at their ragged clothes, nibbling shrimp, sipping bubbly champagne, glad to be alive.

Even as they congratulated themselves, Brit thought of their reluctant rescuer tucked away in that big tent, working. She recalled his large, rough hands and his long, sensitive fingers and how they felt touching her skin when he fixed her shoe. And she simply could not dismiss her feelings of anxiety, or was it trepidation, whenever they were close.

Finally, the group began to move around the

campsite, trying to familiarize themselves with its strangeness. Rudi and Yolanda sat on a slab of sandstone, talking quietly, and Frank stretched out on another boulder. Brit took the nearly empty champagne bottle and headed for the large tent. Jake shouldn't be left out of this. After all, he had rescued them.

She rattled the canvas doorway and squinted inside. "Excuse me, mind if I come in?"

A small battery lamp threw a yellow glow over the shadowy figure of Jake sitting on the floor, typing. He looked up from the portable computer. "Sure. Come on. I'm just finishing some notes I wanted to make on my findings today before I forgot them."

"Notes on your findings, huh? Us?" She stepped inside and sat beside him, crossing her legs Indian-style.

"No, although it might be wise in case anyone wants to make a stink over what happened."

Brit frowned. "You mean, someone might sue you? For what? You saved us."

"That's your opinion. I'm sure the others have a different view of what I did for them. And before the night's over, who knows what they'll think? Or do!"

"You don't honestly think they would actually sue, do you? For what?"

"You never know. From the way they're talking, and acting, I wouldn't doubt anything."

"Well, I wouldn't sue," she declared. "I'm glad you found us. We'd still be sitting down there by ourselves beside the river if you hadn't come along." She sighed and shook her head, trying to reconcile the rapid changes this day had brought. "My friends won't believe . . . all this."

"Your friends in L.A.?"

"No. My friends at work in San Diego."

"I thought you were going to L.A. when you crashed."

"That's right. I have a new job there. Supposed to start tomorrow."

"And what do you do?"

"I used to be a secretary in a large insurance firm in San Diego. That's where my friends still work."

"So, the company's transferring you to L.A.?" He pushed a few keys on the keyboard, closing the program in the computer.

"Please don't stop. I didn't intend to interrupt."

"It's okay. I'm finished. Tell me about L.A."

He turned his attention to her. She was struck by the angled planes of his face, the almost chiseled look of his swarthy features. In the closeness of the tent, she could see that he was not exactly handsome in a model-perfect way, but there were some fascinating qualities about him, like strength and honesty, that were visible in his eyes.

"Well, I'm heading for a completely new job. A new life, actually." She smiled as she considered her rosy future. "I'm going to be a consultant on a movie."

"Oh. Now, there's a logical transition." He

looked at her, puzzled.

"You see, my Great-grandmother Bonnie wrote a book about her life, and it was published many years ago. Now, a movie company is producing it. I've been hired as a consultant to make sure Bonnie's story remains true to her real life. And to add what I can about her."

"Bizarre. Is that how movies come about?"

"Not usually, from what I've gathered. I'm very lucky." She paused and laughed. "At least, until today I've been lucky."

"You all were damned fortunate in the way you came down." His tone grew sober. "They don't usually make it when they crash in the canyon."

"Yeah, I know." She gazed admiringly at his computer. "That's a great little computer. I'm surprised to find something so modern here. I mean, everything else is pretty crude."

"It's great for fieldwork," he explained enthusiastically. "I can make unlimited notes, and they're all stored on disk. Doesn't take up much space. I don't have to bother with much paper. Then when I get back to my office, I'll just print it all out. It enables me to have only the base essentials that I need down here."

"Nothing extra, like blankets?"

"Oh." He snapped his fingers. "Blankets. Everyone will need something tonight."

"And, would you have, possibly, an extra toothbrush?"

He grinned. "Matter of fact, I do. A handful. I use them to clean my artifacts."

"Yuk! They have dirt in them?"

He moved to a box and started digging. "There may be a few clean ones." Triumphantly he pulled up several. "Maybe the Romeros won't mind sharing."

She shook her head. "Don't bet on it. I can't imagine them sharing a TV set, let alone a toothbrush."

"I never bet. The odds are always stacked."

Brit tucked away that bit of information before continuing. "Jake, you must think we're all jerks. The arguments. The fight. I was awful back there about my shoes, but I was just so aggravated that I'd paid so much and they fell apart."

"I understand. You've all had quite a day."

"We're just upset. Tomorrow will be better, I'm sure."

"Yeah. You're going home. No offense, but none of you belong down here."

"You're right, as usual." She poured the last of the champagne into the paper cup and handed it to him. "Here. We had a toast with the champagne from the cooler. This is all that's left. Since you did the rescuing, seems only right that you have a couple of sips."

He started to refuse, but she insisted with a persuasive smile. "Please. We want you to know that, in spite of everything, we appreciate your efforts. We'd really be up the creek, so to speak, without you, Jake."

He moved closer and took the cup from her, his rough fingers brushing hers. "Don't thank me, yet. You haven't spent the night."

"Is it really dangerous?" Brit's eyes widened. "What kind of animals roam around down here?"

"Not dangerous at all." Jake took a healthy sip of the champagne. "I happen to think it's beautiful at night here."

"Tell me about the animals." A part of her wanted to know. Another part didn't.

"Coyotes, javelina, an occasional mountain lion."

"That sounds dangerous to me." She hugged her arms to her ribs and shivered.

"We'll keep a low fire going, and I don't think we'll have a problem." He shifted to a lounging position, propped on one elbow. His long body stretched out, taking up one side of the tent. "I'm sure the Romeros aren't very good at roughing it."

"No, probably not."

He examined her with a gentle, but thorough, gaze. "And you?"

Brit shook her head. "Me, either, I'm afraid. I haven't slept outside in years." She paused then added, "I'll bet you're pretty aggravated with us, aren't you? We've interrupted your work and peaceful life."

He finished the small amount of champagne and handed her the cup without answering her question. "I hope you're saving these."

She stopped short of crumpling the cup in her hand. "Save these paper cups? Why?"

"Because I don't have enough cups, or utensils,

for that matter, for five people."

"But you said you had enough food."

"There's enough canned food to share, but it's nothing fancy, I warn you. I only get food drops once a week, and not much is fresh." He got up and went to another box in the corner and began sorting through it. "I have some leather pieces around here somewhere. Let me have your sandals. I can use the soles as a base for your moccasins."

"I can't believe this."

"They'll do for the interim. Ahh, here's what I need." He pulled out a sizable sheet of finished leather. "This is perfect. Give me your shoes."

She gestured at her one foot tied with the cord. "It works. You're absolutely right. A person needs shoes down here."

"Hiking boots would be even better."

"Right. But I didn't plan to hike to L.A." Brit handed him the tattered shoe. "Are you . . . I hope you don't mind me asking you this, Jake, but are you an Indian? I mean, Native American? Making moccasins isn't an everyday thing most people do. And you do look, sort of uh, like . . . I mean, dark hair and . . ."

"You noticed." He smiled teasingly. "I'm part Zuni. My grandmother was Zuni, and she married a white man and moved away from the village. So I only went back with her to visit occasionally. Never spent much time there."

"Zuni?" The word sounded familiar, but Brit couldn't place it right away. "Is that a branch of the Navajo?"

He chuckled. "No. Completely different tribe. Different location. Different language. Different culture. Not all Indians are alike, y'know."

Brit felt embarrassed. "Sorry, I don't know much about them, obviously." Then she remembered. Bonnie's lover was from the Zuni tribe. Of course, she should know that.

"Not many people know about them or care." He placed her shoes with the leather in the corner. "I'll work on those later." When he straightened and moved closer, Brit noticed a thin leather necklace with a small charm that rested at the base of his throat. The tiny figure seemed to draw her, refusing to let go, and she shifted so she could see it more clearly.

Jake lifted his chin, inviting her inspection. "It's a bear fetish, a good-luck emblem. The Zunis have several of them—toads, birds, sheep, and goats, but the bear is my favorite. A friend carved this and gave it to me for good luck while I'm down here."

"And have you had good luck?" Brit admired the tiny jet bear with a single turquoise eye that nestled against his copper skin.

He gazed into her eyes with a trancelike intensity. "Very good luck so far. It even worked for you."

"How do you figure that?"

"You got out of the crash alive. And with relatively few injuries. That, in itself, is a miracle."

"Right." Spontaneously, for a reason beyond

her understanding, Brit reached out to touch the tiny bear. She rubbed it with one finger, but it was so small she also stroked Jake's sleek brown skin. At the contact, she pulled away as if stung by fire. "Nice," she mumbled, unable to think of anything intelligent at the moment. There was a feeling, a power or energy in the touching, and she wasn't sure if it came from him or the bear. But touching him definitely sent her senses soaring.

Just as her gaze met his, they heard loud voices from the group outside the tent. Loud, arguing voices. Jake reached into a nearby duffle bag and tossed her a pair of thick socks, obviously his. "Wear these around camp until I get your mocs made. They'll keep your feet warm. Next we need to do something about that." He gestured to her torn dress. "Wear these." He pulled out more clothes, dumping a T-shirt and a plaid flannel along with jeans in her lap.

The magic moment between them was gone, and Brit felt let down and deflated. She wanted to be alone with him, to know more about him, his past, and to tell him about herself and her dreams. But they were here, in the bottom of the Grand Canyon, in a strange place for a brief moment in time. "I'm sorry . . ." she mumbled.

"About what?" His tone was sharp. His amiable mood departed. They could hear Rudi's and Frank's voices rise. "Go ahead and get dressed," he instructed. "I'll see if I can settle the children down." He stepped outside, leaving her alone to

53

change clothes and ponder their situation.

Brit listened to Jake as he immediately took charge of the argument. He was, at times, infuriatingly arrogant and self-assured. Maybe his attitude came from being part Indian and that he thought he had a beat on living out here, next to nature. Well, dammit, she'd show him she could be just as hardy as he.

Actually, Brit had never thought much about the Indians as being different from each other before he suggested it. She had simply lumped them all together into one large category: American Indians. It was good that Jake had pointed out the distinctions. She would need to know this while working on the movie.

Like Bonnie's Zuni lover, Jake was a ruggedly handsome man. And tall. Brit couldn't help feeling an attraction to those mysterious dark eyes and that silky jet-black hair of his. Oh! She must be hallucinating after the shock of this day. How could she find such an arrogant, strange man appealing? He wouldn't fit in her world at all. As she pulled on her socks, she could hear Jake's strong voice booming over the others.

"Listen up . . . canned beans for supper . . . no more arguing. No law suits down here . . . all work together."

Brit smiled. He was optimistic. And dictatorial. He sounded like an army sergeant. As a professor, he probably ran his class with an iron hand and expected this group to behave the same way as a classroom of students. A chuckle escaped her smiling lips. He'd actually told Yolanda to shut up. Wouldn't the girls at the office get a kick out of this? She heard a rustle outside the tent.

"You dressed yet, Brit? Frank and I are going to unload this tent so more than one can sleep in there tonight."

"In a minute." Brit made a quick assessment as she undressed. She was a complete mess. This morning, she had been normal. She had looked good. Hair, nails, immaculate clothes, expensive shoes, everything was perfect. That was the way she liked it. Now her clothes were in tatters. Her nails were broken, the polish chipped. Her hair had lost its bouncy curls. And her shoes were ruined.

Hurriedly she slipped out of her torn dress and into Jake's clothes. They were soft and warm against her skin. The cloth smelled like wood and fresh pine, just like Jake. She was surrounded by his fragrance, his essence. It was the most comfortable she had felt all day.

When she stepped outside the tent, a magenta glow from the sunset on the vermilion cliffs gave the entire campsite a pinkish glow. It was unusual and beautiful. Yes, as beautiful as a rock castle whose walls were draped with rich red velvet.

Jake's commanding voice broke into her reverie. "Rudi, gather more firewood. Look down by the river for driftwood. We'll make any campfires in this firepan." He lifted a large metal pan. "Since fires are dangerous to the environment

55

and leave such a mess, they're prohibited in the canyon." He pointed to Brit and Yolanda. "You two open these cans and set them on this rack over the fire. Frank and I'll unload the big tent so there'll be room for sleeping in there."

Everyone responded to Jake's orders, everyone except Yolanda. She had broken a fingernail and now refused to touch another thing. So Brit opened the cans and set them on the rack above the fire. Twenty minutes later, everyone gathered for an adequate supper of canned beans, canned corn, canned green chili peppers, and tortillas.

"With a meal like this, I feel like one of those ancient Indians you're studying, Jake," Frank observed as he rolled the flour tortilla around a generous helping of beans and chopped green chilies.

"Actually, this is possibly what they might have eaten, from all we can tell," Jake responded.

"Probably explains why they died out," Yolanda commented as she picked at her plate.

"It's nourishing enough to have sustained them for hundreds of years. They revered corn and squash," Jake said in defense of the plain food. "They also used sunflower seeds and pinyon nuts in a number of ways. They ground them for flour."

"That must have been real tasty," Yolanda muttered.

"Not bad, actually. My classes make these foods every year in the process of understanding past cultures. And understanding benefits us all."

He glared at Yolanda, and she looked down at her plate without further comment.

It was the first time Brit had seen Yolanda speechless and she had to give Jake credit. He was certainly not intimidated by her celebrity status. Down here, no one had status. Except, maybe, Jake.

"What happened to those Indians who lived down here?" Frank asked.

Jake answered eagerly. It was a subject he obviously loved. "There are theories as to why they left. Some think it was a period of drought which left them unable to grow crops and feed their people. Others think there were wars between the various bands who lived here. That's one of the things I'm hoping to uncover in my research. To see if we can tell why they're no longer here."

"How could you possibly do that?" Brit spread one hand and gestured at the cathedral walls. "They're all gone. There's no one to ask."

"I'm studying what they left behind."

"What did they leave?"

"That's the strange part. In some instances, it's almost as if they were caught by surprise and just escaped. Some of the rooms remain untouched, as if the occupants would be back tomorrow. And they've been that way for hundreds of years."

Brit was amazed. "What's there? Household things?"

"Exactly. Pottery, cooking utensils, toys, parts of clothes made from skins, food."

"Food?"

He nodded toward his plate. "Corn. It's rather dried by now, but preserved enough for anyone to recognize it."

"Good grief!" Yolanda exclaimed, getting up in a huff. "As absolutely fascinating as this conversation is, I must excuse myself. Dinner was, um, unusual, to say the least. Can I dispose of this behind a rock?"

"No!" Jake jumped up and followed her. "That'll attract animals, for sure. All garbage and trash must be contained." He showed them how to clean up the supper dishes and store the trash. Later he handed out the toothbrushes along with instructions for hygiene that wouldn't sully the natural beauties around them.

As Jake had predicted to Brit, the night was very long and relatively sleepless. He brought out two sleeping bags. The extra one had been intended for a colleague who could not make the trip at the last minute. Yolanda and Brit tucked themselves into the bags in the small tent. Rudi and Frank rolled up in blankets in the large tent. Jake made his bed outside under the stars.

Yolanda mumbled complaints to Brit for at least an hour. Then she announced loudly that she was cold and wanted to sleep with Rudi so she could cuddle with someone.

"Please, go ahead! Quickly!" Brit turned over and buried her head in the cover. She actually felt warm and secure and fairly comfortable in Jake's insulated sleeping bag and, if the ground weren't so hard and rocky, she could probably sleep.

"I knew you didn't want me in here with you, all along," Yolanda muttered as she crawled out of the pup tent and made her way to Rudi.

That arrangement lasted about ten minutes before Frank declared that he wasn't sleeping with the Romeros. "I've never seen such spoiled, inconsiderate jerks!" He found a spot beside the low campfire near Jake.

Even after things had quieted again, Brit could hear Yolanda and Rudi grumbling to each other. She could hear Frank snoring. And she could hear other strange sounds that she couldn't recognize. She wondered if animals actually would disturb—or attack—the camp. As she dozed, Brit thought of the elusive, confident Jake Landry She recalled the electric spark of his smooth copper skin when she had touched the bear fetish at his neck. She imagined piercing black eyes with jet lashes, closed against dark skin. And she slept, dreaming of the brush of his lips against hers.

Chapter Three

Brit woke to strange noises. They were unfamiliar, as were her surroundings, and her imagination shifted into overdrive. Maybe it was wild animals; maybe looters, raiding the camp!

Heart pounding, Brit crawled out of her warm cocoon and peered through the thick gray morning air. The noises had come from Jake, looking rumpled and somewhat weary as he knelt before the campfire.

His lean form was outlined by cold blue shadows; his jet-black hair dominated the cool grays of morning. He wore jeans and a longsleeved insulated undershirt. She watched him take a seat on a rounded stone, hunkering over to absorb the sputtering heat of the small fire and to wait for the coffeepot to boil.

Brit was struck by the amazing notion that Jake looked, at that instant, like a man from another era, even from another world. Curiously, he appeared at ease, as if he belonged here. A strange impulse pulled her toward him, toward his ancient and interesting world.

She made a polite noise and joined him. Jake merely nodded a greeting. No words were spoken between them; none were necessary. They sat still and quiet, absorbing the exotic beauty of the early morning. In a short time, an opaque grayness gave way to a silvery glistening which faded into pale shades of pink as the sun rose steadily. Brit had never known there were so many colors in a sunrise.

"It's beautiful here this morning," she said finally in a soft voice.

"Yep," Jake agreed noncommittally. "Always is."

"Is it like this every morning? All these colors?"

"Um-hum."

"What makes so many different shades?"

"Light reflection off the minerals in the rocks. Iron and copper and bits of mica."

"Everything seems to be in layers." Brit's gaze roamed around the mammoth amphitheater.

"Layers of time." Jake's tone was hushed and solemn, as if he had the utmost respect for his surroundings. "It has taken millions of years to reach this point." He handed her a mug of coffee, brewed black and strong.

She inhaled, savoring but not drinking the steamy hot liquid. "It's strange here, almost as if we're in a time warp. Right now. Like we're caught in a place that never changes with time."

He gazed at her, a kind of appraising quality

61

in his eyes. "You noticed. It especially feels that way when I work in one of the ruins."

"The Indian houses?"

He nodded.

Brit looked around. "Where are they? I don't see anything."

He swept his hand around in a vague gesture. "Hidden in caves in these canyon walls."

She stood up to get a better look. "Up there? I still don't detect any openings or caves."

"They're quite remote. I have to climb to them."

"Isn't it eerie to enter these homes where people lived hundreds of years ago?"

"Yes."

"I'd love to go in one of them." Her green eyes glistened as she thought about the prospect. "I would love to see the things you're talking about, Jake."

He gazed at her and pursed his lips. For a moment, she thought he was going to offer to take her to one of the ruins. But before he could say a thing, the morning quiet was disturbed by Rudi's rambunctious greeting.

"So where does a guy get a cup of java around this joint?"

Brit watched sullenly as Jake poured a cup of coffee for Rudi. Another magic moment between them was gone, and she couldn't help feeling some resentment.

"Damn hardest earth I've ever slept on!" Rudi exclaimed with a laugh. "Course, I didn't expect it to compare with my water bed at home."

Jake stood by Rudi while they chatted. "In a few hours, we'll be able to notify the supply plane that you're here, and the pilot will relay the message. By evening, you'll probably be sleeping in the comfort of your own water bed," Jake said.

"Ahh, music to my ears!" Rudi said. "Can't happen soon enough for Yolanda and me."

Brit wrapped her hands around her cup and felt strangely discordant with thoughts of leaving this place today. She squeezed her eyes shut. What in the world was wrong with her? Their one goal, since the wreck yesterday, was to get out of here. Now Jake was explaining how it would be done and how soon it could happen. Suddenly she felt as though the bottom had dropped out of her life. It made no sense whatsoever.

Then a bizarre idea occurred to Brit. She didn't care if she were rescued today. She wanted to remain here, to stay in this alien and beautiful land, with Jake. She wanted to be with him and get to know him. Completely. Jake was an interesting and elusive man, and she wanted to break his tough-guy facade. She wanted to see him laugh, to make his expression soften, to feel some kind of response from him.

Rudi's loud conversation woke Frank, who was sleeping nearby. Before long, the men were eating breakfast of granola bars and canned fruit and planning their hike to the clearing where the supply plane flew overhead.

"Looks like a storm brewing." Frank gestured toward the sky.

Jake agreed. "By afternoon, we'll probably have a whopper of a monsoon."

"Monsoon?" Brit asked. "I thought they only had those in Asia."

"It's the same principle," Jake explained. "Heat builds, pulling moisture from the clouds, turning to rain by afternoon. Our monsoons can be vicious down here, but they don't last long. An hour or so and the storm's usually over. Well, men, let's hit the trail. Got a lot to do before the rains come."

Brit watched them until they disappeared behind a sandstone boulder. Even though she wanted to go with them, hiking without shoes was not a good idea, especially since their destination was a good half a mile away. It was decided, then, that she and Yolanda would remain at camp.

Brit ambled past the large tent where Yolanda was still sleeping. Rudi had declared that Yolanda didn't need to get up at "this ungodly hour" just so she could wave a flag at an airplane. He could do that. Besides, this was way too early for her. She was accustomed to sleeping until noon.

Left alone, Brit decided to familiarize herself with the small camp set amid prickly pear cactus, yucca, cat claw, mesquite, and the shelter of large leafy cottonwood trees. It was a strange ecological mixture. She wandered around the small, neat camp, actually enjoying the peace and quiet of being alone and away from the Romeros' bickering for a little while.

Soon after the men left, Brit heard what she thought was an aircraft. The world at the bottom of the canyon was so quiet, so absolutely undisturbed, that anything as noisy as an airplane was a definite interruption. She tried to spot it, but low-hanging clouds prevented her from seeing the sky clearly. She wandered away from camp and down to the stream's edge. Funny how this whole area seemed nicer today than just yesterday.

She picked up a red pebble and tossed it into a small pool ringed by several strategically located boulders, as if they were placed there by some giant hand. She took a seat on a rock and trailed her own thin hand in the chilly water. This place was more like paradise than a prison. But it held them. They weren't here by choice. That made it a prison, didn't it?

Brit realized with a start that she was supposed to begin working on the movie set today. How often in a lifetime does someone get a chance to do that? This was to be the beginning of an exciting career and a brand-new life. Yet here she was, stuck in the canyon. She couldn't help wondering if the producer realized she wasn't there today. Or if he even cared.

Surely everyone knew by now. The media had probably jumped on the story of Yolanda being lost in the canyon. And Frank had said that search and rescue efforts would begin when their chopper didn't meet the scheduled flight plan.

Michael was probably beside himself with concern over her. And what did she think of him? Of them? The way she felt right now was much the same as yesterday and the day before. Only now she knew she had to officially break with him.

Brit picked up another stone and gazed at it centered in her palm. On one of their rest stops yesterday, Jake had explained that these red ones had lots of iron in them; the black stones were from some volcanic eruption millions of years ago. She tossed the stone into the pool and watched the ripples radiate outward to her.

Peeling off Jake's socks, she pulled the legs of her baggy jeans up and stepped into the shallow edges of the stream. The water was shockingly cold as it crept over her feet, and she realized that she felt dirty and in need of a warm shower. She squatted down and washed her face, scrubbing her complexion with the clear water. It was chilling, but refreshing, and she considered stripping and taking a bath in the stream while everyone was gone. The more she thought about it, the better the idea sounded.

Within minutes Brit had shimmied out of Jake's oversized clothes and was wading into the shallows of the pool. She splashed herself all over, delighting in the crude, but welcome bath. Her skin tingled from the icy water. It was refreshing as well as cleansing.

A hawk swooped overhead and screeched at her in its high-pitched voice. At first startled by the intrusion of a pair of eyes, she laughed and waved at the fantailed bird. Lifting her face, Brit let the gentle breeze caress her skin, drying it. The wind brought songs of unfamiliar birds as well as some familiar sounds . . . people talking.

Suddenly someone shouted her name. "Brit! Brit, where are you?"

The men were returning! So soon? And here she stood, bathing in the nude! She splashed through the knee-high water as she scrambled to get her clothes. But they were out of reach, draped on a rock all the way over at the pool's edge. Inadvertently, she had waded out near the middle of the stream where the water hit her mid-thigh. Scrambling, she reached for the shirt.

Jake's voice sounded alarmingly close. "Brit! Brit?"

Startled, she looked up. He stood on a rock ledge directly above her. Dark and towering, he seemed to dominate his world. Furthermore, he had a full view of the little pool—and of her, in the nude!

"Everything all right?" he called innocently.

Quickly Brit lifted the red plaid flannel shirt in front of her exposed body. "Until a minute ago, everything was just peachy!" Realizing the shirt wasn't covering her completely, she gestured angrily. "Can't I take a bath in privacy?"

"Sure, excuse me. I just . . . was worried

about you. Didn't know where you were."

"Now you know!"

He backed away, with no real apology that she could detect in his devilish grin. But his intense, stern expression had softened for the first time since they'd arrived. She'd gotten a response from him, but not the one she wanted.

Jake turned his back and pretended to be busy when Brit arrived back in camp. It wasn't that he was embarrassed at seeing her naked. On the contrary. He'd been delighted with the sight of her smooth, shimmering skin, still wet from her bath. He turned away because he didn't want her to see that pleasure still on his face. Besides, he knew she'd be furious. And, he admitted privately, rightfully so.

As Brit approached, the group was arguing, as usual. And Yolanda was at the center. "No excuses! How could you let him slip by? You had one thing to do, and you blew it!"

"Look, I didn't see you rolling out of the sack to make sure it was done right!" Rudi countered.

"You're back so soon," Brit said. "What happened?"

"Plane was earlier than scheduled. We missed him," Frank explained.

Brit frowned. "What do you mean 'missed him'? He came by. I heard him."

"Sure, he flew over," Frank said with a futile gesture. "Early. He dropped supplies. But we didn't get a chance to signal anything. Cloud cover was too low, so he couldn't see us, anyway."

"Can you beat that?" Yolanda said, stomping around and shaking her head. "Our one chance outta this hole, and you missed him. What a bunch of bumbling idiots."

Brit felt Yolanda's frustration. How could they have let this happen? She turned accusingly to Jake. "So what'll we do now?"

"Try again in a week when the next drop is scheduled." Jake tried not to let them see that he was as upset at the thought of them hanging around as they were. He ripped open one of the supply boxes and pulled out a couple of items, then left the rest packed. "We can use this cereal. Everybody like oatmeal?"

"Wait a minute. The plane isn't coming back for a week?" Yolanda asked, her voice reaching a shrill, whiny decibel. "If you think I'm gonna stay here a whole week, you're outta your mind, friend."

"Afraid so," Jake muttered, checking the next supply box. "He only comes once a week. We missed our chance this time. So, do you like oatmeal?"

"No! I hate it! My mother made me eat it every morning," Rudi answered, his aggravation mounting.

Jake ignored Rudi and nodded toward Brit. "You like it?"

She shook her head. "I don't eat breakfast."

Rudi stood in the middle of the camp, his fists on his hips. "You mean we've got to stay in this hellhole another week?"

"No. You can hike out," Jake answered smartly, irritated with their attitudes and their complaining. "And what about canned tuna?"

"Agghhh!" Yolanda uttered.

Frank broke into the conversation. "Well, that's exactly what I intend to do. Hike outta this place. You folks can stay here if you want, but I'm going for help. It's the only way."

They all turned to look curiously at the pilot, who stood with legs apart and arms folded. His face was determined. There was no changing his mind.

"Think you're up to it?" Jake asked. "It's a pretty rough climb."

"Of course I can do it," Frank said confidently. "Anyway, it's my fault that we're down here."

"Amen to that," Yolanda muttered.

Frank cut his eyes at her, then looked back to Jake. "I take full responsibility. And it's up to me to go get help. Can you show me the way outta here?"

"Sure. I'll draw a map for you. And there are plenty of supplies. It'll take two full days of hiking. Maybe a little more, depending how fast you go. And the weather. If it storms, you may as well tuck it in and not try to fight it. Mother Nature is vicious out here and she always wins."

Everyone was unusually quiet while Jake

helped Frank load a backpack with food and a blanket. Meanwhile, the wind kicked up occasional strong gusts, and the clouds overhead turned dark. Distant thunder rumbled, threateningly, warning of the impending turbulence. Jake handed Frank a navy blue jacket and a matching cap that read NAU, for Northern Arizona University, above the bill. "I think you'd better wait until after this squall, Frank. It's coming fast."

"Naw, no problem. I've delayed long enough."

"It could be violent. Sometimes they're pretty rough around here."

"I'll manage," said Frank stubbornly. "I'll wait it out, then continue from there. You gonna give me that map?"

Jake motioned and the two men put their heads together over the map Jake had drawn. He explained the exit route along the tributary. "There might be a small cave through here that you could use as shelter. Another around here." Jake could tell that he was much more concerned about the weather than Frank. But it seemed that Frank's urge to get away from his nemeses, the Romeros, was so great that it obliterated his common sense.

While they ate a quick lunch, Jake wrote instructions about their location for the rescue team. "Give them this. They won't have any problem finding our camp."

Finally, there was no more information to relay; the time had come for Frank to leave. He shook hands with Jake and Brit, then turned to

Rudi and Yolanda. "I, uh, I'm sorry about all this trouble and inconvenience. Maybe if I get somebody to rescue you ASAP, you'll forget about this lawsuit business."

"You'd better hurry, then," Rudi said stubbornly. "I'm still thinking about how much you've cost us. Not to mention the risk to our lives."

"Look, I could lose my pilot's license over this."

"Oh, too bad. Then you wouldn't get to dump anybody else into the bottom of the Grand Canyon," Yolanda grumbled.

"You might say that I saved your life by trying to land," Frank responded angrily. "You know we were all damned lucky to live to tell about it."

"I won't comment until I talk to my lawyer," Yolanda vowed.

"Good luck, Frank," Brit said, interrupting the tension-filled moment.

Frank nodded to them all, and with a little salute-wave, was off, following a path along the river. Silently they watched him retreat. Brit had mixed feelings. She understood Frank's need to go, his feeling of responsibility. But she couldn't help feeling that this was a dangerous trip he was undertaking. What if something happened to him? No one would know. What if . . . this were a bad decision? Frank seemed so small and helpless when contrasted to the towering vermilion cliffs.

"I wish someone were going with him," Brit said to anyone who would listen.

Rudi and Yolanda ignored her and walked away.

"He'll be all right. Anyway, it was his decision." Jake lifted one of the new supply boxes and hauled it to the big tent.

Brit caught up with him, still angry over the pool incident. "You know, I don't appreciate you peeping on me earlier."

"I wasn't peeping."

"Looking. Gaping. Staring. Whatever you call it, I call it peeping!" She followed him from the big tent to the supplies, then back again, taking several steps to keep up with his long strides.

"Checking. Call it checking on you," he said firmly, his mouth drawn tight with his physical exertion. "I couldn't find you when we got back to camp. Yolanda had no idea where you were. I was concerned."

"Yeah, sure. Like I might have gone somewhere with no shoes."

He halted and glared at her for a moment. She could be damned pesky, but he wouldn't be diverted. "Like you might have fallen down one of these cliffs. Like you might have done something stupid and—"

"The only stupid thing I did was to think I could have a moment of privacy in this miserable place." She turned on her bare heel and stalked away. The man was infuriating. He was always right, the perfect camper, the perfect man. He knew everything. She hated his type. At the slight touch on her arm, she stopped.

Jake held her for a moment, noting her tremble beneath his fingertips. "Brit, I . . ."

She turned and looked into his eyes. There was a spark of sincerity in their dark depths.

"I'm sorry I embarrassed you. When I stepped to that ledge, the last thing I expected to find was you taking a bath that, uh, way."

She hesitated long enough to study those dark eyes of his. Here was the apology she wanted. Was it enough? "I . . . hadn't planned to bathe," she offered as an excuse. "It was just a spontaneous act. I didn't expect you back so soon. Nor standing on a ledge watching me."

"I didn't watch. Just a glance." He tried to make it sound casual, as if he hadn't seen much of her. But he'd seen enough . . . enough to know that she was beautiful and sexy . . . enough to know how much that brief sight of her affected him. Even now, just remembering her slender feminine form bending to scoop the blue-green waters and letting it cascade over her body made his throat dry.

Thunder shook the ground and reverberated around them, reminding Jake of the rising storm. "Storm's coming on fast," he muttered tightly. Almost before he finished speaking, lightning flashed across the rocks behind them. "It's close now. Gotta put all my equipment back in the tent before it hits."

"Do you need help?"

"Yeah, but they're heavy for you. I'm running out of time."

"I'm sure Rudi'll help." Brit headed across the camp where the Romeros sat, talking low. "Hey, Rudi! Jake needs your strong arms."

"What does he want?" Rudi asked, not budging.

"He has to carry those boxes back into the big tent before it rains."

"Sure, Rudi'll haul stuff." Yolanda pushed Rudi's brawny shoulder. He gave her a menacing look and lumbered reluctantly in the direction of the stack of boxes. "He used to be real good at it. See if you can remember how to haul, honey," she taunted.

"I remember more about my past than you do," Rudi countered.

"And what's that supposed to mean?" she yelled.

"Whatever you think," he flung over his shoulder.

"Jerk!" Yolanda turned her back to him, and said to Brit, "I wonder if Frank is taking cover."

"I'm sure he knows the dangers of this kind of storm and will take cover."

Yolanda looked around uneasily. "I hate to admit it, but I'm really concerned about Frank. For some strange reason, I have bad vibes about his trip."

"What do you mean?" Brit frowned and gazed involuntarily in the direction that Frank had walked out of camp.

"Oh, I don't know. This sounds funny coming from me, but I just have a strange feeling about him taking off by himself."

"Good grief," Brit moaned. "Why didn't you mention it before he left?"

"What would I have said? 'Hey, Frank, I've got these vibes about your trip? Could you hold off a few days?'" She pushed her dark hair behind one ear. "How sensible is that? Anyway, Rudi would laugh his head off at me. I've never done anything like that before."

Brit was angry at Yolanda's belated admission. "You might have warned him."

"I'm sure he wouldn't believe any kind of warning coming from me."

Brit, too, had been leery of Frank's solo journey. Now, Yolanda's confession stirred her anger. Something inside her snapped, and she just wanted to lash out at Yolanda. They all had a responsibility to each other, and that included Frank. They were all in this mess together. She challenged Yolanda's intentions. "What do you care about Frank, anyway?"

Yolanda's eyes widened and she returned sharply, "How do you know what I care about?"

"It's pretty obvious what you care about. Yourself! And only you!"

"Why, you little goody-two-shoes twit!" Yolanda shouted.

"You self-centered motor-mouth!" Brit yelled. "You, with all your complaining and threatening, practically pushed Frank down that path. And now, now that he's gone off by himself, you claim to care? Ha! Big deal!"

"I didn't push anybody to anything. Frank has a mind of his own. Besides, he got us into this mess, didn't he? He should be the one to get us out."

"No! It was an accident! He couldn't help it."

"He even admitted guilt when he left."

"Not guilt, responsibility. Of which you obviously know nothing!"

Yolanda leaned her face close to Brit's. "There you go again, telling me what—"

A thick body squeezed between them, and Rudi's voice interrupted the women's verbal battle. "Hey, babe, what's going on here?"

Brit felt a pair of hands on her shoulders, whirling her around.

"I'm getting damn tired of this," Jake muttered. "Leave you alone for two minutes and you go for each other like two wildcats."

"Well, she's so . . . so—" Brit looked at Jake's stony face and her voice trailed to silence. "Oh, you wouldn't understand."

"What I don't understand is, why you?" he yelled above the whine of the wind. "The others are bad enough, but now, you, Brit! I just can't believe it."

She folded her arms across her chest. "Don't give me one of your college class lectures."

"It's going to rain buckets any minute and we're standing here, arguing." Jake grabbed both Yolanda's and Rudi's arms and asked, "Please, help me. We—you—can clear the air later. Right now, everything, including the camp kitchen, has to be stored in the big tent."

The wind pushed and pulled at them, whipping their hair and muffling their voices. In the frenzy of the moment, they had to forget the argument and work together. The storm wouldn't wait, and storing Jake's equipment was important. The task kept them busy, and they didn't have to face each other, which was fine with Brit. By the time huge cold drops of water started to fall, the tent was loaded again.

The wind was blowing so hard, it bent small trees to the ground. Jake rushed Yolanda and Rudi toward the large tent. "Any more room in there?"

"It's pretty crowded," Rudi said, assessing the cramped space. "We could all stand."

"The pup?" Brit yelled above the howl of the wind.

"Too risky! It's in the water path. How are you at climbing?" Before she could answer, he spoke to Rudi. "Hand me a blanket." Jake grabbed it and shoved it into Brit's hands. "Follow me!" he yelled above the wind's roar.

Brit scrambled blindly behind him, climbing, taking his strong hand for assistance, not looking where they were going, just climbing upward with him. Midway up the wall of rocks, he pulled her onto a ledge and pointed toward a shallow cave. "In here. It's cold, but dry."

They sat on the ground and looked down on

the camp, which was being pelted by rain and whipped by a gale-force wind. Brit flattened herself against the sandstone wall and felt amazingly safe from the storm. She wondered about their pilot, who couldn't be very far away yet. "Do you think Frank found shelter?"

"I hope so. Yeah. I gave him the locations of several caves like this. They're usually safe enough."

"This is quite an attack. Now I see why you tried to discourage him from leaving. You knew."

"This is just the beginning. It doesn't take much of a downpour in this country to create flash floods. They're more dangerous than anything because there is no control. You're completely helpless, a cork in a vicious sea."

Brit's thoughts shifted to what had happened between her and Yolanda. "I can't believe I yelled at her like that," she muttered.

Jake chuckled. "I thought you two were going to start throwing punches any minute."

"Heavens, I would never do anything like that."

"But I didn't know. When people get out of their elements, they do bizarre things. And you're definitely out of yours."

Suddenly a feeling of remorse, of actual sadness, ripped through Brit. "What's happening to me? I'm becoming just like her, and I hate it. I don't know what made me act like that. I never argue like this. And yet, that's all we've done

79

since we landed."

"Yep, sure is."

"It's the money. Ever since the money. First Michael. Now Yolanda and . . . everyone."

"What money? And who's Michael?"

"The money for the movie rights to my great-grandmother's book. And Michael is my—" Her lips hesitated at the words.

"Boyfriend?" Jake finished for her.

"Yes," she murmured in a bare whisper.

"How could it be the money?"

"Because it changes you. It changed me. I quit my job; Michael and I argued over what to do with the money. I started indulging every whim that entered my head, including renting a helicopter for this trip when I couldn't get a regular flight. I even paid for Vegas. The gambling. The losses. Everything. I wonder if it changed Yolanda, too."

"Well, I wouldn't know about that. But the way I figure it, there's only one thing to do."

"What's that?"

"Apologize."

"To Yolanda?" Brit groaned. "I don't apologize well."

"You and Yolanda have a week to spend together. You'll both be better off, and so will everyone else, if you air it. And clear it up."

Brit stared into space. The red rock walls were curtained with misty sheets of rain. Barriers. A giant prison keeping them all inside, together, to bicker and pick at each other like animals. Like wildcats, Jake had said.

Silently she admitted that Jake had a point. She had to settle this problem that had developed between her and Yolanda. He was right, and, dammit, she despised him for it.

She leaned forward to watch anxiously as the strong wind tugged at the big tent. "Are Rudi and Yolanda safe down there?"

"I think so. That tent is on higher ground, protected by the rock wall." A piece of the little tent began flapping and Jake yelled, "Hey! The pup's going!"

In the next moment, he was dashing through the rain and lightning, scrambling down the precipice they had climbed, splattering through puddles, and slipping through the mud. Just as he reached the flapping pup tent, it gave one last whiplash and, like an angry kite, fluttered away.

"Dammit, come back here!" he yelled, and his words spiraled through the small stand of cottonwoods, down to the stream and disappeared like the tent. In frustration, Jake pivoted in the slippery mud and climbed back up to their dry little cave, heaving down beside her again. He was drenched.

He breathed heavily after the run, his large frame moving with each gasp. He brushed his hair back and yelled out in frustration. "Dammit! We're a tent short now!" The wind slammed his exclamations against the cave walls.

Brit didn't move away from him, even when his shoulder rubbed hers, even though he was wet and getting her wet. His cotton shirt was dark where the rain had soaked through, and it clung to his muscular angles. His hair hung like a silk fringe, and dripped water onto his shirt.

Spontaneously Brit grabbed a corner of the blanket and applied it to his head, drying the moisture. Gingerly she wiped the excess water from his hair, then dabbed at his ear and cheek.

He turned to her, sitting perfectly still, letting her dry his face. She touched his forehead, and he closed his eyes while she stroked his nose, cheeks, and chin. At that moment, Brit was overwhelmed with the desire to kiss those sensuous lips, so inviting and unguarded as she hovered near.

"You have nice lines," she murmured, barely aware she was speaking. Softly she ran the blanket edge down his cheek to the angle of his jaw.

He opened one eye, then the other. "I could say the same about you, and you'd be offended. Probably scream something about harassment."

"I meant that your face has nice lines." Brit cleared her throat and sat a little straighter.

"So's yours," he said softly. "Lovely face." With one finger he traced down her cheek and under her chin, lifting it slightly.

Their bodies were touching; their faces only inches apart. She looked into his dark, mysterious eyes. They promised more than she'd ever experienced. More adventure. More emotion. More desire.

She shivered and smiled faintly. His touch sent

ripples of excitement through her, a feeling she'd never had with Michael. She wanted to experience the touch; the promised kiss, the heat of Jake's mouth on hers. Her lips parted ever so slightly. "Jake . . ."

"Brit . . . you're beautiful. How do you expect me to . . ."

She could feel his warm breath on her cheeks, her lips. "I don't know . . ."

His finger left her chin, and he turned his face. "No, we shouldn't . . . can't—"

"Jake . . ." she mumbled and felt the cold air of rejection when he moved. Brit dabbed feverishly at his arms and shoulders with the blanket and started talking rapidly in an attempt to grasp some reality. "If I didn't know better, I'd think you enjoyed that run in the rain."

"What makes you know better?"

"Well, I assume you didn't want to lose that tent."

"Yeah, we need it. But these storms are part of what makes this place so exciting to me. Being here is . . . it's hard to explain why I like it. But I always return to Flagstaff and teaching refreshed." He took a deep breath. "It's great down here."

She caressed his shoulder. "Aren't you cold?"

Before he could answer, thunder crashed overhead and rumbled all around them, like a hundred metal garbage cans. Brit ducked her head and cringed against Jake. "Ohmigod! What is that? Is this thing falling apart?"

83

His arm went around her naturally and he pulled her close to his chest until the rumbling stopped. "Rock slides. We'll be okay. Don't worry."

At that moment, another rumbling preceded a series of rocks tumbling down the cliff, bouncing and rolling right through the spot where the small tent had been.

Brit sat up and peered over the side. "Did you see that? If we'd been in the little tent, we'd be dead right now."

"Nature, especially in this place, can be violent."

"What about Yolanda and Rudi in that big tent? Are you sure they're safe?"

"I think their tent's okay because it's located close to the rock wall. When rain softens the mud and loosens the rocks, they start to tumble. They tend to bounce outward, though, rather than dropping straight down. You cold? Come on in." Jake pulled the blanket around his broad shoulders and opened the other side, inviting her inside.

Brit slid under his arm and felt an immediate inner glow with their closeness. Something about this man had attracted her from the beginning. His masculinity, his authority, his sensuality, even his arrogance appealed to her. Being close to him was thrilling and satisfying; she felt as though she were right where she belonged. While the storm raged outside, she was warm and safe with Jake.

After a long time, he spoke softly. "From the looks of things, we're going to be stuck here all night."

Brit stiffened. "What?"

"Even if the storm lets up, it's too wet to do anything. Anyway, there's a danger of flash floods. We're safest right here where it's high and dry."

"Won't it be cold up here?" she choked, trying to imagine sleeping in a cave with Jake.

"Don't worry. We'll get the extra sleeping bag. I'll make sure you stay warm enough."

"Oh. Good." She swallowed hard, thinking of spending the night with the man next to her. It was a dream come true.

Chapter Four

Brit woke the next morning feeling rested and alert. She had slept amazingly well, considering her bedroom was in a cave and her bed, an insulated sleeping bag. Last night, she hadn't even minded the inevitable pebbles beneath her. Maybe she was so tired that she could have slept anywhere.

She blinked in the daylight and snuggled deeper under the covers, smiling to herself. The girls back home would not believe that she had spent the night with a hunk of a man who never touched her. Brit wasn't even sure she believed it herself. But she knew she had definitely remained alone. And she was still dressed in jeans and Jake's soft shirt. Besides, she would certainly have remembered if anything remotely affectionate had happened between her and Jake. The closest they had gotten was when he had curled toward her, wrapped in his blanket, and rested his head near hers. Even though he had been sound asleep, she had been conscious of the sounds of his soft breathing and the warmth he exuded.

Brit had been tempted to turn over and pull him to her so they could share that warmth. Oh Lord, she had wanted to touch him and to feel his sensuous lips on hers. But she kept her back turned toward him and could only imagine how those lips felt . . . and it was frustrating, especially this morning!

Suddenly, in the light of day, Brit realized why he left her alone as she stared wide-eyed at the sandstone ceiling of her cave bedroom. Jake was keeping her at arm's length because of Michael. She had mentioned arguing with him, so Jake assumed she and Michael were a couple. Brit knew in her heart how she felt about Michael, and she would just have to figure a way to convey that to Jake.

She sat up, savoring the unusual fragrances—both familiar and unfamiliar—in the air. Apparently Jake was already up and making coffee. It didn't take her long to climb down from the cave to camp and join him. This time, there was no campfire, only the single-unit gas stove. Jake wore a rainbow-colored Mexican poncho over his shirt and jeans as he worked on his breakfast in the morning chill. The turquoise, green, and yellow stripes of the poncho contrasted his dark shaggy hair and gave him the look of a bold ancient explorer who might be pictured in a history book.

"Morning." She gave him a chipper smile even as she shivered in the chill.

Jake glanced at her, surprise in his expression. "You up so early?" He handed her a blanket, the one he'd used last night, and indicated that she should wrap it around herself. "This'll help until you get some hot coffee in you."

Brit gratefully pulled the blanket over her shoulders, relishing its warmth and the erotic idea that it had encircled Jake all night. "Mornings are so beautiful down here, I hate to miss them." She wondered if he could guess that her true reason for crawling out of the warm sleeping bag was to be with him, not necessarily the morning's special beauty.

He let her comment pass and continued stirring a pan on the tiny stove.

Undeterred in her effort to converse with him, Brit inhaled deeply. "What is that interesting scent? It's wonderful. So unusual . . . not mint, not exactly pine."

Jake poured her a steaming cup and handed it to her. This time he did not let their hands brush. "That's the creosote bush, peculiar to the desert. Rain brings out its unique fragrance."

She accepted the cup with a smile, which he didn't see because he had already turned back to his cooking. He was trying to avoid her, she realized while sipping her coffee. What had happened after they had snuggled together under the blanket during the rain last night? She only knew what had *not* happened, and that she regretted it. Determined not to be ignored, Brit moved closer and appeared interested in what he was doing. "What are you fixing?"

"Oatmeal. Want some?"

She shook her head. "No, thanks."

"I didn't bother with a fire because I didn't expect any of you up so early. But you can use some of the dry wood I have stored in the rock crevices behind the tent if you want a fire for warmth."

As she watched Jake's graceful movements, Brit was certain that without him here, she would be entirely miserable. As it was, she was already dreading their rescue when she'd have to leave him.

"Sure you don't want some?" He lifted the pan toward her.

"No, no thanks. Coffee's enough for me."

He dumped a couple of packets of sugar into the oatmeal and started to eat directly from the pan. "Coffee isn't enough breakfast for me when I'm climbing around these rocks."

Brit's eyes widened with interest. "Are you going to the cliff dwellings today?"

"Yep. That's where I work. It's the real reason I'm down here, remember." He walked away and sat on a stump.

Brit poured herself more coffee and followed him. As she walked across camp, she could feel her thick, warm socks getting wet from the damp earth. "Jake, I know you aren't here to entertain or to rescue us, and we've taken up a lot of your time already. But I would really love to go with you to the ruins."

"You would?" He gave her a glance, then continued eating.

"Oh yes! You even said I could go sometime."

"I did?"

"Yes, I think you did. Or you were about to when we were interrupted. I would hate to miss something like that while I'm down here."

He looked steadily at her for a moment, his dark eyes reflecting his distant heritage. She thought that, perhaps, some Native American relative of his had lived in a camp like this, minus the tent and modern equipment, of course.

"Well, okay," he relented finally. "But you can't go without shoes. There's no way you could hike out there."

She looked down at her muddy socks. They were impossible. "Maybe I could borrow some boots."

"Whose? Mine?"

She nodded, then shrugged.

He looked directly at her, made eye contact and laughed. Jake actually threw his head back and laughed. Brit smiled uneasily. "What's so funny?"

"My boots are size eleven." He shook his head, still chuckling. "You really want to go, don't you?"

"Yes." Brit knew she was appearing overanxious, but there was no other way to let him know how she felt.

"Okay, tell you what. Soon as I have a chance, I'll fix those moccasins for you. They'll fit and be better for climbing." He finished eating and headed back to the supplies.

Once again, Brit followed. "Okay. Great. That'll be wonderful."

He washed the pan he'd used for the oatmeal and turned it upside down on the box of utensils, leaving it to dry in the sun. "Fix whatever you want to eat today," he offered as he finished loading a backpack with tools and a camera and small note pad. "Have a good day, Brit. See you later." He seemed too busy to look at her and started away as he spoke.

Brit felt desperate for his attention. "Jake?"

He paused, finally, and looked back over his shoulder at her.

"I'm . . . uh," she halted and stared down at the empty coffee mug in her hands. "Michael and I aren't . . . we argued a lot because we aren't making it."

"Michael?"

"My ex," she explained quickly.

"Your ex-boyfriend?" Jake turned to face her. He hooked his thumbs into his jeans' pockets and rocked back on his heels. "Why are you telling me this, Brit?"

She raised her chin and gazed directly into his

dark eyes. "I want you to know, that's all."

"To know what?" he challenged.

"To know that there's no one in the way, if you're interested." Brit couldn't believe she was saying this, but now was not the time to stop. "I mean, no one on my side. Maybe on yours."

He took a step toward her and the rope looped to his belt rustled against his thigh. "No, no one in the way on my side, if you're interested."

"Not even the one who gave you the bear fetish? A Zuni girl, perhaps?"

"A Zuni grandmother. A very good friend."

"Oh." She flashed him a smile. "That clears up some things."

"I suppose."

"Well . . . are you? Are you interested?" When he didn't answer right away, she thought she'd made the biggest mistake of her life. She felt exposed and stupid. And she wanted to turn and run away as fast as she could.

Slowly Jake nodded and a sly grin spread across his lean face. "Sure. Could be, now that the Michael issue is cleared up. Are you interested?"

She stomped one foot and nearly slid in the mud. "Dammit, Jake! That's why I told you, if you can't figure it out."

He pressed his lips together to hide a smile. "I think I would have, in time. But it's nice to know."

"It is?"

He nodded, and a small grin broke his usual stern expression. "Very. I'll be in before dark and we'll work on those moccasins together. See you."

"Okay." She smiled happily and watched him turn to go. The backpack seemed small on his broad back and the loop of rope flopped against his thigh with every step. She admired the self-assured way he strode across the rocks and the masculine amble of his gait. Caught in his spell, she was unable to turn away from the sight of him until he disappeared down the path and behind a sandstone boulder.

Brit replayed their cryptic conversation in her mind periodically during the next hours, and it gave her strength to face another day with the Romeros. Things would be better when Jake returned, she repeatedly told herself.

Brit spent a great deal of the morning inspecting the changes in the landscape around the campsite after the violent storm. "Mother Nature" was definitely in charge of the canyon. Not only was the small pup tent gone, but rocks had been rearranged, evidence of the powerful forces of this wilderness. Around the camp, there were small piles or lines of stones made by streams rushing down the canyon walls.

There were remarkable changes at the river.

Several of the boulders damming the water into the shallow pool where Brit had bathed yesterday had shifted or been moved entirely, so that the pool was no longer a separate entity from the river. Most amazing, though, was the water level. What was once a peaceful pool and shallow stream had doubled in size and now raged with remarkable speed and strength. Little whitecaps decorated the ripples.

It must have been nearly noon when Rudi and Yolanda emerged from the tent and began poking around the campsite. Brit ignored them and stayed away as long as she could. Facing Yolanda after yesterday's yelling match was the last thing she wanted to do. But, eventually, she decided she must. And she had to do the thing she most despised. Apologize.

Brit approached Yolanda stiffly. "We need to talk, Yolanda."

The always-confident TV star looked uncomfortable. "I have nothing to say to you."

"Maybe not, but I have something to say to you. Believe me, this is hard to do, but I feel it's necessary. We have a ways to go together, and it would be a shame to spend it like this."

"I thought it was pretty peaceful without us talking at all today to mess things up."

"You're right. And it'll be peaceful again soon," Brit promised and took a deep breath before she launched into her mini-speech. "Look, I'm sorry about the argument, Yolanda. I guess

94

I was in a bad mood. Like you, I was worried about Frank and upset about our own hopeless situation. Still, I shouldn't have yelled at you yesterday, and I'm sorry."

Yolanda stared at Brit a moment, then smiled slightly. "I did my share of yelling, too." Her dark eyes softened. "I like somebody who can apologize, Brit. That takes some guts."

"Not really. I just had to do something about it."

"Believe it or not, this whole thing has me pretty upset, too. I know I'm hard to get along with; Rudi lets me know that all the time. So for others, outsiders like you, it's especially tough. You don't know or understand me. I'm temperamental. That's just the way I am."

"That's no excuse. What if I told you that's the way I am, too?"

Yolanda shrugged. "I guess we'd have some problems, huh?"

"You expect people to make exceptions for you because of who you are. But down here, everybody's the same. We're all in a bind until we're rescued."

Yolanda looked contrite and sat down on a rock. "I remember being sort of demanding when I was a little girl back in San Antonio. Even then, I wanted attention. Craved it. My papa would say that in our family of eight there was no room for one to be special. We all had to pitch in together. And we did. I didn't like it, but I did what was necessary. So, you see, I can." She grinned sheepishly. "I just haven't done it in a long time."

"Hey, I know you're accustomed to things being better back in Hollywood," Brit conceded. "You're used to having your way. This is hard for you, I know. But my life is better and easier, back home, too. That doesn't change the hard fact that here we are. Stuck together."

Yolanda toyed with a wet leaf that she picked from the rock. With a little chuckle, she suggested, "I'll bet I could write a doozie of a routine about this. About us and our arguments and our generally rotten situation down here."

Brit laughed lightly. "I'm sure you could."

"So, babe," Rudi broke in. "Do it. Go ahead and write it. That would be great."

Yolanda looked from Brit to Rudi, then back to Brit. A new gleam lit her brown eyes. "You wouldn't get offended if I made jokes about this? I mean, it hasn't always been funny. We've been in a dangerous situation. Still, it could be hilarious."

"We wouldn't mind at all," Brit said honestly. "I think we might enjoy a laugh or two at ourselves. We haven't done much of that lately, either."

"That was how I got attention in our family. We were very poor, and I made jokes about it. We laughed, and it was better." Yolanda's smile revealed a hint of the little girl who laughed her way out of poverty. "If I could get my hands on some paper, I would do it."

"I'm sure Jake has a spare notebook he'd share." Brit motioned toward the large tent. "Plus he has that laptop computer. Maybe he'll let you use it."

"Okay. I'll ask him. I'm glad we had this little talk, Brit." Spontaneously, Yolanda gave her a quick hug.

"I feel better," Brit said.

"Me, too. Now, what's available for lunch? Rudi and I are starved."

Rudi responded as he sorted through the box of food Jake had left out for them. "There's oatmeal or canned tuna."

"Uggh! Come on, Rudi. Let's find something more appetizing." She motioned for him to follow her into the tent where they could go through more supply boxes.

Brit laughed, knowing that they wouldn't find anything more exciting than a jar of crunchy peanut butter or packaged noodles.

Feeling a sense of relief after her conversation with Yolanda, Brit climbed back up into the little cave that had been her shelter from the rain with Jake. Actually it wasn't such a bad place to curl up with a book. There were some warm memories associated with the place, like when Jake had snuggled close to her. She brought a soda and some peanut-butter crackers to nibble and her only book.

Brit was always surprised at how the chill of the early morning melted into extreme heat by midday. She removed Jake's long-sleeved shirt and rolled it up for a pillow. Then she slipped Jake's baggy jeans and mud-coated socks off, and wearing only his T-shirt, stretched out her legs, and wiggled her bare toes in the sun. Ahh, she thought as she settled back. This is much cooler.

She had tucked Gran Bonnie's book into her purse with plans to reread it on the flight to L.A. Fortunately the old book had survived the crash, which made it more special than ever. Soon Brit was transported back to another era. A young woman named Bonnie was trying to resist, but helplessly falling in love with a handsome Indian named KnifeWing. So engrossed was she in Bonnie's life that she didn't notice when Jake returned to camp.

Unable to concentrate on the petroglyph handprints or chipped flint artifacts he found in the Indian ruins, Jake quit work early. He could only think of creating a pair of moccasins for Brit and how it would feel shaping the leather to her slender, bare feet.

When he entered camp, the place appeared deserted. But it didn't take him long to find his trio of charges. He could hear Rudi and Yolanda talking and laughing down by the river. And he spotted Brit tucked away, high in the little cave. He smiled to himself and grabbed what he would need for the moccasins from the tent.

Brit looked up, startled, when his boot scraped a stone. The expression on her face was absolutely peaceful, almost as if she were mesmerized or possibly asleep. Her delicate, doll-like features were relaxed, seemingly on the verge of smiling, but not quite. Her blond hair was rumpled after a couple of days of being tossed about and combed with only her fingers. It was, to him, quite sexy that way. Admittedly, he was intrigued with her. She was the most appealing woman he'd met in a long time. And, with her bare legs stretched out beneath his T-shirt, her appeal was definitely sexy.

"Hi." He tried to sound casual as he climbed up beside her. But the sight of her knotted his stomach and he felt slightly nervous and tight. "Can I join you up here in the eagle's nest?"

She smiled softly, and he wanted to touch that gentle face. "Sure. The eagles have flown, and it's just me."

"Did I wake you?"

"No, I was reading." She checked her left wrist out of habit, then grinned at herself. "My watch broke in the crash, but aren't you off work early?"

99

He leaned against the sandstone wall which arched above them. "That's one of the 'bennies' of this job. No time cards to punch."

"No clocks, therefore no time. Only the sun."

"And the moon," he added. "The natives moved by the earth's natural rhythms. Sometimes that's best. Your body adapts to it quickly and easily." He took the sheet of leather and began cutting it to the shape of her ruined shoes.

"What are you doing?" She peered curiously at his handiwork.

"This will be the flat part that fits your sole. Then I'll add a curved piece to cover your foot. Last will be a tube for your ankle."

"How neat," she marveled as she watched his careful hands measuring and piecing. "Seems so simple."

"Except for this part." He began stitching the sections together with a thin cord. "The Indians usually bead these pieces for decoration before they start. And they use leather strips for sewing instead of cotton thread. But this is all I have, and I think they'll suffice as long as you're here."

"I really appreciate this, Jake. How many people get handmade moccasins?"

He shrugged. "How many crash-land in the Grand Canyon and live to tell? What are you reading?"

"My great-grandmother's book." She held it

up so he could see the title. "This is the one they're making into a movie. I happened to have it in my purse to read on the trip, so I could be familiar with it when I got to the set. I'm supposed to be a consultant on the movie." She chuckled ruefully. "Funny thing happened on the way to L.A."

"You fell into a great hole in the ground." Jake took a stitch and pulled it through the leather.

"It's been an interesting experience," she admitted. "And, contrary to what you might believe, not altogether bad."

"Oh yeah? You like camping with no adequate clothes or equipment?"

"True. It would have been better if this had been a planned trip. But life doesn't always work that way."

"You're learning." He finished the shoe part of one moccasin and started on the ankle section. "Where did your great-grandmother's story take place?"

"Not so far from here, actually. Bonnie ran a trading post somewhere on a remote stretch between Arizona and New Mexico."

"Is it a good story?"

"Very. It's mostly a love story." Brit thumbed through a section she'd just read. "What's strange is that she writes about their monsoon rains and her descriptions are quite similar to the very storm we had yesterday. Violent and cold.

101

She even mentions the way everything smelled afterwards."

"What does she say? Read it to me."

"You sure you want to hear it?"

"Yeah, I like history. I explore it every day."

"Yeah, I guess you're right." Brit scanned several pages until she found the one she wanted to read aloud. *"KnifeWing warned me about the dangerous monsoons."* Brit paused to explain. "KnifeWing was a Zuni leader and friend who saved her life that first winter by bringing food. I don't think they're lovers yet at this point."

"They become lovers?"

Brit nodded.

Jake motioned for her to go on.

Brit cleared her throat and read. *"But I thought I would have enough warning before a bad storm, so I took Sara, who was almost two, in the wagon to a small canyon to gather sunflower seeds. Before I knew it, the sky turned black and a cold, vicious wind blew away the summer's heat."* She looked up at Jake and smiled. "Sound familiar?"

"Exactly." He let the moccasin rest in his lap while he listened. "It's been that way for centuries. The weather patterns, the sight of rain or lightning in the distance, the rainbows arching from horizon to horizon, all are part of what gives us our connection with the people who lived here in the past."

"In a way, knowing gives me a connection

with Bonnie, too. Now I know exactly what she's talking about. And I'm glad so that I can understand her better." Brit turned back to the book. *"I tried to reach the wagon, but it was too late. Ice pellets beat down on us, and I couldn't see the road. Out of the cold mist KnifeWing appeared and hid us in a small cave where we were protected from the storm. Rocks crashed around us as if they were a scourge sent from the heavens."* Brit paused to smile at Jake, then went on. *"And when it was over, our world was washed clean. Even the bushes gave up their sweetest fragrances in thanksgiving for the much-needed water, and the creek swelled with happiness."*

Jake returned to his crude sewing. "That's great, Brit, a real part of history. What I wouldn't give for an account like this from the natives I'm studying who lived in this area."

"There's nothing?" Brit let the book rest in her lap.

"Nothing written. Only petroglyphs."

"Petroglyphs? What are they?"

"Etchings in stone that depict animals they encountered or killed and certain elements of their lifestyles, like tribal or religious figures, enemies, or symbols."

"I'd love to see them."

"You can. When we go to the ruins tomorrow." Jake snipped the last thread and held the finished product up for her inspection. "One down."

"Hey, that's remarkable. It actually looks like a moccasin." Brit sat up and scooted closer. "Let me try it on."

"Let me help." Jake reached for one foot and slipped the soft leather sheath over her toes. Cupping her heel gently with his hand, he worked the body of the boot snugly onto her foot. "There, how's that?" As the moccasin slid over her ankle, his hand naturally moved to her smooth calf.

"Feels wonderful." She admired the hand-crafted boot. "And it fits. I'm impressed."

"So am I." When she raised her leg to inspect it closer, his hand slid further upward. He tried to concentrate on her foot, but his imagination surged to other parts of her anatomy as his fingers touched her knee.

"Are they your first?" She didn't move her leg away from his touch.

His throat constricted and normal conversation was difficult. "I made myself a pair, but these are the first for someone else."

"They're wonderful, Jake," she said softly. "I like them much better than those expensive Italian sandals. Thank you." Spontaneously, she leaned forward and kissed his cheek.

Her warm lips brushed his skin, kindling the embers of a smoldering, well-tended passion. Jake had prided himself in never letting go, never giving in to the desires that once drove him over the brink and into a mistaken relationship and marriage. But today, in the remoteness of this cave, in the sun, touching Brit's smooth feminine skin made him want to gather her to him, to hurl himself into her life without a backward glance.

Jake knew, though, that Brit was different. She was sensitive and smart and beautiful beyond question; she respected him, responded to him; she was here, warmed by the sun and willing. He turned his face so that their lips paired, and he pulled her roughly against him. He couldn't lose her, not yet, not until he'd tasted those sweet lips, that smooth skin, and quenched his masculine thirst with her eager and willing femininity.

Brit had waited for those lips, had dreamed of them caressing hers, yet nothing had prepared her for the jolt of desire that permeated her body, radiating to every limb and culminating in the center of her being. She curved against him, feeling the muscled ridges of his chest on hers, the firm strength of his leg bracing her side. His hand slid up her bare thigh, and she thought she would explode before he even touched her intimately. His lips traveled a sensuous path around her face, her eyes, her cheeks, her chin, back to her lips, murmuring her name with every soft pause. She leaned back against his arm and lifted her chin to give him better access to the pulsing stretch of her neck. His lips created a sweet, leisurely path, assuring her of his loving skills and silently promising more fulfillment than she had ever known.

Brit dropped the book and forgot everything except for Jake's lean, hard body capturing hers and the intensity with which she was responding to his sensuous promises. She wanted more, wanted him to touch her, wanted to know his body and if they could possibly get closer.

"Jake . . ." she murmured, arching her back and urging her aching breasts to him.

"Oh God, Brit . . ." He pressed himself to her and kissed her lips again, this time probing them with the tip of his tongue and sending shock waves through her.

She opened her mouth, allowing the easy, rhythmic thrusting of his tongue, savoring the sweetness and losing herself in a remarkable overflow of passion. She was out of the crude cave, out of the Grand Canyon world, existing only with Jake, her body moving with his, her emotions surging with his. Every thrust sent shock waves through her and excited her senses to the highest point. She wanted him, badly.

They moved and shifted together, wrapping themselves in each other, kisses fiery, breathing heavy and hot. Closer. He buried his kisses against her neck, and she pressed the small of his back, relishing the masculine swell that teased her through their clothes.

His jeans were tight and uncomfortable. Only

one thing would relieve that pressure; only one act would fulfill them both.

He slipped his hand between them, touching her feminine softness. "Brit, I need you."

"Oh Jake . . . yes . . ."

"Are you . . . protected?"

"Yes, are you—" She was thinking of the pill.

She felt, rather than heard, his sigh. He was quiet a moment. Then, "Hell, no! I hadn't planned on this—"

"I have something for you," she admitted shyly. "In my purse—" It was a precaution she had always taken, even with Michael.

He cradled her head, rubbing her cheeks with his thumbs. "You are amazing."

She smiled, feeling flushed and warm, anticipating the culmination of the most intense sensuality she'd ever experienced. Ever. She could hardly wait. "Touch me, Jake." She closed her eyes.

In the moment of silence, of heavy emotion, of the highest anticipation, a sound echoed against the cave's sandstone walls. A frantic sound. A yell. The panicked yell of fear. A man's voice shouting, "Help! Help!"

Jake raised up and listened. All of his other senses were focused on the woman in his arms. But he heard something out of the ordinary. Something unusual. Something that rang deeply in his subconscious.

"Jake! Help us! Somebody! Quick! Oh God, help—"

107

With one quick breath, Jake turned away from Brit and to his feet. "That's Rudi! Something's wrong!"

Brit lay there for a second, cooled by Jake's sudden departure, unsure of what was happening. Except that Jake was gone; another magic moment was destroyed. She wanted to scream, "Jake, come back!" but something logical clicked into her passion-muddled brain and she realized that there was trouble. Rudi needed help. Jake already realized it and was on his way down the rocks to the camp.

In half a minute, Brit was scrambling, barefoot, down the rocks and toward the distraught sounds.

Jake felt a rush of adrenaline that was precipitated by arousal, then fueled by Rudi's frantic calling. When he reached the camp, Rudi was standing on the perimeter, waving with his whole arm for Jake to join him down by the pool.

"What is it?" Jake demanded.

"It's Yolanda! She's washed away in the high water!"

Jake paused only long enough to grab the looped rope.

Chapter Five

Brit was horrified at how quickly the river had turned rampant. The current was much worse now than it was earlier. It was hard to recognize this as the same calm, safe spot she had bathed in yesterday before the storm.

Water, the giver of life, had changed into a violent villain. What once was a lazy stream, ambling through canyons, had become a spirited racehorse, thundering ahead. What once was a wading pool had turned into a runaway wagon, crashing its way over the cliff, taking its passengers along for the wild ride.

At first, Brit couldn't see Yolanda in the expanse of choppy white-capped waves. She feared Rudi was right, that the wild river had swallowed Yolanda and washed her away!

But Jake pointed out the dark-haired woman clinging to a rock, just before the rushing water turned into a raging rapids and proceeded downstream at breakneck speed. Apparently Yolanda had grabbed onto a half-submerged rock at the last minute and now, she desperately clung to it.

"There! There she is!" Jake yelled and started to run around the bank to get closer to her.

"All right!" Rudi yelled, following Jake and waving frantically. "Yeah, babe, hang on! We're coming to get you outta there!"

Brit chased the men to the shore closest to where Yolanda was stranded. They stood on the side, all of them calling frantically to her. "Hang on! Don't let go! You can do it!"

Jake fiddled with the rope for a minute and, aiming carefully, threw it toward her. The looped end fell short. He tried again and again, but each attempt missed her. "Damn! I . . . can't do it!"

Rudi's red hair stood on end and he bounced around as if attached to a rubber band, bounding, waving and calling to Yolanda, urging Jake to "Try again, try again, man!"

"It's no good. This isn't working," Jake muttered. He feared that Rudi would dive into the raging river any minute. And he knew he couldn't rescue them both. "Got to try something else."

Yolanda clung stubbornly while rough water splashed around her shoulders, tugging and pulling at her.

"She can't stay like that," Jake said tightly, knowing full well the tragic consequences if she let go. "We've got to get her off that rock. The danger is that she'll get tired and lose her grip. If she gets caught in that current, we won't be able to keep up with her." He gritted his teeth and didn't utter the other possibility, that of her being pulled under, as he retrieved the rope for another attempt. This time it brushed her shoulder, almost lassoing her, then fell into the water.

Yolanda remained glued to the rock, an expression of absolute fear on her face.

Frustrated, Jake stood still for a moment and studied the situation. He could see that fear had paralyzed her. "She's afraid to move, Rudi. Afraid she'll lose her grip and fall. Afraid to do anything."

"But she'll lose it, anyway," Brit wailed, voicing what everyone knew. "It's only a matter of time. She can't hang on there forever."

"My God, what can we do to help her?" Rudi begged frantically, continuing his rubber-band bouncing from Jake to Yolanda, then back again. "Something. Do anything, man!"

Jake tried to remain calm. "We have to think of something else."

"I've never seen her like this, Jake," Rudi said. "It's like she's frozen to that position."

"Then we have to hurry," Jake decided as he recoiled the rope. "Before she falls."

"Oh God, no! We can't let that happen." Rudi's voice was thick with emotion.

Brit suspected that he was near tears, and near to losing all control, as well. Her heart went out to him. "How are we going to get her?" Brit asked Jake. "The water's too high and wild. It's impossible!"

"There's no other way. We're all the hope she has," Jake said with conviction. "We'll just do it, that's all."

For a moment no one said anything. Only the clamor of the river could be heard, the roar of nature's rage and power. Then, from the distance, Yolanda called in a weak voice, "He-elp me!"

That feeble sound was the impetus they needed. Brit could feel the electric energy spark between them. Emotion welled up to choke her. They *had* to do something quickly for Yolanda and crying wouldn't help at all. Brit forced her own swell of tears back down. They needed brawn right now, raw muscle to overcome the might of the river. But none of them had that kind of strength. They were only human against a vicious force of nature. She looked at Jake and saw something in his face that could combat anything: grit, determination, and resolution. He would not be defeated, and she believed it with all her heart.

"We have to work together on this, or it'll never happen," Jake said as he began unbuttoning his shirt. There was no one who could go except him. He knew it. Rudi was frantic, almost hysterical. Plus, Jake knew that he was probably in better shape than Rudi for such an effort. Besides he would need both Rudi and Brit here, on shore, to help.

Fortunately Brit seemed not as panicked as Rudi and might help calm him.

"I'll go after her." Jake had already decided and his tone left no room for argument. "You two will have to hold the rope and keep us from being washed away. I need to be able to depend on you. So does Yolanda."

"Yes, yes! We'll do it!" Brit confirmed.

Rudi blinked hard and nodded. "Yeah, man. Anything! I'll do anything for her. Hurry!"

"Good." Jake wasn't sure how Rudi would function in this crisis. Right now, he didn't look so hot. Bending down to drag off his hiking boots, he said, "My tennis shoes are in the tent—"

"I'll get them." Brit sprinted off before he even finished the sentence.

Good sign, Jake thought. At least Brit was alert and capable of following orders and reacting. He hoped Rudi wouldn't collapse under the stress. They needed his vigor to pull off this nearly impossible feat.

Rudi stood with his big arms dangling helplessly by his sides, his normally ruddy face pale. "Want me to go out there for her, Jake?"

"No, definitely not! I need you here. You'll have to provide the muscle to hold both of us. Can you do it?"

"Sure. Whatever you need, I'll do it."

"Good. I'll depend on that. Yolanda, too."

Jake stripped down to his briefs while Rudi bounced around again, yelling encouragement to Yolanda.

"Hang on, babe! We're going to get you! Jake's coming out there after you! He'll help you back safely."

Jake glanced at Yolanda. She probably couldn't hear everything Rudi was saying, but his voice and actions would encourage her, showing her that they were doing something positive to rescue her.

Rudi's words sounded so simple. *Jake's coming after you.* But the rescue would not be simple. It was risky for both of them. Anything could happen to plunge them into the swift current. But now wasn't the time for evaluation. They had to act. *Get her,* he repeated to himself. *Get her out.*

Brit moved as fast as she could, slipping in the mud but managing to stay upright as she raced back with the tennis shoes. She halted before an almost nude Jake, a man with a lean body framed with taut muscles and sleek tanned skin from the width of his chest to the length of his sinewy legs. "H-here," she stammered, shoving the shoes into his waiting hands.

"Thanks," He tugged them furiously onto his feet.

Brit tried not to notice the intense masculinity of the man, nor her own stomach-knotting reaction to the sight of him so scantily clad. Get a

114

grip, she told herself firmly. We've got a job to do! And yet, this view of him convinced her that Jake indeed had the ability they needed to combat the dark, swirling waters; he was the only one who could rescue Yolanda. He just *had* to do it. Feeling a mixture of emotions, ranging from pride to fear, she turned away from the magnificent man, back to Yolanda, back to the subject of their rescue.

"Listen up!" Jake grabbed Rudi's and Brit's arms. "I can't do this without your assistance. Both of you will have to hold on with all your might. Rudi, you will have to keep me upright. Wrap the rope behind your back so you can use your body as leverage. Brit, use this boulder to brace yourself and pour all your strength into the pull. Got it?"

Rudi nodded eagerly. "I will, man. Just get her, please."

Jake knotted the rope around his slender waist. "Okay, when I get out there, I'll be your responsibility. I intend to support her, assist her on the way back here, but there's no way I can completely carry her. She'll have to walk with me. Think she can do that?"

"I don't know, man. She's scared of water."

"Does she swim?"

"Nope. Not a lick."

Jake breathed out a curse. "Oh, great. Another strike against us. That's why she's totally panicked." He was already figuring how he

115

might have to force her to move, if she wouldn't come voluntarily. And he wouldn't use gentle encouragement. It might be pretty rough, especially for Rudi to witness. Jake pressed his lips together. He would just do his best and hope it worked.

Brit stared anxiously at Yolanda who continued to cling to the rock.

"Okay, let's do it," Jake said, plunging into the muddy swirls. "Rudi, keep that rope stretched taut, especially when I grab her. Brit, don't let up. Rudi needs you."

"Right." She wanted to hug Jake or give him some sign of her support, but he was already moving into the engorged river. There was no time for emotion. Only action.

As she watched him, Brit was struck by the notion that although Jake was anything but small, right now he appeared vulnerable and frail. A mere man versus a world gone berserk. The waters swirled up Jake's body, past his thighs, hips, waist. When the water reached his chest, he stumbled. Rudi struggled with keeping the rope tight until Jake regained his footing and moved onward. At this point, he seemed to be swallowed by the nemesis, a part of the greater mass, lost in the depths of the universe.

Brit and Rudi watched anxiously in lip chewing, breath-holding silence. Their hands laced side by side on the rope, alternating their strength, pooling their resources for one concentration. Their legs braced together to form one strong base. Mentally and emotionally, they took every toiling step with Jake.

Just before he reached Yolanda, a deep current grabbed him and whirled him around. Brit gasped and loosened her grip.

"Hold it! Don't let go! Steady, man, steady." Rudi kept up his encouragement to Yolanda. All the while, he created a buttress with his legs set far apart to keep the rope tight. As Jake lunged and stumbled, Rudi maintained the line that kept him on track toward Yolanda.

"Keep going," Brit murmured and renewed her grip. She released her breath only when Jake started moving forward again.

Finally, he stood before Yolanda, wavering a little in the push of the current. Neither of them moved for a long minute, and Brit wanted to scream with the tension. Yolanda's attention was glued to Jake. He was probably talking to her, instructing, persuading. She shook her head.

"Come on, babe," Rudi muttered to his wife. "Come on."

Yolanda shook her head again.

"Go with him, babe. Go." Rudi's voice rose and he bellowed, "Go, dammit!"

"What are they doing?" Brit asked. "Why won't she go?"

"Too scared. Too scared to budge."

"But Jake needs for her to walk. What'll he do? How'll he get her—"

"Go on . . . you can do it, babe . . ." Rudi seemed mesmerized. He spoke as if in a trance, a direct communication with Yolanda, commanding her, pleading with her at some other level, for she certainly could not hear him.

Abruptly Jake raised his fist in a signal to them. This was it. No more waiting.

"Hold on!" Brit commanded, knowing instinctively that he was going to force Yolanda. Rudi tensed as Jake grabbed Yolanda, pulling her into the water with him.

She struggled frantically and fought him. Arms and legs flailed above the high water line. Yolanda bobbed underwater, then popped up again. The two of them teetered, Yolanda clambering onto Jake's body, trying, it seemed, to climb onto his shoulders.

They grappled. Jake grabbed her roughly and, pinning her arms to her sides, forced her back against his chest, keeping her from clutching at him. She had little choice but to walk—stumbling and struggling—through the water with him toward shore. Jake leaned against the rope, depending almost entirely on the muscle power of Rudi and Brit to pull him across the deadly currents.

It took them about twenty minutes to reach safety. It seemed to Brit like hours. When they were close enough, Yolanda's verbal barrage directed at Jake could be heard. She was furious with him, and left no doubt about her feelings or her future actions toward him. Finally they stumbled ashore and fell, exhausted, onto the pebbles.

Rudi grabbed Yolanda, hugging and cuddling her. "Oh, babe, my sweet girl, thank God you're safe!"

Gasping for breath, Jake looked at the two in dismay. "Sweet? Ha!"

Brit knelt beside Jake, tears streaming down her face. When he turned his weary eyes toward her, she laughed, unable to stop. "You did it!" She felt overjoyed and relieved and weak and exultant all at once. She wanted to hug him but tentatively placed a hand on his shoulder instead. "Terrific . . . great rescue . . ."

He shivered at her touch and tugged at the wet knotted rope at his waist. "We did it together. All of us. I did nothing alone."

Feeling a little rebuffed, she bent her head and helped him untie the knot at his waist. Her shaky fingers brushed his wet muscled waist. "You're cold. You need . . . to get warm."

"Yeah." His devilish dark eyes met hers. "Only one sure way to prevent hypothermia. Body heat to body heat."

"I'm sure a blanket will do nicely." Brit quickly reached for his clothes. How could he think of anything else at a time like this? "Here's your shirt."

Jake nodded at Yolanda. "She's going to need some warmth quickly, or she'll go into shock.

She can wear some of my clothes. You gather the blankets, and I'll gather some wood to start a fire." He skinned off the wet tennis shoes and slid his legs into the dry jeans.

"You scum!" Yolanda yelled when he stood to zip his jeans. "You hurt me out there! You forced me against my will and hurt my arms. I'll bet I have bruises all over from your manhandling! When we get out of here, I'll sue—"

"Nothing like a little heartfelt gratitude," Jake murmured to Brit.

"Yolanda!" Rudi yelled. He grabbed her shoulders roughly and shook them. "Yolanda, shut up! Jake saved your life, And he risked his own to do it. If you're going to sue anyone, sue us all, including me! Because I was a part of this life-saving effort, too."

Brit was amazed at Yolanda's outburst, but even more astonished at Rudi's uncharacteristic assertiveness with her. His defense of their rescue, including Jake's necessary roughness, impressed her.

Yolanda glared at Rudi, shocked into silence by his reaction to her complaints.

"It's true, babe," he said in a quieter tone. "I love you so much, I was scared silly. And I'll admit, I wasn't worth much. Brit helped keep me in there. But Jake's the one who saved you. So leave him alone. You aren't going to sue anybody here."

Sudden tears filled Yolanda's eyes and, in an

120

emotional switch, she began to cry. She also started to shake all over.

Jake nudged Brit. "That's it She's going into shock. We've got to get her warm—quick. Come on. Let's get busy."

They all worked steadily for the next hour with one goal: to keep Yolanda from going into shock. They dressed her in Jake's insulated underwear and a heavy flannel shirt, wrapped her in a blanket, and filled her with hot chocolate and warm soup. Jake started a small fire, and the four of them huddled around it, sipping hot chocolate and eventually rehashing the events of the afternoon.

"Man, we were so lucky today," Rudi said, kissing Yolanda's hand repeatedly. "I'm sorry about the way she acted. She didn't mean what she said out there, Jake. She just didn't understand—"

"Thank you, Mr. Rudi Romero," Yolanda interrupted, giving him a commanding glare. "But I can speak for myself. Never had any problem with the mouth." She turned a timid smile toward Jake. "Rudi has helped me to realize that I put everyone at risk today, especially you, Jake. And I know now why you had to rough me up today. In spite of the inevitable bruises, I do fully appreciate what you, and everyone, did. And I'm sorry I cussed you out!"

As usual, she had everyone laughing.

Jake put another piece of wood on the fire.

121

"Aw, shucks, Yolanda." He continued her banter with an effective drawl. "I had to do something. You might still be perched out there on that rock if I hadn't dragged you off."

"No," she answered seriously. "I wouldn't still be there, and you know it. I couldn't have held on much longer. We all know what could have happened today. That was pretty close. In fact, that's two close ones in less than a week."

"I'd say you're damned lucky, Yolanda," Brit said. "Jake didn't mean to bruise you, but you fought him pretty hard. I know a lot of women who would fight like that to get *into* his arms!"

She grinned. "Quite a trick, huh? Still, I'll admit I was damned scared."

"I guess you still have more to accomplish on this old earth, babe," Rudi offered philosophically. "A mission not yet done."

Yolanda ran her fingers through her still wet hair, trying to dry it. "Do you really believe that?"

"Sure. My grandmother used to say that everyone has a mission on earth." Rudi served everyone more hot chocolate. "And when there's a close call like that, the mission hasn't yet been accomplished."

"I can't imagine what in the world my mission could be," Yolanda scoffed.

"Why, you make people laugh," Jake said. "It keeps the human spirit up. For some, it's even proven to be physically as well as emotionally healing."

"Oh yeah? Cure your heart attack with a routine from Yolanda!" she joked.

"Or, cure your heart *ache* by laughing with Yolanda," Brit corrected.

"Think I could do a routine about this . . . about what happened to us today?" Yolanda asked.

"From my perspective," Rudi grumbled, taking his seat next to hers, "it wasn't very funny."

"From my perspective, perched on a rock," Yolanda began teasingly, "you guys were like the Keystone Kops, running around, jumping, yelling, finally getting a rope. It's amazing you got anything done!"

Brit recalled her peaceful bath yesterday witnessed only by a bird until Jake came along. "What about the perspective of a hawk watching us today? I'll bet he thought we were strange, running around like that."

"Yeah," Yolanda chuckled and lapsed into her story-telling voice. "Hey, how about this? A couple of hawks are up there spinning around, catching air currents over the Grand Canyon when they spot a couple of humans diddling around in an overgrown swimming pool." She paused and looked at Rudi with a girlish giggle. "When all of a sudden, one of those humans starts floating away. The one who's left gets his buddies, and they lasso the one who fell in." She paused again, testing her punchline timing.

"Which shows that diddling can be dangerous . . . unless you've got a rope." Although the group laughed, she dismissed them with one hand. "Aw, it needs some work, but maybe . . ."

"You forgot about the part where you wouldn't leave the rock," Rudi added. "I thought for a few minutes that you'd laid an egg out there and didn't want to abandon your nest."

"Hey, that's not bad," Yolanda said. "You want to be my writer? But seriously, folks, I want to thank you all for making it possible for me to be here, planning a goofy version of what happened today."

"Only you could make us laugh about it," Brit said.

Yolanda yawned and stood to warm her backside by the fire. "After this most eventful day, I'm pooped. I think I can sleep tonight even in that cold, uncomfortable tent."

She approached Jake. "I think a hug is in order for the hunk who saved my life." Before he could react, Yolanda swept her arms around him in a big bear hug. When she stepped back, she wiped a tear from each eye. Then she hugged Brit, too. It was a tender moment, and obviously a rare one for Yolanda, so she quickly made light of the situation. "Hey, better catch my beauty zzz's. Tomorrow might be the day we're rescued. G'night all."

Rudi shook Jake's hand with his big mitt and hugged Brit, too, then followed Yolanda into the big tent.

Jake nursed the small fire, which sputtered with damp wood.

"I'm glad everything turned out okay," Brit commented.

"Um-hummm. Of course."

"You did an admirable thing today, Jake."

"As I said earlier, I couldn't have done anything by myself. It was a joint effort. We all did it."

"Well, Rudi and I couldn't have saved her by ourselves, either. I was very proud to know you today."

Jake stood up and stretched. He felt uncomfortable listening to Brit's compliments and knew only one way to stop them. "I'm tired, too. Are you ready for bed?"

"Sure." Brit stood and turned to pick up the sleeping bag she'd wrapped around herself.

Jake caught her arm and slipped it over his shoulder, pulling her against him. His arms curved around her waist. "To bed in the loft?"

"Yep," she nodded, leaning into the warm masculine strength of his body. It felt good to be in his arms. "It's as safe as any place around here. Safer than most."

"Together?"

Her heart pounded, and she smiled in the darkness. "Are you asking permission?"

"It isn't my usual course of action, but down here, I feel that everything is at risk. Including us. Except for tonight."

"I hate risk," she whispered. "I prefer a sure thing."

"Sorry, no promises. Except one."

"Yes?"

"It'll be good. Tonight."

Brit's breath caught in her throat, and she turned her face down. She could feel his breathing, the steady rise and fall of his chest. She'd never done anything like this, with someone she knew so little. But she'd never known a man she'd been more attracted to, anyone she'd respected more. Anyone she'd wanted more.

This afternoon, they'd come close, so very close to intimacy. She'd been willing then. Oh, so willing.

"Brit . . . beautiful Brit . . ." His voice was low, almost a whisper.

She raised her eyes and looked at his shadowed face. The angles picked up the flickering light from the campfire with hints of the shaded slope of his jawline. His eyes were dark, inviting, sexy. The man was mysterious in some ways, bold in others. She desired him more than she had desired any man. She wanted him, completely and thoroughly, wanted him tonight.

"Yes, Jake?"

With one finger under her chin, he gently lifted her face until their lips met. Firm and cool, they pressed against her mouth. His tongue slid across her lower lip and she opened for his

126

delicious invasion. The sensuous stroking of his tongue against hers sent tides of passion flowing fresh and new between them.

"Yes, Jake," she murmured breathlessly when he took his kisses to her cheeks.

"Hmmm?"

"Sometimes you have to go on intuition," she murmured as his lips brushed hers. "My intuition says yes tonight."

"Yes, yes, yes," he murmured and picked her up, sleeping bag and all, and carried her to the foot of their rocky loft where they had to begin their climb to the cave.

Chapter Six

She took his hand and kissed the palm, then placed it on her cheek. The warmth from his body radiated to hers.

Jake spread his hand beneath her chin and his fingertips stroked her cheeks, her neck, the sensitive area between her breasts. He kissed her lips lightly. "Hmmm, Brit, I want to know the real you, the beautiful you. Let's get rid of this shirt."

The backs of his fingers nudged her responsive skin as he unbuttoned the flannel shirt. Her creamy breasts stood high and firm, their nipples erect as if proudly acclaiming her womanhood. Unable to resist their rounded allure, he caressed them lightly as his hands scooted the shirt off her shoulders.

She was fair and breathtakingly beautiful with a special feminine charm which, in itself, was a minor miracle here in his rough world. He appreciated her, cherished her as he would a gift, an unexpected pleasure in his life. He had expected to work this summer, work with no relief, no companionship, no beautiful woman. Now he had more than he could deal with, much more than he could resist in Brit. He was beyond trying. He had dreamed of her sleeping alone, and longed for her next to him. But, it had been a fantasy.

Jake had forgotten how he could feel in the arms of a woman, especially one who appealed to him on all levels, not just sexual. And here was Brit, eager for him, a blond delight who wanted him as he wanted her.

She stood trembling before him, both from the exposure of her partial nudity to the cool night air and from the erotic strokes of Jake's admiring hands. Making low murmurs, he left no doubt that he adored every inch that he touched. She thrilled to that knowledge and yearned for more. Much more. His hands drew along her ribs, fingers spread wide, then moved lower. She loved the firmness of his touch.

"Take these off, too," he breathed, unsnapping the jeans she wore. His jeans. One hand deftly unbuttoned the fly with easy familiarity while the other slid behind her and forced the jeans slithering to the ground.

She shivered, and he took delight in her reactions as his palms roamed her soft curves. He was like a potter, molding her body into the perfect female image. The perfect creation was at his fingertips. The darkness magically transformed her into willing artist's clay — soft, pliant, moist. With every caress, she became, in his clumsy hands, exactly what he wanted her to be. Perfection.

"My turn," she said with a certain eagerness, starting at the bottom shirt buttons at his waist and working her way up his chest to the pulsing V at his neck. She opened the shirt and kissed the muscled stretch of his chest, traveling from one tight male nipple to the other.

His skin was sleek, and kissing it was like pressing her lips to silk. Free of any but the faintest of body hair, her lips skimmed lightly, tasting and savoring with every kiss. He smelled fresh, like a walk in the desert rain when the earthy fragrances mingled. She ran her tongue around his nipples, and he tasted faintly of moss and nutmeg. The unusual combination was heady and erotic.

After discarding his shirt, Brit slowly unsnapped the front fly of his jeans and proceeded to remove them, too. Not daring to look at him, actually unable to see much of him in the dark, she settled for touching. Shy at first, Brit reached around him and covered each slender buttock with her palms, pressing him to her. The swell of his masculinity urged against her belly, exciting her, thrilling her with anticipation.

"Oh yes, Jake," she murmured, holding him firmly to her. He quivered against her and she thrilled to his reaction.

130

Jake held her, running his hands down her back and over the curve of her fanny. "You'd better get into the sleeping bag before you get chilled."

Brit followed his directions and watched Jake get himself ready for her. His actions were sensuous for, at this angle, his lean, smooth body caught just enough flickers of light from the campfire to reveal the masculine shapes she so desired.

He slid into the sleeping bag with her and, for a moment, there was no contact. Neither touched the other. But their expectations were strong, almost tangible, and the height of desire bridged the small space between them. The moment was filled with an increased tension, a homage to the basic elements of physical attraction between man and woman when they both realized the dominance of passion.

Then the modest separation was closed as Jake moved to encompass her length with his. Brit felt his body with every alert fiber of her being. From top to bottom, chest to pelvis, shoulder to thigh, they met and mingled. Even their legs and feet entwined. His energy reached out to her, surrounding her. She rejoiced in his masculine embrace and melded her body to his boldness.

His lips captured hers with urgent passion. There were no more hesitant nor gentle brushes. His mouth took hers, trying different angles, drinking in her sweetness as if he could never get enough. He was instinctively teaching her how to kiss him, how to respond to, how to please him. She was thrilled and somewhat amazed with the new sensations cascading through her body. And the kisses, each and every one, increased the level of desire coursing through her veins.

"Tell me," he said between delicious kisses. "Tell me how you feel right now."

Brit nearly laughed out loud at his outrageous suggestion. How could she think at a time like this? She'd never been asked how she felt in the midst of passion. But she'd never felt such powerful passion as at this moment. She'd never realized it could be so good, *this* good.

Now that Jake was asking, she was curious to examine her feelings, and willing for him to know. "Excited . . ." she began tentatively. Then she added, breathlessly, ". . . and a little nervous, maybe."

"Nervous? Why?" His hands caressed her breasts, rubbing the tips with a gentle rhythm of his thumbs.

She could hardly think past her body's reactions to his caressing. "Nervous that we're finally here, just you and me, alone. That the moment's now."

"It's what you wanted, isn't it?" His hands traced her ribs and explored her back, massaging gently.

"Yes . . . didn't you?"

"Wanted you from the beginning," he confirmed as he stroked her hips, then her thighs. He relished touching what he had only watched until now.

"Yes, oh, yes—" She took a quick breath as he ventured to more intimate parts of her body.

He spread one large hand over her belly, digging his fingers into the curls at her feminine juncture. "Me, too. I want . . ." His hand went lower, fingers slipping between her thighs. "You. Want you now."

"I want . . . you, too. Want to please you, Jake." She'd never thought of lovemaking in this way.

Michael had never asked how she felt, never seemed to want to please her, just her alone. And she had never felt the urge to please him, either. They just went at lovemaking like anything else they did together, each seeking an individual pleasure from the experience. Nothing was shared. Michael usually took the lead, and she followed without question or examination of her own feelings.

Now that Jake was asking about her feelings, she was forced to examine why they were here and what was their purpose. Was this just a sexual experience, merely for the pleasure, or was there more to this encounter between her and Jake? She wanted to believe the latter.

Miraculously, any inhibitions she harbored with this man she hardly knew fell away like their discarded clothes on the cave floor. There was nothing between her and Jake; their relationship was merging, both physically and emotionally. *Together*. And that was all that mattered.

Brit felt free, as if she were just now discovering her true nature, both her sensual nature and her inner self. These intensely personal elements merged to become one Brit, one liberated, thoroughly alive woman, reveling in her own awakened passion, in her sexuality. She could be herself and enjoy this relationship with Jake.

While she savored the erotica of the moments, enhanced by her own imagination, he slid between her legs and pressed himself into her with such a sudden thrusting that it took her breath away. Curiously, this joining with Jake seemed to be the culmination that her mind and body craved. Together they were fire and spirit, emotion and senses, man and woman. They were together, the way they were meant to be.

Her desires rushed to the ultimate brink that she had so often missed in her relationship with Michael. Her head reeled, her body sang with a new vibrancy. She dug her hands through his hair and moaned low, hoping the wind would carry their sounds of love away, to the towering walls of stone, and on to the sky.

His hands circled her waist, reaching under her hips, lifting, forcing himself fully into her until she moaned again with abounding pleasure.

Again and again he drove into her, rocking

them together to the ledge of sensibility. She clung to him, pressing herself to him, going with him all the way. She reached higher and higher, ascending to the wildest heaven she had ever known. She wanted this experience, this marvelous encounter never to end. *Together forever!*

And when the rapture gripped them, it sent them over the edge and into a swirling of intensity and sensation that combined lust and joy and zeal and . . . love. Love of everything and everyone; love beyond description; love of life.

Brit had never known such depths of feeling. She wanted to cry or shout or laugh wildly for joy. Tears burned her eyes and she squeezed them shut, just as she held him tightly to her, in her.

When it was over, a radiant glow warmed them, and they lay in each other's arms for a long time. Jake held her tenderly, still kissing her occasionally, but gently now, and lovingly.

Brit returned his sweet kisses, sometimes pressing her lips to his neck or chest. She wondered if, for a moment, she had lost consciousness in the intensity of her sexual frenzy. She felt as if something had carried her out of this world, away from this sleeping bag in a cave and to some warm, wonderful cloud-like heaven.

They had flown away together. And now they were back, bare bodies heated, the cold night air on their faces. Together.

Brit felt like a different person. Not only had

she been introduced to the most terrific sex she'd ever experienced, but she had been freed to experience life and love at its ultimate. The highest and the best. And they were hers to take, hers to have for this night. With Jake.

She nestled in his arms, comfortable in their new relationship, feeling no regrets nor doubts. It had been right; she would always believe that. Sleep came like a solace, a blanket of contentment in a life of turbulence and ruggedness. Her confusion was gone. Jake gave her a new self-worth and ultimately, a new self. That was liberating to her soul. She would always be grateful. She would always remember this encounter, and Jake.

"Do you want to go . . ."

The lightest feather-breath tickled her ear, and Brit fought the heavy sleep that tugged at her subconscious. Still that feather pestered her ear. She brushed at the pest.

"Hmmm?" she mumbled, not awake, but automatically pulling the covers over her head.

Something skimmed her ear again. "Brit . . . go with me?"

"Go home?"

"No. Not that." His voice rumbled in her ear. "Not yet."

Something in the tone, or perhaps the sound of her own voice, woke her. Brit opened her eyes to the dim light of morning. The cave. The Grand Canyon. Jake. "Jake?" She turned to find him smiling down at her.

His dark, hooded eyes contained traces of sleep, and his touchable jet hair was still disheveled from a night of tossing on the pillow with her. His voice sounded hoarse in the early morning quiet. "Do you want to go to the cliff dwellings with me. If not, you can sleep all day. It's okay." He said it with a smile, as if he expected her to turn over and close the shades on the day.

After last night, though, Brit was inspired not to miss a thing, even a moment, with Jake. He was too vital, too involved, too interesting. Her eyes widened. "Of course, I want to go with you. I told you I did."

"But I thought you'd forgotten. Or lost the urge."

She smiled sexily. "I'll never forget. And I haven't lost any urges."

"That's reassuring to know," he said as he stretched out beside her on top of the sleeping bag. Propping his head on one hand, he stroked her hair with the other. "You're beautiful in the morning. You still have a little glow after last night . . ." One masculine finger drew a light line down her cheek.

Brit blushed. "I'm still breathless after last night."

"So am I," he admitted with a slight grin. "But I'm glad to know all your urges are still intact." He brushed a strand of hair from her forehead, kissed the cleared spot, then her nose and lips. With slow reverence, he peppered kisses over her face until their lips made contact.

Amazingly, the power of passion clicked on again and they kissed deeply, tongues battling, senses awakening. When he finally raised his head, she realized that one of his legs was draped over hers and she was breathless again. She pushed against his chest and her finger tapped his nose. "Give me a chance to wake up and catch my breath." She meant, "I need time," and he seemed to realize it, for he shifted to give her some space.

"This is all your fault, you know. You cast a spell with those green eyes. And when I look into them, I see myself . . . falling."

She laughed at his verbal images. She couldn't imagine Jake Landry falling anywhere, much less into her spell. If anything, he was the one with the magnetism, and she was the one drawn. But she was determined to refrain, for now, until she had sorted out this sudden relationship, if that's what it was. Even if it were just a fling for both of them, that was okay, too.

"How long have you been awake?" she asked.

"Long enough ago to make the coffee."

She squirmed and tried to sit up. "Coffee sounds great."

"And oatmeal." He sounded hopeful. "I worked up a powerful appetite during the night.

So did you."

"I'll settle for coffee."

"No appetite?"

"Not for oatmeal." She ran her hand under his shirt and over his chest.

He shuddered beneath her fingertips. "Shall we stay awhile?"

"No. You have work to do. And you promised to take me along. You aren't getting out of that."

He shifted and lay with one elbow propping up his head. "If you're going with me, you'll do best to dress in layers. As cool as it is now, it'll be scorching by midday."

"Right. I'm learning about this strange country down here. And about the people, too. Do you happen to have a clean T-shirt I can wear?"

"Sure." He motioned for her to wait under the covers until he brought clean underwear for her. When he got back, he also had half a cup of coffee for her.

"Ah, warm sustenance," she said, gratefully clutching the cup.

"How about a quick cold bath before we dress?" he suggested as he gathered items he thought they might need today.

"Good idea." Brit scrutinized Jake while she sipped her coffee. She watched his careful hands, and remembered how her body responded to his touch when they were making love. *Making love*. She liked the way that sounded. Especially when she thought of lovemaking with

Jake. It sounded as it felt, just right.

He was the most knowledgeable and interesting man she had met in a long time. And now that they were lovers, she knew that he was the sexiest man she had ever known. No, the most sensual; the most romantic; the most . . .

"Ready for a cold dousing?"

She nodded bravely and, wrapped in a blanket, followed him to the river's edge. The place looked different now. It was calmer and the water level was lower. And it was, as Jake promised, cold.

They dressed warmly, in layers, and shared a breakfast of coffee, oatmeal, and camp toast. Brit ate a little to satisfy Jake, and they headed for the cliff dwellings.

"Where are they?"

"Not far. About half a mile."

Brit eagerly took off, not even considering the distance they would walk. A week ago, she would have grumbled and complained that half a mile was a long way. She followed Jake wearing his clothes, his underwear, his handmade moccasins. And strangely, she felt absolutely content, completely at ease with the world.

For the first time in her life, she had made love with a man she had known less than a week. And yet, she felt closer to Jake than to anyone, even Michael. Closer emotionally. She was attuned to Jake, confident in him, and interested in his life and the way he worked and made decisions.

Yesterday, watching him orchestrate Yolanda's rescue, was a marvel, she realized in retrospect. He had been amazingly calm and confident. He'd known exactly what to do, what would work with the people and circumstances. She admired someone who could take a bad situation and make it better than expected. Jake had done that. She didn't care what he said about the rescue being teamwork. She knew he had been instrumental in saving Yolanda's life. And she was fascinated by him, so fascinated that she'd made love with him, an almost-stranger.

Those moments in his arms would not be forgotten. Ever. She would never forget him, even when they were far, far away from each other. Her thoughts jerked to a halt. Whatever made her think of their parting? As much as she wanted to go home, the thought of leaving Jake, especially after last night, was overwhelming and depressing.

Back home . . . to what? No real job. To whom? Michael? Brit shuddered at the thought and knew she could never make love to him again after last night. Michael was history.

Here, everything was simple, basic, and natural. Even she was natural. She had worn no makeup all week, and yet Jake had found her beautiful. She had not done her hair all week. No conditioners. No styling lotion. No crimping. No hair dryer. And yet, Jake had found her irresistible. With him, she actually felt beautiful.

He halted ahead of her and pointed to what looked like a sheer wall. "There it is."

"Where?"

"Way up. The cliff dwelling. See it?"

She looked again, closer. There, wedged into a large arch in the tan sandstone, was a network of crumbling brown bricks. Their colors blended with the stone walls, and she would never have noticed them if he hadn't pointed them out. The entire construction was large, perhaps two or three stories high.

"Looks like an apartment building," she said. "How do you get up there?"

"No elevator for this old-fashioned apartment building. There probably were ladders here at one time. Fortunately, those resourceful early fellows chiseled steps into the wall. We'll use them."

Brit moved closer and narrowed her eyes at the worn niches in the stone wall. "You've got to be kidding. This is a mountain-goat path."

"Nope. It's for people. I use them all the time and my feet are bigger than yours."

"Why did they build way up there? Why not here, closer to the stream?"

"For protection."

"From whom? Big-footed people with a fear of heights?"

"Damn! I forgot the rope. Can you follow me and hug the wall?"

142

"Yeah. Right. I have a feeling that hugging will never be the same for me." Brit eyed the sheer barrier with skepticism as Jake began to scale it easily. "Jake . . ."

She had trusted him completely until this moment. Now she wasn't sure. This looked tough. The most athletic endeavor she ever accomplished was riding the stationary bike in the gym.

And yet, he encouraged her, instructed her every step. "Come on, Brit. It isn't as bad as it looks. The wall slants, so it's easy to lean into it. And, with your moccasins, you should have pretty good footing. Just don't look down."

Brit observed with apprehension as Jake placed one foot, then the other, in the tiny steps. "Looks so simple when you do it," she murmured.

He called down to her. "The Anasazi did it. You can, too."

"Who're the Anasazi?"

"The ones who lived here first, over seven hundred years ago."

Brit propped her hands on her hips and glared up at him. The gauntlet had been tossed. The challenge offered. And Brit wouldn't be bested, especially by the unknown Anasazi. She would climb that damn wall. Or else. She placed one moccasined foot in the prehistoric step and heaved herself up.

Slowly, carefully, one foot above the other,

143

leaning against the wall as Jake instructed from above, Brit managed to make it to the ledge where Jake waited for her. "Do I dare ask how we get down?" she muttered, taking his offered hand and stepping up beside him.

"Don't worry about that now," he advised, smiling proudly at her. "You did great, Brit."

She clutched him. "Tell me I don't have to go down that way! I'm too scared to even look down."

He pulled her close to him. "You can sit on your butt and slide down," he teased. "Now, take a look from here. It's a great view."

"Hold me." Nervously, Brit leaned against Jake and gazed tentatively over the ledge that she had just climbed.

Her hawk's-eye view revealed the trail they'd taken along the stream. The water level had gone down considerably since yesterday, so that the incident with Yolanda now seemed almost like a nightmare fantasy. In the distance was also a low roaring sound. "Do I hear a waterfall?"

"Come over here and you can see it." Jake led her to the far end of what amounted to a small patio in front of the ancient cliff dwelling. Standing behind her, hands poised casually on her shoulders, he pointed between a pair of crimson boulders to a silver spray of water leaping into a turquoise pool.

"Magnificent!" she breathed, caressing the hand that rested on her shoulder. The tall red and buff buttes had a certain fluidity about them, as if they had been molded in mud by some giant hand and left to harden. The water that fell between them was tinted blue and made the whole scene appear to be a well-designed movie set for Shangri-la. "I wish we could get closer."

"We can take a dip, if you want to. Later. After work." He knelt down and began unloading items from his backpack.

"I would love to swim, if it's safe." She couldn't forget the risk Yolanda and Rudi took yesterday with the water so high.

"We'll check it out. Should be okay today."

Gaining some degree of confidence, she walked the length of the patio. "This place is like a fortress. I can understand how it was so secure for the Anasazi. You can see everything in every direction. Can I go on inside, or should I wait for you?"

"Sure, go on. Just don't touch anything. Leave everything as it is, so I can document it as we find it."

"Why are the doors so small? Were these people very short?"

"They were a few inches shorter than today's average American. The doors were purposely made small so that a visitor or enemy would have to stick his head in first, identifying himself, or back in. Either way, the dweller would have a chance to protect him or herself."

"Pretty clever." Brit stepped through the open doorway of the Indian ruin and into another era. Seven hundred years ago was before the Pilgrims landed, before the Jamestown settlement, even before Columbus's voyage to America. She was both awed and humbled by the nearly unfathomable stretch of time since the Anasazi had built this little fortress castle and lived here with their families.

The rooms were eerie and quiet, occupied by leaves and litter of the present and whispers of the past. She walked carefully past a smoke-blackened wall, stained by an indoor grill or fireplace. Apparently this had been the kitchen. In a corner, she spotted fragments of a basket containing a few pieces of dried corn. Could it be possible? Corn that was over seven hundred years old? He had told them of finding dried corn, but she couldn't believe it.

"Jake? What about this corn?"

When he didn't answer, she knew he was too far away to hear. She bent down and wandered through the next doorway into the adjoining room. To one side, as if it had been recently abandoned by the owner, stood a huge clay pot, too big for her arms to encircle. It was reddish brown and undecorated, obviously a utilitarian item. She paused, thinking she heard something. "Jake? Check out this pot."

She glanced around and saw that Jake was not there. Just the wind, she decided, and continued her exploration. The next room was low-ceilinged and actually built against the back wall of the cave. The entire cave wall served as a prehistoric mural and was covered with ancient drawings. Brit was amazed as her eyes scanned images of recognizable animals, human figures, several clear handprints, and many unfamiliar symbols that probably completed the ancient story on the wall. These must be the petroglyphs he had told her about.

A flicker of blue on the heavily littered floor caught her eye. As she stooped to pick it out of the scattered potsherds and debris, she heard a faint noise again. Thinking it was Jake finally coming to join her, she called, "I'm in here."

She held the object in her palm and examined it closely. A large scalloped seashell was decorated with a mosaic of turquoise and coral chips. Brit was amazed. In her hand, she held a seven hundred-year-old ornament! Perhaps it was a gift between lovers; maybe a mother gave it to her daughter as a keepsake. It had a history, a story. What was it? Where did it come from?

How would a seashell get here, at least five hundred miles from the nearest ocean. And a mile deep in the Grand Canyon wasn't exactly on an ancient trade route. Brit's heart pounded. Even she knew that this was truly a remarkable find.

That noise again.

"Brit, what do you have?"

She looked up, startled to suddenly have Jake so near. In her excitement to show him what she had found, she stumbled and the ornament slipped from her hand and fell to the floor.

He lunged forward. "Hey, I told you not to touch anything."

"Oh, no!" She knelt to retrieve the ancient treasure among the litter, praying that it wasn't broken.

Jake knelt with her. "What is it? Did you break it?"

Brit hadn't seen him look so intimidating since the day they arrived and he had stopped the fight between Rudi and Frank. With a shaky hand, she picked up the mosaic shell. Miraculously, it was intact. "Sorry, so sorry," she murmured, again and again.

Jake reached for it, cradling her hands in his. "Let's see."

"I should never have touched it. I . . . don't know what happened. I was hearing strange noises. And when I saw this colorful thing on the floor, I just couldn't help picking it up. It drew me, like some kind of magic. I hope I didn't ruin it with fingerprints. Anyway, I was hearing noises and, for a minute, I thought that image on the wall was making sounds, like warning me to leave. Does that ever happen in these ruins? Do you ever feel like the spirits of those who lived here are coming back to haunt the place?"

He squeezed her hands affectionately. "Oh God, Brit! Looks like you've discovered a real treasure in here."

"I'm sorry I touched it."

"It's okay." He bent his head and looked closely at the shell. Then he looked at her and smiled. "Beautiful . . ." Before either of them knew what had happened, his lips were on hers, pressing, searching, tasting, feeling. Excited . . . happy.

Another noise, something hissing.

She squirmed. "Did you hear that, Jake?"

He raised his lips from hers just enough to mutter, "Yeah, old Kokopelli's jealous."

"Who?"

"Kokopelli. The fellow with the flute on the wall. He's the god of fertility, and I think he's jealous of me, getting your kisses." Jake bent his head for another.

Lost in time, they embraced on the floor of the cave room, letting the kiss carry them away. Abruptly, the rustling noise interrupted them and couldn't be ignored any longer. It was too close.

This time, they both looked up and around for the intruder.

Brit gasped as she stared into the beaded orange and black face of the largest, ugliest lizard she had ever seen. She closed her eyes and screamed.

* * *

149

Brit agreed to return to the interior of the ruins only when Jake checked and assured her the lizard was gone, and the room was safe.

"That was the biggest lizard I've ever seen. Like one of those things on fantasy-horror movies."

"It was just a clumsy old Gila monster. And he, or his kin, has probably been the prototype for plenty of movie monsters."

Brit was not amused. She continued to anxiously watch the large hole in the corner where Jake claimed the lizard had disappeared. "I don't know when I've ever been so scared."

Jake laughed aloud. "I'm sure we scared him out of a year's growth, too. Gilas are certainly ominous creatures, but they aren't aggressive. Unless provoked, they usually stay away from humans. We just happened to disturb his private habitat."

"Well, Gila disturbed my regular heartbeat," Brit muttered with a little groan. "They can bite, can't they? He had a huge mouth."

"Oh yes, and they emit a poison from the back teeth, but they don't attack like a snake. It's rare that someone gets bitten. Only if you decide to pick him up or get very close."

"Well, not to worry! No way would I ever pick up that big ugly creature!"

Jake turned the mosaic shell over in his hand. "This is a major find, Brit. It's fabulous."

"I thought you'd be angry because I touched

it." Brit looked over his shoulder at her ancient treasure.

"It's hard to keep your hands off something this beautiful. Of course I'm not angry with you."

She kissed his earlobe, then traced the broken lines on the shell with one finger. "Where and how did they get such a large shell?"

"Trading."

"But this could hardly be a trade route," Brit reasoned. "It's too far from everything."

"Well, they probably traded a couple of times with several different travelers. We don't know precisely what they did, of course. But it isn't entirely unknown to find items here in the southwest that were only produced on the west coast, or even Mexico. The ancient ones had quite a barter system going." Jake took a couple of photos of the colorful shell.

"Imagine," Brit theorized. "This may have been made by a young woman on the Mexican coast as a gift for her lover. But they had an argument, and he sold it to the first traveling salesman who came along."

Jake gave her a long look. "Quite an imagination you have there."

Brit grinned and shrugged. "Well, it isn't an everyday item."

"Right." Jake walked to the middle of the room. "Now, I need to reconstruct this area exactly as you found it. Where was the shell?"

"Minus the Gila monster?"

"Yes. Just the facts."

Brit placed the shell on the floor. "It was here, half-covered with debris."

Jake took a small pad from his back pocket and began making clumsy lines on the page.

She looked curiously at his work. "That's this room? Here, let me sketch it for you."

"It doesn't have to be a masterpiece, just accurate in terms of contents within the space. This, along with the photographs and reports, will go into the surface survey."

Brit took the pad and began drawing loosely, with a long-forgotten, easy skill. In a matter of minutes, she had reconstructed the room, complete with all artifacts, debris, and broken pieces of pottery.

"Hey, you're good at this. I should use you as a sidekick more often. My sketches leave a lot to the imagination."

"I'd love to work with you, Jake." Brit knew that he was teasing. But she was serious. Working with Jake would be the most wonderful job in the world.

For the next few hours, she assisted him in taking notes on all the recently discovered artifacts, ceramics, non-ceramics, fragments, and the general site condition. They listed and detailed everything they found at the cliff dwelling, which they named *Casa Patio*, meaning patio house. They even named flora, fauna, dried food particles, and live animals or lizards.

Later, they took a break and sat outside on the stone patio ledge. Brit was curious about everything. "Tell me about the people who lived here, Jake. Who were they? What did they do here?"

"These were hunter-gatherers, not farmers. There obviously wasn't much good land for farming, so they had to forage for what they could. They also became basketmakers. I propose that they moved out when food sources became scarce."

"Where did they go?"

"Probably developed into some of the Pueblo tribes. Amazingly, there is still a group of Indians who live on the other side of the canyon floor."

"Really? Where?"

"The Havasupai have a reservation in Havasu Canyon that can only be reached by foot or horseback. Or, of course, by helicopter."

"I can't imagine living down here all the time."

"They've been here since the twelfth century. Imagine that."

She shook her head. "I can't. It seems so remote, you would think no one was here. And yet, a civilization has been here longer than America has been settled."

"The fact that so much still remains of their civilization, real material that we can study, is what fascinates me and keeps me interested,"

Jake said. "It isn't a dead science. We're still discovering new information every year."

Brit was impressed with Jake's knowledge and enthusiasm for his subject. He was like no other man she'd ever known. Intelligent, introspective, and dedicated to his work.

"You know so much about these Indians, Jake. I would love for you to be a part of Bonnie's movie. Would you do it for me? When we get out of here, would you go to Hollywood with me? I want to make sure everything they do is accurate. And authentic."

He looked at her strangely and shook his head. "That's something I could never do."

"I . . . I could try to get you a job as a consultant."

"No, no. I mean that I have no desire to be a part of . . . entertainment." His dark eyes grew intense. "Don't you understand, Brit? Education and uncovering knowledge is what I'm all about. Not . . . fun and games."

She stared at him. He was serious. Too serious. Unrelenting. How could she persuade him? His eyes said, "Never." And she feared his heart did, too. This was a Jake she didn't know at all.

Chapter Seven

When work for the day was finished, Jake took Brit to the most perfect place. They lolled on a flat sandstone, eating tuna sandwiches and soaking up the late afternoon sun like two smooth lizards. A faint spray from a small nearby waterfall reached them occasionally when the wind kicked up, and it felt refreshing and cool.

"Up there." Jake lay back on the warm rock and pointed at a corner of the blue dome above them. "See where the treetops edge the sky? That's the north rim."

Brit gazed at him lazily, admiring the way his T-shirt stretched across the breadth of his chest when he moved. They were a matched pair, sort of, she mused. They were both stripped down to their T's in the heat of the afternoon. His fit snugly, framing his muscular torso in white. But on her, the too-large shirt hid her body and hung down to her thighs like a large tunic.

Although she would rather evaluate Jake's attributes, Brit tore her eyes from him and squinted in the direction he pointed. "Is that the way out?"

"The northern route."

Brit didn't respond for a while. Their exit seemed a thousand miles away and, she hoped, eons in time. It was unusual for her that she felt so contented down here in such a rugged environment. She did not even mind wearing Jake's sloppy clothes, whereas at home she wouldn't be caught dead in something like this.

"All we need is wine and bread." He passed her a water canteen.

She took the plastic container and her fingers laced with his and lingered. They felt warm and erotic, reminding her of his intimate touch last night. "I have thou. What more could I need? Just us, alone in the whole world, Jake. It's almost perfect here. Beautiful. So completely quiet. Like a little Shangri-la tucked inside the Grand Canyon, if you pretend."

He chuckled. "You certainly have an active imagination, woman."

"Thank you," she murmured smugly.

"I like the quietness here." He laced his hands beneath his head and studied the sky. "It's hard to find this kind of silence in our lives today. There's always something, the hum of some motor or distant sonic boom or, worse yet, a blaring radio. I thrive on this quiet. It gives me time to think." He paused. "To sort things out."

"What do you think about when you're alone down here?" She finished her sandwich and lay back, pillowing her head on his chest.

"Nothing monumental, really. Being here just calms me down, *slows* me down, and helps me put my life in perspective."

"And what is that? What makes you tick, Jake? Professor Landry." She giggled at the thought of Jake, so regular in basic jeans and a T-shirt, back at the university and attired in a three-piece pin-striped suit with a pair of bifocals propped halfway down his nose.

He thought seriously about her question and was slow to answer. "I guess I'm work-driven; some say I'm a workaholic. Almost everything I do is related to learning or teaching. It's my whole life, I'm afraid." He slid one arm across her upper chest, and his fingers gently stroked her shoulder. "No kids. No wife. At least, not anymore."

"Well, that's a relief. Not the kids part, but about the wife. You've been married?"

"Oh, yes. Married almost four years. Been divorced three."

Brit waited, wanting to ask more details of the failed marriage but not sure how to do it without sounding as if she were probing.

"What about you?" he asked before she could

form another question. "Were you ever married?"

"Me? Oh, no. I, uh, Michael and I have been together almost a year. We discussed the possibility of marriage a couple of times, especially lately. I think the movie contract had something to do with it, though."

"Why should it?"

"Oh, because my financial status changed. I went from being a secretary, dependent upon my job and living paycheck to paycheck, to being able to do basically what I want. That's a big difference."

"So you quit your job?"

"Yep. As soon as I had the first money in my hot little hands. Of course, it doesn't mean I'm set for life, but I can take my time before deciding what to do next. I'm sure Michael found my financial security appealing. He even talked about quitting his own job and helping me manage my career." She turned her face toward Jake's. "None of that would matter if I . . . if I really loved him. And if I felt that he really loved me. I wouldn't care if he took over everything."

"Do you? Love him?"

She shook her head against Jake's ribs. "It just never was right between us. We look at everything differently. And I'm very disturbed by his compulsive gambling. I used to think it was just an occasional thing. But he plans every vacation or time off so that he can gamble." She paused, then finished strongly. "No, I don't love Michael."

"You're lucky you found out now, before you took the next step. I . . . wasn't so wise." Jake stroked her neck and face with gentle fingers. Brit could barely concentrate on their conversation as his fingers worked some kind of magic on her skin. Although she wanted to strip his clothes from his body and make wild love right here on this rock, she restrained herself. She also wanted to know more about this man who turned her on and captured her wild imagination, but would have nothing to do with her life back in California.

"What do you do in your time off, Jake?"

He gestured with his free arm. "What I'm doing right now is a good example of my lifestyle. This is my vacation from teaching."

"But you're working down here." She bent one leg and propped it on the opposite knee, tapping her foot in the air. "We just spent hours documenting that cave ruin. That's work."

"To you, maybe. Not to me. I enjoy every aspect. But the project isn't finished. Nowhere near. We have to assimilate the material and include necessary documentation. Then, it has to be collated and printed in a document."

"This is your vacation time? That's crazy."

159

"Maybe. But what better place to be? Or to work? It's like a travel agent who goes to Bora Bora to see if it's worth recommending. All part of the job." He laughed and her head bounced on his taut stomach. "I don't even know how to play golf. Furthermore, I don't care to learn."

"Don't you ever fish or play baseball or do some sport in your spare time?" She couldn't imagine anyone being so work-driven. In her experience, almost all of the men and many of the women in management levels of the business world played golf. It was a necessary skill for making good business contacts and, ultimately, for climbing that all-important corporate ladder.

"Those pasttimes don't really interest me." Jake considered her question for a minute. "I hike. Down here, I hike a lot. But usually, even the hiking's related to something else I'm doing." He sighed contentedly. "I guess I enjoy being a loner."

"Is that why you're here at the Grand Canyon? So you can be completely alone to work?"

"No, not at all. This just happens to be where the project is. Cole Washburn, a colleague at NAU, and I've been interested in these undocumented ruins for a long time. So we wrote a grant to get funding for a study. He and I had planned to make this trip together, but at the last minute, his wife became very ill and he couldn't leave her. That's why I have

160

more equipment than one person needs."

"I'm sorry about Cole's wife, but his stuff sure came in handy for us."

"When I get back to Flagstaff, Cole will help me organize the information and write the reports. It's still a joint project." Jake's entire body vibrated and seemed to grow animated as he talked about his venture. "You see, Brit, the whole story of the canyon isn't yet told. There were people here, people like us, and we don't know much about them."

"And we should?"

"Oh, yes. Their reasons for being here, their methods of living, and the reasons they left are all unanswered mysteries. I want to help solve some of those dark holes in the history of man. And the exciting thing is that here, in the canyon and other parts of the southwest, we have proof of their existence and clues about their lives. In other areas, those clues have been buried by housing projects and swimming pools or cemented over for freeways and parking lots, destroyed by man and development. Here, they remain. It's up to us to fit the puzzle pieces together and learn about their lives. I want to be a part of that discovery."

"You make it sound very important."

"It is. But not just to me. Historians, anthropologists, and other archeologists are waiting for this information, so they can do further studies.

161

Someday the links will form the complete story."

"You're amazing, Jake. Always thinking . . . and always thinking about your work." She reached up to caress his cheek. "I could tell we had interrupted something important when we arrived."

"Oh, mostly my peace was interrupted. What a bunch of characters to drop out of the sky."

"We were a pretty unconventional bunch, weren't we?" She laughed, remembering the chaos.

"Hell, the first thing I had to do was to break up a fight between the two men. I was really ticked about that. I expected to find broken bodies everywhere at the crash site. Instead, they were fighting over some petty thing."

Brit stroked his hand. "It was peculiar. Once we found out that everyone was safe, everything fell apart and anger took over. I was glad you appeared to break it up. I don't know what I would have done alone. Let them fight it out, I guess."

"Well, it was obvious to me that the group was reacting in some sort of shock to the crash." Jake stroked her face with the hand she had been kissing. "No one wanted to be here and I suppose you considered yourselves stuck, which you were. Then you couldn't seem to adjust to the rigorous camping lifestyle. I think that's one reason Frank decided to take out on his own.

162

I know it's hard, when you aren't used to it."

"Do you think Frank is okay?"

"I hope so. There were several places where he could rest or take shelter along the way. I'm sure he'll be out by tomorrow or the next day."

Brit did not want to talk about the possibility of being rescued soon. "The Romeros are still struggling with this whole scene. Not that I'm used to it, either. I like a warm shower and regular bed as much as the next one. And Lord knows, I was so scared yesterday. I really thought we were going to lose Yolanda to the river."

"Yeah, we came damn close."

Brit squeezed his arm. "You were great, Jake. The hero of the day." She turned over and kissed his lips, then laid her head on his chest again.

"Aw, there was nothing else to do but try to get her. We were just damn lucky, that's all." He stroked her arm, letting his fingers trail softly down the sensitive inner skin. "Brit, you've been the ballast, the stabilizer for this whole episode. You've helped keep the Romeros steady. And you've made me forget work. Forget everything." He lifted her hand to his lips and kissed the palm, then moved his lips to the pulse point inside her wrist. "Everything but this."

Warmth fluttered deep inside her as he continued to kiss the sensitive inner strip of her arm. Unable to resist him another minute, she stretched up and sought his mouth for a long, hard kiss. Their lips matched, meshed, provided a source for satisfying a lusty thirst. Their tongues mingled and exchanged fresh sweetness. "Everything but us," she murmured softly against his lips.

He shifted and pulled her over him so that she lay on his chest and wedged between his long legs. "This is everything, Brit." His arms wrapped around her, his hand cradling her head and pressing it toward him. "Everything important."

She settled her lips on his again. For her, time was silent and still, filled only with Jake's kiss and the touch of his entire erotic body against hers. The only thing in the world that mattered right now was the way she felt when he kissed her, when they were together, completely and fully. She wanted him again.

A sudden draft sprayed them with cool water, and she shivered. "See what you do to me," she murmured laughingly and pushed away from his embrace before she gave in to the elemental urge to rip his clothes from his virile body. Scooting to the edge of the sandstone, she slipped her moccasins off and wriggled her toes in the sun. "Who would ever dream there was such clean white sand in the Grand Canyon?" She hopped down and began frolicking on the tiny beach.

Jake removed his hiking boots and socks and

joined her. "Virgin sand. Never been touched by human toes." He took her hand and pulled her close for a quick kiss.

"Never? I don't believe that. I don't know much about those Anasazi folks who lived here, but if they were real people like you and me, I'm sure they walked along this beautiful little beach. At least, walked." She led him forward in a zig-zag path, laughing at their drunken footprints in the pristine sand.

"Of course, they were real people. We have proof."

"Then they must have played here. And more."

"How clever of you to deduct that. You're probably right. They probably found it as beautiful as we do." He laughed and kissed her again. "Maybe they did this, and more."

"They probably waded in the pool." Brit stepped into the cold water and pulled him along with her. They shrieked and laughed and ran in and out of the shallows kicking water up into high arcs that glistened in the sunlight.

"They probably bathed here." She shook her head and an energetic zephyr caught her hair and tossed it around her head like a golden halo.

Unable to resist the sexy sight of her, Jake pulled her into his arms for another kiss, holding her close so that he could feel her breasts through the thin T-shirt. "Would you like to take a bath here, like the Anasazi undoubtedly did?"

"Of course." She swayed against him, enjoying the playful moments. "If I get whisked away by the current, will you rescue me, Jake?"

"I'll go with you, every inch of the way." He undulated his hips softly against her, and, even through their clothes, she could feel his arousal teasing her groin. "We'll experience the current together."

"Sounds inviting." She mimicked his motions, rubbing herself against him.

The cool water rippled over their feet, and they reacted at the same time. Without even breaking their embrace, they laughingly danced to warmer sand, trying to kiss but not succeeding until they stood still again . . . still and quiet, admiring and loving, in each other's arms.

"This seems to be a good place for my research," he murmured finally when he lifted his head.

"What research?" She felt slightly dizzy and wanted more of his intoxicating kiss.

"I think we should explore your creative theory that the Anasazi did more than walk this beach." His kisses roamed over her face and down to her neck. "We've already deducted that they must have waded in the pool."

"It was only logical," she responded weakly as his hands drew the shape of her face and lifted it for another long kiss.

"It's only logical, then, that we take the next step."

"Yes?" Desire rippled up and down her body as his words fell in hot spurts on her skin. She felt giddy and clung to his shoulders as she tried to follow his thinking.

"My theory is that they made love here. We should research the possibilities."

She threw her head back and laughed as his kisses explored her breasts through the T-shirt. "This is research?"

"Absolutely. In order to write convincingly about my findings, I must experience what the Anasazi experienced. Playing, wading . . . making love. That way my report will be scientifically accurate."

She kissed him again. "I wouldn't want to stand in the way of pure scientific research."

"Then let's not stand at all."

They dropped to their knees in the sand and helped each other remove their remaining clothes. Laughing as their fingers fumbled the familiar task, they discarded jeans and T-shirts and underwear.

In the silence of the setting, with only the hypnotic splash of the waterfall in the background, Jake's senses soared. His admiration of natural beauty had never been taken so far as when he knelt before Brit. She was golden in the sun, her sleek body shiny as it reflected glossy highlights.

Her shimmery blond hair was tousled and so touchable. He splayed his hands through it as he angled her head for a kiss. Her breasts brushed against his arms. The full globes were adorned with erect dusky tips. He bent to kiss them, letting his lips pay homage to their feminine splendor as his hands slid down her body to grip her ribs. He pulled her to him and kissed her stomach and navel, then moved lower to the enticing, inviting mound of femininity.

She made soft sounds when he touched her, showing him her impatient, unmistakable delight. "Jake . . . oh Jake . . . You're driving me crazy!"

Jake felt as though he had been lifted to another level of pleasure, something beyond desire, beyond simple lust. He felt wild and free, as if he were breaking loose for the first time in his life. Free to enjoy; free to love her to the fullest.

"Brit, Brit, you are . . . so special," he murmured, trying to express his feelings and knowing as soon as the words were out, they were inadequate. He lowered her to the sand and kissed his way up her body.

She laughed playfully and swung her leg over his hips, shifting her weight until they rolled over and over in the sand, laughing, kissing, teasing.

"I'm covered with sand." She lay back onto the gritty bed. "I know practically nothing about you, Jake. And yet I want you like I've never wanted any man."

"I want you all the time, Brit. Even when it's impractical."

"And when's that? Tell me," she begged.

"When the others are there. How can we get rid of them? Can we send them away tonight?"

She giggled. "You're terrible!" But she loved hearing that from him.

"Terrible to want you? I disagree." He kissed her again and settled over her, careful not to give her his full weight. She seemed so slight, so pale and fragile against his growing strength. "You're the best thing, the best woman, to happen to me in a long time. Maybe ever."

Jake gave himself to destiny in her arms. Their divergent paths had turned inward, and merged, as if this were fate, planned and sanctioned by God. Their bodies came together with a never-before richness of physical and spiritual beauty. He entered her swiftly, powerfully, unable to control his urge to make them complete.

With a delicate tenderness, she opened her soft body to him, reveling in their union as she clutched his back with digging fingers. Jake rocked in her quiescence with a harmony he had never known. Here, in her, was his own inner truce. Time turned fluid as they flowed together, mutual currents of desire softening the hard gray edges of life and dissolving away reality. Jake felt a surge of power as their two bodies and two hearts swelled together.

Every part of him, every cell, cried out for satisfaction, but more. For love and caring, for the calm serenity of mutual desires fulfilled, for loving and being loved in return. These were feelings he had fought over and finally discarded long ago in exchange for purely physical satisfaction and devotion to his work. In the end, he cared only about himself, and that was not enough.

But this . . . this woman who made him laugh and who now rode with him in wild abandon, was such a refreshing, exquisite person, he released former thoughts and pledges. And he freed it all for this glorious moment in time with Brit.

Only the sun knew how long they remained locked in the essence of love. And only when the sun's intensity flicked at Jake's backside, did he move, ever so slightly. He felt completely relaxed, transposed to another plane of ecstasy.

"Are we still on earth? I dreamed we rode to heaven," Brit sang softly.

"We rode to Shangri-la in the sand," Jake murmured in her ear.

"My, my, you have a vivid imagination."

"You taught me everything I know."

"And all the time, I thought we were researching the Anasazis' ways."

"Ummm-hummm." He nussled her neck. "I think we've made some new discoveries."

"Oh? What are they?"

"That you are spectacular." He rolled beside her in the sand.

"So are you." She baited him with a smile and ran a fingernail lightly down his belly. "What else?"

He shivered and turned to her. She looked thoroughly ravaged, tousled, well-sanded. And undeniably happy. His next observation scared him because it matched his own feelings, and he hesitated before he said, "That together, we're perfect." Quickly, he suggested, "Let's go for a swim."

Jake ran toward the pool, ran from Brit and from himself, from thoughts and feelings he hadn't let himself entertain in years. Like a sleek brown otter, he plunged into the chilly waters without a pause, diving deep into the blue velvet.

Brit got up slowly, feeling the gritty sand that was stuck to her legs, back, and shoulders. She watched Jake disappear beneath the surface and wondered what had happened between them so suddenly. Did she say the wrong thing? Or do something that he could construe? No, it had been so fleeting, so imperceptible that she doubted herself now.

Across the pool, he surfaced. He shouted and

beckoned to her. You're paranoid, she told herself. He seems perfectly happy. Everything is fine, she confirmed silently.

She stepped into the cool water and a chill raced up her back. Her heart didn't lie; she knew now that she was crazy about the ruggedly handsome Jake Landry. He was the boldest, most interesting man she'd ever met. Intelligent and introspective, yet she'd seen that he could loosen up and be fun. Today she'd seen both sides of him, the one who worked almost all the time, and the one who could tease and play. She found him a powerful lover, someone to dream about, a man to love completely.

Oh, yes, the man had taken her heart by storm, and she sailed into the hurricane willingly. Until a moment ago, she thought he had been telling her the same with his body, that he cared deeply for her, too. But all he'd said was that he couldn't resist her. Well, at this point, maybe that was all she could expect from him. She followed Jake into the icy brink.

They did not stay in the water long. It was too cold for playing, and the current was still strong. They washed quickly, then sat nude on a smooth rock until they dried in the sun. Leisurely, in no hurry to return to camp, they began picking up the clothes they'd scattered along the beach, dressing in one item at a time, as they found it.

Brit felt content and happy. Even with her

doubts about their relationship, she couldn't contain her overall glow, for it came from inside. And she wished with all her heart that this moment, this day, this time with Jake could last forever.

Jake loaded his equipment and notes into his backpack and they started down the trail. "We aren't finished with this ruin. I have much more to do here. Are you willing to help?"

"Sure. What else do I have to do?" She grinned. "This has been one of the best days I've ever spent, Jake. I mean it."

He nodded and met her gaze. "Yep. It's been outstanding."

"I'll help you finish. I feel a kinship with the Anasazi, even if I don't know much about them. We've both enjoyed this spectacular place."

"It is special," he admitted.

As Brit walked behind him, she couldn't help wondering what would happen to them when this odyssey was over and she was rescued. Would she ever see Jake Landry again? Or would she disappear in Hollywood and he retreat to Flagstaff?

They walked in silence. Suddenly Jake stopped. "I hear a plane."

Silence. Dead silence. Then, a distant buzz.

"I hear it, too!" Brit felt a stab of panic in the pit of her stomach that traveled like cold steel up to her throat. She thought, for a panicky moment, that she would burst into tears. She knew she should be happy and hopeful, wanting to be rescued from this prison. But things were different now. This location was no longer a prison; it was Shangri-la. And she was in heaven in Jake's arms. She wanted to stay here forever.

But even the Anasazi left Shangri-la.

The now-definite buzz of a plane's motor had interrupted their beautiful silence.

Rudi spotted Yolanda on one of the rocks beside the camp pool and yelled as he made his way toward her. "Hey, babe! I've been looking for you. What are you doing here?"

Her head was bent over a book. "Reading," she said, not looking up.

"Reading? You?" he said with a chuckle when he got closer.

Yolanda lifted her head and glared at him defensively. "So what's that supposed to mean?"

"Well, it's just that you never do."

"It's because I don't have time," she retorted as if he didn't know what filled every hour in her life. "Now I do. And I like it."

Rudi shifted and looked around uneasily. "Why don't you come closer to the camp to read?"

"It's nice here, Rudi. Nice and quiet."

"It's even quieter over there. No water rushing around."

She frowned. "What's wrong with you?"

"I just don't like this spot, that's all. Don't trust it, especially after yesterday."

"Oh, how sweet, Rudi," she said with a smile. "It's perfectly safe today. The water's down. Anyway, I'm not going in, just sitting beside it. Come on, sit here with me. See how nice it is." She extended her hand to him, and he reluctantly took it.

"I'll keep an eye on the water level. You never know when the damn stuff is going to rise."

"Now, Rudi, don't be paranoid. It's nearly back to normal and perfectly safe. Jake said it would go down almost as quickly as it came up. And it has. We just weren't careful. Next time—"

"There isn't going to be a next time!" Rudi almost shouted. "I will make sure of it."

"Okay, okay. Calm down. Listen. Let me read to you."

"What?"

"I want to read a passage to you."

"Isn't that Brit's book?"

"Yes, it's the one her great-grandmother Bonnie wrote. It's very good."

"What's it about?"

"Sort of a love story."

"Humph! No wonder you women—"

"Hey, there's also a murder mystery. And adventure. They're making a movie of it, so it has to have something for everyone, right? Hollywood's got to make its profit from violence and sex."

"You got that right." Rudi shifted so he could be comfortable and watch for any rise in the river at the same time. "So this book is about violence and sex?"

"No! Course not. Just listen," Yolanda said softly. "Bonnie's Indian lover is KnifeWing."

"An Indian?"

"Yep. He's from the Zuni Pueblo Indians."

"Brit doesn't look like she's got any Indian heritage."

"She doesn't. This is about her grandmother's lover, not Brit's grandfather. He left Bonnie a widow and she took over running the trading post. Brit's mother was Bonnie's grandchild, daughter of Baby Sara in this book."

"Okay. Got it." Rudi leaned back on the rock and folded his hands beneath his head. "Go ahead. Read."

"I'm not going to read you the whole book. You can do that for yourself." Yolanda turned back a page. "Just this one beautiful part. *KnifeWing and I were alone for the first time last Sunday. Always before, the trading post customers, family, neighbors, or most certainly, Baby Sara had been with us.*" She paused. "Does that sound familiar, Rudi? We've always got somebody with us. We're never alone."

176

"You've got that right," he mumbled. "Go on."

She continued softly. *"On Sunday, his sister, Tuni-wa, kept Sara, and he took me to a small lake hidden in the sacred mountains beyond the Zuni village that he called Place of Still Waters. It was completely tranquil and quiet, and the water was like brilliant turquoise. KnifeWing said his people had been coming to this place for hundreds of years for purity and renewal. I could see why, because it was quite spiritual, as if it had been made by the hand of God, just for us."* Yolanda stopped again. "That's kind of like this place, Rudi, don't you think so?"

"Hummm, I guess."

Yolanda turned the page and continued reading. *"We tried not to disturb the silver-smooth lake when we swam. We whispered while we ate our picnic lunch, so we wouldn't disturb the beautiful silence. Later, as we sat beside the still waters, KnifeWing whispered 'I love you' for the first time. And a special peace came over us, and I knew that God meant for us to be together.* Isn't that sweet, Rudi." Yolanda closed the book and gazed at her husband. "We used to feel that way. Remember when we went to Madina Lake?"

"Babe," he said, touching her cheek. "I still feel that way. I just don't tell you enough. I get this chill up my back when I think that I almost lost you yesterday to this damn river. We came so close, too close for me."

"But it makes everything more valuable now. The beauty around us. The quiet. Each other. Isn't it nice?"

"Yeah. But I can't wait to leave here."

"Me, too. But that doesn't mean we can't enjoy it while we're here."

"Yolanda, I don't think you realize how valuable you are to me. How very precious."

"Why, Rudi, you haven't said anything romantic like that to me in a long time." She smiled sweetly.

"I want you to know how much you mean to me." He kissed her hand. "You mean everything to me, babe. Everything in the world."

"Rudi . . . you're serious." She reached to stroke his face. The man she had married years ago had turned into a hard-nosed businessman who managed their affairs and manipulated others around her, even manipulated her at times. But this man, sitting on the rock next to her, was more like the old Rudi. The one she had first loved.

"I'm serious about loving you, needing you." He sat up and, scooting closer, bent his head for a kiss, taking her lips with such fervor that he almost knocked them both off balance.

"Ummm . . . I think I'll read to you more often," she murmured as she settled into the security of his arms and smiled into another kiss. They were lost to time and motion, locked in each other's arms in a soundless, beautiful world where love, though timeworn and battered, still flickered.

The soft shushing sounds of the water provided a soothing backdrop for the kiss that continued, long and hard, jolting Yolanda clear through to her toes. She was a young girl again, heart fluttering because the dark-eyed, handsome Rudi Romero had given her the attention she sought. She was that young girl, giggling with her girlfriends as she told them how he'd claimed she was the prettiest girl at San Antonio High. She was, again, the girl who joked about him and with him until the night he asked her to marry him and she had cried with emotion, from utter happiness. This man, who kissed like a million bucks, still loved her and she had never felt so fulfilled.

Above the white sounds of the water, came a different sound, low and rumbling.

Yolanda tried not to notice, tried to remain lost in the beauty of the moment. But the noise continued and grew into the definite sound of a motor. She moved, and Rudi lifted his head slowly. He had heard it, too.

"What is that?" she whispered, as if saying it aloud would interrupt what was happening between them. But they'd already been disturbed.

"A plane. Maybe our—"

"No!" She pressed her fingers against his lips, those precious, beautiful lips she loved to kiss. "Please, no!"

"Why? You wanna get rescued, don't you?" He sat up and strained to see something in the heavens.

"No, Rudi! I can't! You know I can't fly any more! My dreams!"

"Babe, you wanna leave this place, don't you?"

"Yes, but—" Fearfully she gazed upward. The sky was a clear blue dome with no sight of a foreign object. Nothing, but the drone of a plane.

Chapter Eight

Jake strode into camp with more energy than he should have, considering the day's activities with Brit. But he felt revived and enthusiastic for whatever lay ahead. With Brit's help, he had been able to accomplish much today and make up for time lost dealing with the rescue and his new charges.

The campsite appeared deserted at first. The Romeros were nowhere in sight. He turned around and called to Brit, "Don't see them." She trudged along a hundred feet behind him and did not look nearly as lively as Jake felt.

"Where are they this time?" Brit knew she couldn't rest until the always-snipping couple was found. She was tired and simply wanted to put her feet up and relax until supper was ready. In fact, what she would really like to do was curl up in Jake's arms and forget eating.

From beside the river, Yolanda yelled and waved. She scurried toward them, talking as fast as she could. "I thought I heard an engine! Did

181

you hear it, Jake? It was a plane, wasn't it? Or maybe a helicopter coming after us?"

Jake heaved his backpack down on a stump and raised both palms toward Yolanda. "Don't get excited, now. As I explained to Brit, that was just a tourist plane. They fly over whenever weather's good, taking their chances with the air currents. So don't get your hopes up."

Yolanda halted in front of him and stared for a minute. Then a slow smile spread across her face. It was probably the first occasion she'd actually smiled at him since they had arrived. "A tourist flight? Oh, good. Great, in fact! Of course, I should have known." She called to Rudi, who was making his way toward them, and clapped her hands a bit frantically. "Tourists, honey, tourists like us!"

Panting from the exertion of hurrying uphill to the campsite, Rudi joined them. "Hope they don't have our same experience and end up down here."

"Well, Jake dear," Yolanda said sweetly. "Don't get your everloving hopes up, either, because even if they send a rescue plane or chopper or whatever can land down here, I'm not flying out of this hole."

"What?" This time, Jake was the one who stared. "Am I hearing right? You don't want to leave? Why?"

"I didn't say that. I just said I'm not flying out of here. I'll walk, with you as my guide."

Jake gave her a long look. "Okay, Yolanda, where did you get that notion?"

"I figured it out."

"Without consulting me?"

"I'm consulting you now." She grinned and moved her hands expressively as she talked. "No, I haven't lost my mind. You're right to think that I've wanted to leave from the minute I set foot down here in this giant hole in the ground. But not any more. Not flying straight up, at least. Going down once was enough for me. You aren't getting me out of here that way."

Jake folded his arms and eyed her narrowly. "So, what's your plan?"

"Nothing specific. Whenever you're ready to go is fine with me."

"I have work to do before I leave, Yolanda."

She nodded as if she understood perfectly. Obviously she had given it some thought. "I trust you, Jake. You saved my life yesterday, and I believe you can get me out of here safely. I've decided that I want to walk out, not fly."

Jake was stunned into silence. He realized that he had been looking forward to their departure almost as much as they were. Now, Yolanda was saying it wouldn't happen. He couldn't believe what he was hearing from the person who complained the most and loudest. Now she was changing her tune. Puzzled, he glanced at Rudi.

"Hey, this is almost the first I've heard of it, too." Rudi shrugged. "She's got some problems with this flying business. But, you should know, I'm staying with my honey. We're together through thick and thin, always have been. So if they send a chopper for us tough cookies. I'll remain with my lady, here." He hugged Yolanda and kissed her cheek.

Yolanda made some soft remarks in response to Rudi's outspoken support and patted his face.

Brit was amazed. As if Yolanda's bombshell about refusing to fly out weren't enough, there was this sudden display of affection between the two who had kept a running banter the whole trip. Then she realized that they were all looking at her. She was completely surprised by Yolanda's turn around. Although she and Jake had joked about getting rid of the Romeros, they both knew it was a fantasy. She had come with them and it was only logical to expect that they would leave together. But she hadn't even considered hiking out. And with Jake?

"Well, I . . . don't know what to say."

Jake shifted uncomfortably and addressed the three of them. "Now, look. It's entirely possible that Frank could reach the rim within the next few days. Then the authorities will know exactly where to find you. I'm sure they will send a rescue chopper down."

Brit felt torn. What was she to do? Leave Jake just when they'd become lovers? She couldn't imagine it. Nor could she imagine flying out when Yolanda and Rudi had refused.

"Well, if they're staying, so am I, of course." Brit's confidence in the idea grew as she spoke. "Hiking out sounds . . . interesting and . . . fun. That is, if Jake doesn't mind."

"All right! We're together on this!" Yolanda seemed happy, strangely happy.

"Hey, wait!" Jake paced in front of them. "This is not an easy decision. First of all, I have more work to do. I'm not ready to leave yet."

"We know, Jake," Yolanda said sweetly. "We'll wait with you. We'll help you."

"Oh, great. Secondly, hiking out of here is a hard two-day journey. From what I've seen, none of you is up to that."

"We'll work on getting in shape," Rudi promised, self-consciously patting his belly.

"Um-hum. That'll be interesting." Jake shook his head and walked around with his hands jammed into his back pockets, into trying to assimilate the new plan. He couldn't believe what they were saying. This was the first time the three of them had agreed on anything. And they wanted to stay with him! It was absolutely crazy. "Mind if I ask why?"

"Oh, she's had these silly dreams—" Rudi began.

"Silly? Are not!" Yolanda protested stoutly. "I'll tell you about them. They're really weird and have me spooked. Ever since we've been here, I've had nightmares. Mostly, they're about crashing. Maybe it's because of what happened to us, but to me, it's a warning. I'm not taking any more chances. I'm keeping my feet on the ground. I'll never get in another helicopter or plane again. You even said, Jake, that the tourist planes were taking their chances with the air currents."

"Yes, but I didn't mean . . ." Jake gazed around the group. He could tell, by their expressions, that they were in compliance with Yolanda. And they were staying.

He realized that if he did not get some organization and cooperation, they would occupy all of his time. This new plan of theirs could ruin his work. Neither his time nor his camp would be his own. He absolutely could not tolerate that. Hands on hips, he began his tactic, as diplomatically as possible.

"Okay. If this is what you want to do, I'll agree. I really have no choice, do I? But we must get some things straight. I have one goal: finish my project. I'm here to work. That's it. You have two goals." He glared at each of them. "Everybody has to chip in with the work necessary around this camp. This is a wilderness area and we are expected to leave it exactly as we entered it. That requires effort. Next, I want you in better shape in order to walk out of here."

The three of them stood before him, gazing up admiringly like obedient puppies. He knew that they weren't obedient at all, but for now, it seemed that they were willing.

"We'll help you. We're game to do anything you need, Jake. We'll get organized. Just tell us what you want." Brit knew by his determined expression that he was about to lay down the law. And she was curious as to how he would handle his unruly cohorts.

"The main thing I want from you is harmony and accord in this camp. In fact, I demand it. I'm tired of breaking up arguments and fights." He glared at Rudi, then the other two. "I encourage you to enjoy this place. It's beautiful and you have a rare opportunity to be here. But please don't do anything stupid and risk your life." He gave Yolanda a quick nod. "This is a dangerous area. Respect it."

"You've got that right. I'm staying away from danger and water," Yolanda vowed with her right hand high in the air.

"It would be nice to have some camp organization. There are four people here, and we need somebody to cook and clean and be in charge for the day. It isn't too much to ask. You'll still have plenty of time to do your own thing. Like exercise to improve your physical condition."

"You're absolutely right," Rudi agreed. "We should all contribute. And we'll start getting in shape first thing in the morning."

Jake could see a spark of enthusiasm click into the group. "Great. I knew you'd come through if you wanted to stay. Look, I figure I have another few days' work on *Casa Patio,* the

187

cliff dwelling that Brit and I explored today. She has agreed to help document the artifacts. There are two other ruins that I've been working on, and I need to make sure they're completely documented. Maybe, if we all pitch in together, we can head out of here in a week or so. Agreed?"

"Yes!" they chorused, like first graders on a field trip.

"First thing is cooking. What's for supper tonight?" He knew the answer. He just wanted to make a point.

Everyone looked at each other and shrugged. They had been waiting for Jake to decide.

"What's available?" Brit asked him.

"It's in the supplies. With this many people to feed, we need to plan meals and maybe ration some food." Jake gestured toward the tent. "He's only dropping enough food for one, remember. That may mean lots of peanut butter and crackers."

"Uggh!" Yolanda said with a groan.

"We grew up on peanut butter," Rudi claimed. "We can live on it for a week."

"This sounds like more material for a comedy routine," Yolanda quipped.

"You write comedy, and I'll get us organized," Rudi volunteered. "I'll inventory the supplies. Then we can schedule meals and divide everything up."

"Good idea, honey," Yolanda cooed, clasping his hand. "That's an excellent job for you." She

188

nodded at the others. "Rudi takes care of everything for me, from booking to hiring. He's really good with figures, too."

"What about you, babe? What's a good job for you? Besides the usual funny stuff."

Brit stepped forward. "I may not be a gourmet, but I can cook. Opening cans is my specialty."

"I guess I'm stuck with cleanup detail." Yolanda propped her fists on her hips and glared at the jovial group. "That's just great. My favorite chore."

Rudi patted her back. "Hey, that's something useful you can do, sweetcakes."

Jake could see trouble with that assignment. "Actually, cleanup is a chore that we should alternate."

"You can help me with cooking," Brit suggested. "You can choose opening cans or stirring the skillet."

Yolanda brightened. "Now that all my fingernails are broken, I don't mind opening a few cans."

"You folks are adapting nicely to camp life," Jake said. "Just to get some basic chores handled will help me get my work done faster."

"Jake, honey," Yolanda murmured warmly. "We're going to make you so proud of us, you might want to bring us back on your next expedition."

"Hum, we'll see," he answered diplomatically.

He was, after all, stuck with them. He, as well as they, needed to make the best of it.

"I've heard that before," Yolanda said. "It means, 'Don't call me, I'll call you, maybe never.' "

Her comment drew a laugh from everyone and seemed to pull them together with some degree of goodwill. Jake was impressed with the new attitudes exhibited. "This could work, folks. Sounds like you're willing to do what's necessary. Now, what's for supper tonight? I'm starved."

"Bring us a few choice cans, Rudi," Yolanda instructed. "We'll whip up meal in a skillet in no time. Tomorrow I'll have dinner ready when Jake gets back in camp."

"Right on." Rudi started toward the tent.

"Tomorrow . . . what . . . what is tomorrow?" Brit asked with a sudden interest.

"Why? Do you have an appointment?" Yolanda drawled. "Somebody check the schedule. I think I missed an appointment or ten."

"The date?" Brit looked around the group, ending with Jake.

He shrugged. "I have no idea. But I have a calendar in the tent. I'll check." He and Rudi disappeared into the large tent and in a few minutes, he called, "Tomorrow's the fourteenth, Brit."

"Oh."

"So what are you missing?" Yolanda asked.

"Nothing much. It's just my birthday," Brit

muttered with a wry smile. "I certainly never dreamed I'd be spending it down here." She and Michael had planned an evening out on the town in Hollywood. But that was before . . . the crash, before . . . Jake, before . . . her whole world changed.

"Tomorrow's your birthday?" Yolanda put her arm around Brit's shoulders. "That's great! This'll be one to remember."

"It sure will."

"We'll do something special. Have a party, maybe. What a rarity! It isn't every year that you spend this occasion in the Grand Canyon. Thank God!"

"Yeah, right."

"I mean it. We'll have a celebration." Yolanda clapped her hands like a kid as the idea gained momentum. "A Grand Canyon fiesta! It'll be great. You just wait and see."

"Yolanda, it's nice of you to suggest it, but down here, everything's so limited. All the food's in cans. Why, we're even wearing Jake's clothes."

"So? That just makes us equal. We women have been after that for a long time, and down here, we made it! We'll have to be creative for our gifts, though."

"Don't go to any trouble," Brit said with a laugh.

"How can we? There's no place to go?" Yolanda rubbed her hands together. "Oh, how I love to give parties!"

The two women started opening the cans that Rudi brought out for supper. "Canned potatoes!" Brit exclaimed. "I didn't even know they made such things."

"I guess they can most anything." Yolanda drew closer to Brit as they worked. "I read part of your great-grandmother's book today. The one you left for me? Well, I'll tell you, I was really surprised. It's very good. No, it's better than that. It's beautiful. A beautiful story and life. Bonnie had a great deal of insight, didn't she?"

Brit gazed at Yolanda strangely. Was this the woman who hated everything? "Glad you liked it."

"It's going to make a great movie, too. I wish I'd invested in it!"

"They started production this week," Brit said wistfully. She could be working on the movie right now. Should be. But she would not take anything for this experience, for this feeling of abandon and exhilaration that she felt. And she would never regret these joyous days and nights with Jake.

"Hey, guys! Guess what!" Yolanda yelled excitedly to get the men's attention. "Tomorrow's Brit's birthday!"

The next day, their new plans began to take shape. Brit was surprised to see that Yolanda didn't sleep until noon. She and Rudi were awake before Jake had finished shaving. They worked together making breakfast, while Brit and Jake packed for the day's excursion. Yolanda even helped Brit fix a small lunch, all the time wearing a silly grin and humming. She even cornered Jake for a whispered conference while Brit was finishing her coffee.

"It isn't personal," she assured Brit with a mysterious smile. "Just about the, um, uh, later."

"If it's about me, it's personal." Brit pretended to be offended until Jake returned and gave her a quick kiss on the cheek.

"It's none of your business," he murmured. "Besides we all have work to do today. That's what it's about."

Brit helped Jake load the day's supplies into his backpack. This time, she would take along his laptop computer. "I spent many years being a secretary. I can type almost as fast as you can talk. We'll cut the note-taking step."

"Great idea," Jake said, delighted at the concept. "Nice to have my own personal assistant." He helped her shoulder the computer carrier strap.

"I prefer the title Special Assistant," she insisted.

"How about Very Special Assistant?" He hooked the rope loop to his belt, slipped the backpack on, and led the way down the path toward the cliff dwelling.

"Tell me what Yolanda is up to," she demanded when they were out of earshot of the camp.

He turned and gave her an innocent, wide-eyed look. "And risk Yolanda's wrath? Not on your life!"

"Jake!" Brit grabbed for him, but he moved ahead quickly, barely out of her reach. She had to step lively to keep up with him.

Casa Patio ruin became an escape from the camp as well as the real world. Just getting there moved them back in time, both mentally and physically. This time, Brit was not the least bit intimidated by the sheer wall leading up to the cliff dwelling with the tiny ancient steps carved in its side. She watched as Jake negotiated the climb. His sinewy leg muscles flexed against his jeans as he skillfully heaved his body up, up, upward to the rock ledge. The lariat to haul up their equipment hung from his belt and flopped against his thigh. When he reached the top, he threw one end of it down to her.

"Attach the hook to the backpack."

She watched as he carefully pulled the loaded backpack to the ledge, then the portable computer. Now it was Brit's turn to climb. Before she could mount the first step, Jake tossed the rope down again.

She looked up, puzzled.

"Put it around your waist."

"I don't need it. I can climb okay."

"Just to be safe."

"Jake, I did this yesterday without any assistance."

"But it was risky. Do it for me."

Brit sighed and clipped the line around her waist. Then she began the climb, stepping carefully, determined not to make a mistake. She grinned triumphantly as she neared the top. But suddenly, just as she was taking the last step and was reaching for Jake's hand, she slipped. Her foot missed the carved notch and scraped the wall, throwing her whole body off balance. Bouncing hard against the sheer rock, she scrabbled and clawed for a hand or foothold in stone that seemed suddenly as smooth as wet tiles.

Abruptly, the rope cinched her waist, jerking short her descent. Jake grunted with exertion as he held tightly and tugged until she found a foothold. Then, hand over hand, he hauled her to the top. Gasping for breath, she clutched him, burying her face in the sanctuary of his chest.

His arms encircled her, drawing her tight against him. "Oh God, Brit! Are you all right?" he kept repeating.

"Yes," she said, her voice muffled against him. She tried to gather her wits and stay calm, but the realization that she could have plunged twenty feet down a rocky cliff left her quaking.

"I'm okay. Just a little shaky in the knees. Thank God you were here, Jake."

"Thank God you used the lifeline."

They stood there for a long time, arms wrapped around each other, clinging to their own private security. Finally, she lifted her head and, still leaning against him, murmured, "Thanks, Jake. You always seem to be there when one of us needs you."

"What an ugly birthday this could have been. A fall like that would have netted you a broken leg, at least. I'm still weak-kneed."

"You? That's hard to imagine." She managed a little laugh.

"Imagine me scared through and through." His dark eyes were serious. "I'm quivering inside like jelly." His hands stroked her hair as she nestled against him. "The thought of you getting hurt tears me up inside."

"Thank goodness you made me use that noose around my waist. It saved me. Everything happened so fast, I don't even know what I did wrong. One minute I was okay, and next, I was dangling."

"You must have missed that last step. Disaster can happen fast here."

"It's a very dangerous place," she admitted softly. "Both Yolanda and I have discovered that the hard way." She kissed him heartily. "Now you have two women who are forever grateful for our lives."

"Wonder how I can use that?" He returned the kiss with one on her earlobe. "You owe me . . ."

"Now, is that any way for a hero to talk?"

"You can tell I'm a reluctant hero."

"Does that mean you don't want to be a hero, or you don't want to act like one?"

He brushed his nose against her. "I don't want to be called one. I'm just an ordinary guy, doing what anyone else would have done under the same circumstances."

"Not true," she protested and reached up with both hands to grasp his lean face. "You are not an ordinary man at all. You are . . . rare, Jake. Very rare, indeed. And I am very lucky." She stood on tiptoe and kissed him again, hard and long.

Finally, they got down to work documenting the remaining rooms of *Casa Patio*. Amidst the potsherds they found remnants of a turkey-feather blanket, shoes made of woven reeds, and a clay doll. Jake lifted it carefully and handed it to Brit. "Nearly a thousand years old. What a find! I think we should take this back to the museum, along with the mosaic shell, for safe-keeping."

Brit cradled the crudely-made figure in one hand. "Is it a child's toy or a ceremonial statue?"

"Looks like a toy. It isn't a deity shape, more like a baby or a child. And there are no indications that it's for anything other than play. There are even traces of clothes." He picked up a tiny

197

piece of fluff found nearby. "This might be a scrap of fur."

"How amazing!" Brit examined the figure. "Imagine that a child played with this and actually lived here in this room."

"Many families lived here. Whole families, Brit, not just adults or men on a hunting trip. This was their settlement, their community."

Brit grew somber. "The dangers they faced daily must have been tremendous. Just getting up here, then living here is dangerous."

"Good observations." Jake walked out to the patio ledge where he'd left his backpack and equipment. Taking out a special cloth, he began to wrap the doll.

Brit joined him and sat down on the rock patio. She peered over the edge to where she would have fallen. "Jake, the Indians who lived here had the same problems, didn't they? If one of them slipped . . ."

He gave her a long gaze. "Yes. They suffered the inevitable consequences. We've found skeletons of early peoples with broken legs or backs, and you can assume what happened to them."

Brit shivered. "Maybe that's one reason these people left. It's too dangerous for families. Okay for sturdy, careful adults, but not for children."

Jake packed the doll away in his backpack and sat next to her on the ledge. "You've got a good point. The Anasazi were a social culture. They worked together. And raising healthy children meant their own preservation. If their children couldn't make it where they chose to live, I suppose they changed. It's possible. Anything logical is possible."

Brit's gaze drifted to the turquoise pool and silver waterfall. Then she looked back at Jake. Is anything possible with us? she wondered. What about love? Is it logical?

They worked through lunch, nibbling peanut butter crackers and drinking sodas while they finished documenting the rooms. Brit's fingers skimmed over the computer keys as Jake dictated what he wanted in the report.

"I can't believe you can type that fast," he marveled.

"I'm just getting your words down. We'll work on the format and spelling later."

"We should have this ruin finished in a few days at this rate."

"Really? Then we can go home?"

He nodded without meeting her eyes. Neither of them wanted to face that prospect. And yet, they knew it was coming.

When they had finished working for the day, they went to the pool. Brit slipped off her moccasins and socks and began wading in the shallows. The sun was warm on her skin and sparkled off the water. A multicolored spray radiated from the waterfall and occasionally gave them a chilling sprinkle. Brit turned her face up to a perfectly clear blue sky. Not a cloud was in sight. With arms outstretched, she danced by herself, feeling thoroughly happy. "What a glorious day for a birthday!"

Jake left his shoes and socks on the beach and joined her. "It isn't over yet."

She whirled to face him. "What's Yolanda planning? Come on, tell me, Jake!"

"No way!"

She took after him. "Tell me! Please!"

He caught her in his arms and bent her back for a kiss. "A canyon party, like none you've ever had."

"Then I need to wash my hair."

"Wash it?" He stroked her hair. "Why?"

She fluffed the blond curls. "My hair hasn't been done all week. It must be a mess."

He mussed it purposely with one hand. "It's great. Very natural."

"But, it'll be better when it's washed. Did you bring shampoo?"

He laughed and set her upright. "No, but I brought soap."

They ran to the beach and began to strip. Jake finished first and dug into the backpack for the soap. "Here. Come with me. I'll do your hair."

"You?" She laughingly followed him back into the water.

"Of course. Nothing to it." He knelt in the shallows. "Come here, Brit. Lay your head back in my lap."

She eyed what he called his lap. Tightly muscled thighs. "I don't know if this will work."

"Just watch. This is the native way. Another research project. I'll bet the Anasazi washed their hair this way."

Giggling with the newness of the experience, she lay back in the water, resting her head on his sinewy thighs. He cradled her head with one hand and dipped cold water over her scalp with the other.

Making a rich lather between his palms, he started by digging his fingers through her hair, scrubbing alternately roughly, then tenderly. He covered her head, his fingers working, touching, rubbing, applying soothing pressure.

She closed her eyes and let his fingers work their magic on her. Ripples of euphoria ran from her scalp down her back to her toes. Brit felt entirely relaxed, felt as if she were floating through thousands of fingers that caressed her entire body. Abruptly he dipped her head into the cold water.

"Eek!"

"Gotta rinse it good, right?"

"Do you have any conditioner?"

"Nope. Only this clear, pure water."

He rinsed her hair with the same scrubbing motion that he used washing it. His fingers spread across her scalp and squeaked through her hair. Then she felt his lips on hers, his hands turning her in the water, his legs bracing her, supporting her thighs as he slid her across his body.

She became lost in the kiss and unaware of her body until she realized that they were out of the pool. He lay on the beach and she was sprawled over him. She could feel his taut male body beneath her breasts and thighs. He was hard and ready for her. The sun warmed her back, sending the radiation through her body, setting her on fire for him.

She moaned and planted her knees on either side of his hips, bracing herself on his chest. Brit watched Jake's face change from seriousness to ecstasy as she lowered her body over his, slowly taking him fully into her. She sat up, feeling a certain mastery, a kind of dominance over this strong brown man who submitted so willingly to her. And, unexplainably, she felt a growing joy that spread through her as they started to rock together.

She moved closer, faster, furiously. She found the position a good place to watch him, to admire his physique, to observe his expressions. She lurched and lunged, reaching her climax with a high yelp of elation that echoed against the rocks and water. As she slumped on his chest, arms and legs entwined with his, she felt a complete and fulfilling exhilaration. She and Jake were a continuation of the ancient societies of the canyon and joyful participants in the bliss of this beautiful Shangri-la.

They remained in each other's arms. Being

alone together was all that mattered now. Brit felt a happiness and fulfillment like she had never known. Before Jake, she would never have dreamed that love could be this wonderful. It was a warmth that permeated her life and made her days joyous and her nights glorious. Oh Lord, she never wanted this to end. But, end it must.

He stirred. "We should be getting back."

She wiggled. "I know. I just hate to move."

"Me, too. A bath in the pool?"

"Yeah."

They bathed each other in a most sensuous, loving way. Brit scrubbed his back. Jake combed her hair gently with his fingers. She'd never known a man who was such an excellent lover, who cared for her enough to wash her hair, and could be so very gentle and rough at the same time. Every day he taught her something new. Every day she learned something remarkable about him. Every day she cared more for him and dreaded the time when they would have to part.

When they were finally dressed, the sun was setting.

"Hurry. It'll be dark soon." Jake heaved the backpack onto his shoulders and started walking. "Come on. Almost party time."

Brit caught up with him. "Jake, tell me what Yolanda's planning. I don't like surprises."

"Just that a Grand Canyon party is like none other," he warned with a teasing grin. "One has to be so creative and inventive down here."

Brit followed behind Jake, wondering what in the world they had planned. She would always remember this day, not because of a party, but because of what she and Jake shared.

Chapter Nine

When Brit and Jake reached the camp, it was nearly dark, and there was a different spirit in the air. Brit could feel the anticipation, even before they arrived. Something was going on, and she found it exciting. The first thing she noticed was a dull clanking that disrupted the eternal quiet of the place.

"What's that noise?" she demanded.

"You'll have to wait and see," Jake responded mysteriously. Yolanda had told him not to be surprised at anything, but he was as curious as Brit about this strange clanking.

"Sounds like . . . cheap wind chimes."

"Hold on, now. Nothing down here is cheap. It's probably all natural."

As soon as Yolanda saw them, she waved and called loudly, "Hi, you two! All right, Rudi, the birthday girl is back and it's party time!"

When they got closer, Brit could see that draped in the trees and around the tent were decorative streamers made of tin cans strung together with socks and T-shirts and briefs. They had to be Jake's since no one else had extra underwear. "They've raided your duffle bag, Jake!" she said, shrieking with laughter.

Jake hooted at the festive streamers. "Cheap wind chimes indeed! So that's why she wanted my clothes."

While Yolanda grabbed Jake and pulled him away to confer in whispered giggles, Rudi ushered Brit to a lounge chair, which proved to be an arrangement of pillows and sleeping bags. "This is for our guest of honor. Sit down, put your feet up, relax. And refreshments will be served forthwith, m'lady," he announced with a flourish and a little bow.

Brit curtsied and complied with a giggle. She couldn't believe Yolanda and Rudi's transformation. Gone was their constant bickering and sharp bantering. They were actually working together on something, in agreement, calling each other "honey" and "baby" and oh Lord, "sweetcakes."

Brit waited with growing curiosity. She knew that there was a limited amount of food, and it was all packaged or canned. None of it was very exciting; they didn't even have beer. Since Jake had planned to work alone, he hadn't bothered to order any.

Soon Rudi brought her a tall, cool drink. "In lieu of champagne, m'lady, sparkling raspberry."

She tasted it delicately. "Strange, but nice. What is it?"

"Concocted from an old family recipe," Rudi continued in an affected voice. "A tad of soda water, a squeeze of Cool-Aid, and a generous helping of clear, natural springwater."

"Cool-Aid?" Brit winced and took another sip. Nodding slowly, she admitted, "Pretty good, actually."

Yolanda appeared next with hors d'oeuvres that looked like a plate of cactus pieces.

"Is this what it looks like?" Brit asked, hesitating before taking one.

"When you're desperate, Yolanda said, you'll make do with whatever is at hand."

"What? We're supposed to eat those?" Brit pulled her hand back and looked skeptically at the dish.

"They're a delicacy. *Nopalitos* are a certain type of cactus similar to prickly pear, only different. These don't have the usual stickers. You roast the tender new pads or leaves and remove any stickers that you find. My sweet lil' grandmother used to make them from cacti in our yard. Go ahead, try them."

Brit took a tentative bite and nodded in approval. "Surprisingly good."

"Supposed to be good for you, too. Lowers the cholesterol bad guys," Rudi added, helping himself. "Maybe we should go back to the old ways." He gave Yolanda a wink. "Naw, babe, we have a great life. I wouldn't go back for anything."

Jake joined them with a small machine tucked under his arm. "How about a little music?"

"Music!" Brit exclaimed. "You have a radio?"

"No. It's a battery-operated tape player."

"Why didn't you tell us earlier?"

"You didn't ask," he said simply, pushing the button and turning on a bouncy tune by Gloria Estevan.

"What else do you have hidden in that tent?" Brit asked.

"Just be patient." Yolanda grinned slyly. "You'll see in time. Or should I say, you'll hear?"

"Yolanda!" Rudi exclaimed, grabbing her for a quick kiss. "Watch your mouth, babe! Don't ruin it now!"

"How can I when you're attached to me every second?" Laughingly, she headed for the campfire. "Now don't you two spoil the future surprises while I'm fixing the main course. Rudi, you never could keep a secret! Please don't leak this one."

"To preserve the secrets, then, I'll help you with dinner," Rudi said generously, leaving Jake to entertain Brit.

They fed each other strips of *nopalitos* until the plate was empty. Jake licked the herbal dressing from her fingers, then kissed it from her mouth. Brit teased his lips with her tongue until

208

he captured her, kissing her breathless. The music was loud and lively, and they both swayed to the beat without being aware of their movements.

Brit could see a different Jake tonight. He smiled at her in the shadows, his white teeth contrasting with the darkness. Putting aside the steely, serious professor, he became a charming, fun-loving man whose sole purpose was to make her happy. And oh, she was in paradise.

His familiar blue shirt was opened at the collar just enough to reveal the Zuni bear pendant. For a moment she felt slightly envious of the tiny jet emblem that nestled against his smooth tan skin. Then she remembered that later tonight, she would have that choice opportunity of snuggling against his broad smooth chest.

He touched her shoulder, then slid his palm down to the small of her back. "Dance?" he asked softly as he nuzzled her hair.

As if on feathers, Brit floated into Jake's arms. She was in heaven under the stars as they wove a tight circle, wrapped together, pressing breasts and waists and thighs. The steamy hot day had melted into a cool evening. A breeze rustled the cottonwood leaves and jumbled her hair.

Jake buried his face in her blond curls, revering the moment and memorizing the fragrance. He would always remember her this way. She was like a pixie in his arms, light and blond in his T-shirt and baggy jeans rolled up. Her green eyes captured him with their sparkle and her body seemed ripe and ready for him. How he wanted to seduce her all over again, as if they hadn't made love in the sand a few hours ago. He'd never had so much energy, nor so much love for anyone. Not anyone.

Brit kissed his earlobe. "This is one birthday I'll never forget."

"This is just the beginning."

"Really?" Her heart jumped. Did he mean the beginning of *them?* Of their relationship?

"The festivities are just starting." He whirled her around. "Canyon parties are notorious for ingenuity. Our choices are limited, so we have to be clever. Our wishes are all for you, beautiful birthday girl," he whispered, then nibbled at her earlobe as he hummed along with the music.

They danced until dinner was announced. Brit knew, from Jake's comments, that she'd better savor every moment because the end would come soon. Too soon.

The meal, while not elegant, was indeed special. The main course consisted of packaged noodles and canned chicken mixed with mushroom soup. Yolanda murmured an apology as she served the meal. "Jake wasn't exactly prepared for a celebration of any kind, so the gourmet items were scarce, but we hope you'll remember this birthday as something special, Brit. Just like you."

210

"From what I've seen already, you all are the most enterprising and creative people I've ever known." Brit smiled happily at everyone. "I'll remember you always, especially tonight." She felt on top of the world, which was odd, since they were a mile below the surface.

Yolanda lit a couple of candles that Jake had stored for emergency and, with the addition of the small campfire blaze, the whole atmosphere was transformed into a lovely candlelight dinner.

When they finished the main course, Rudi rose. "Time for more. One birthday cake, coming up!"

Brit clasped her hands in anticipation. "Rudi, you baked a cake down here? How on earth?"

Rudi blew her a kiss and went to the single-burner stove where he worked with his back to them. Though she tried, Brit couldn't see what he was doing. Finally, he was ready.

Jake stopped the taped music. Yolanda and Rudi slowly approached Brit carrying the cake and singing, *"Feliz cumpleanos para ti . . ."* Together they sang the complete "Happy Birthday" in Spanish.

Brit clapped delightedly. When Rudi lowered the cake toward her, she saw it was a giant pancake. In the middle flickered a red candle.

Brit jumped up and gave both of them kisses. "Rudi, Yolanda, how brilliant. And beautiful. I've never had a birthday pancake."

Rudi beamed with pride and happiness. "This

211

was the best we could do, considering the ingredients available."

"This is perfect," Brit assured him. "I love pancakes."

"Okay, blow out your candle," said Yolanda. "And don't forget to make a wish."

Brit gave Jake a shy grin. "I have only one."

"We know what it is, too," Yolanda teased, laughingly. "And I'll bet you get your wish, too! Later tonight!"

Brit blushed and tried to hide her face in the darkness. She knew that Yolanda was referring to what was happening between her and Jake. It was no big secret, she supposed. But her deepest wish was that she and Jake wouldn't lose each other when this whole trip was completed. She didn't know how they would resolve their present differences, but couldn't imagine parting with him. She took a big breath and blew out the single candle. Would she get her wish?

After they had all shared the giant pancake dribbled with syrup, Yolanda announced what would happen next. "My gift to Brit is a preview of something I've been thinking about the last few days and working on today. So, watch out, it's still pretty raw."

"Raw humor is my favorite kind," Rudi declared enthusiastically. "Especially Yolanda's."

"Before the, uh, the big time," Yolanda continued, "I used to gather my friends and brothers and sisters in the living room and try out routines on them. They were my toughest critics. If they laughed, I kept it in. If they didn't, I axed it. I haven't done that in a long time, but I think it's a valid test. So, tonight, you're the test group for my new routine. Remember, it's rough, but I hope it gives you a laugh or two."

The audience of three waited eagerly.

Yolanda started by introducing two women friends, thinly disguised as Yolanda and Brit types. The humor came as the two friends discussed experiences with husbands, lovers, mothers, children, and society's expectations of the liberated woman. As usual, Yolanda presented a stinging wit, with comments that were barbed at both ends.

When she had finished her routine, the three-member test group applauded wildly. Yolanda accepted the accolades gratefully, as a seasoned pro would.

"Babe, that's the best routine you've written in ages. It's great! Just great! This one's a winner!" Rudi jumped up and grabbed her, swinging her around in a giant bear hug.

"You really think so?" Yolanda's vulnerability surfaced, along with her self-doubts.

"I do. As soon as we get back home, we're going to work that one into the next appearance. They'll love it. You'll see." Immediately Rudi was her advisor, coach, and agent. He was her business manager, thinking of audience reaction and how to profit from the material.

"Thanks, honey." She smiled at him, then turned to Brit. "I hope you aren't offended that I used you."

"I'm honored," Brit assured her. "I will be so proud if you use this material in a skit. I'll tell everyone I know to watch. I agree with Rudi. It's good material. All I know is that I laughed."

"That's the main point," Yolanda said, then nodded to Jake. "Okay, stud. Your turn to perform."

Jake rose slowly. He was, obviously, not as accustomed to having an audience as Yolanda. "My gift is . . . a little music. This is something that I do chiefly for myself and a limited audience. I don't even know if you'll like it, because the flute is such an old and odd instrument. The sound is pretty weird to the modern ear. Hope you enjoy, Brit. This is for you."

Brit watched with pounding heart and glistening eyes as Jake moved into the shadows. He lifted the flute to his lips, and as he stood before the campfire, his form made a black silhouette against the yellow blaze. Brit was beguiled. His image looked like one of the ancient Anasazi drawings they found on the cliff dwelling's wall. What had Jake called him? Kokopelli . . .

Even in ancient times, there were those who played this instrument, producing these same eerie sounds, enchanting audiences in this same way. Jake's music immediately transcended time and ignited the imagination of the group.

The notes of the flute seemed to re-create the hush-shush of wind filtering through the trees and slipping around the huge rocks, the rush of water in the stream, the scurrying of small animals, the wail of coyotes, the rugged echoes of mountain lions. The song was intrinsically primitive and had the unique qualities of nature. Brit had never heard such music. The performance was like magic, pulling them into a time warp. Jake was a man spanning the generations, imitating the wind and wild animals as did his ancestors. Strangely, it was as if he were communicating with the ancient dwellers of the Grand Canyon.

When he finished his mini-concert, his audience stood up and cheered and applauded wildly. The cacophony broke the silence of the night and bounced off the rocks, off the river, frightening away the night spirits, which was the purpose of the music.

"You really make that thing talk, man," Rudi said. "I've never heard anything like that."

"For a while, I thought we were surrounded by wild beasts and birds," Yolanda said. "You're pretty good, Jake. Have you ever thought about going public with it?"

"No way!"

"I think I heard the Anasazi slipping around us," Brit said. "You resurrected the lost tribes of the canyon, Jake. It was great!"

Jake, embarrassed by their enthusiasm, mumbled, "It was nothing, just a few strange notes," before slipping away to the tent to pack away his flute.

When he finally returned, Yolanda teased him about not staying around for their full appreciation. "You've got a lot to learn about performing, Jake. The first thing is to take your bows graciously. Give your audience plenty of time. And an encore is always a nice gesture."

"I'll leave the performing and the extra bows to you, Yolanda. It's not really my thing."

"But, Jake, you had the ghosts rumbling around these old rocks," she responded with sincerity. "That's something special. For your ancestors, performing is traditional. That's where you got your ability. Don't hide it."

"I guess you're right," he admitted. "I'm just not a performer by nature."

"What happened to those lost tribes in the canyon, Jake?" Rudi asked, suddenly aware of what Jake had told them about other people who lived here. "You say they lived right down here? Are you talking about whole families, or just bands of hunters and rovers?"

"We have proof of whole families who lived here. Why, just today, Brit and I found a clay doll that I estimate was almost a thousand years old."

"No kidding! Why don't they still live here?"

"No one really knows why they left. Logic tells us that it had to do with survival, food, and

216

water. But maybe something else influenced their passage."

"Like what?" Yolanda asked. "Maybe a bunch of them got swept downstream, like I nearly did."

"That's entirely possible. It could have been an epidemic that wiped out a great number of the tribe. Or a hostile tribe could have attacked them, killing and taking slaves, leaving the rest vulnerable. All of that was common in the ancient cultures. It's why we're investigating. To see if they left any clear signs that would explain their disappearance."

"I think you're doing something pretty interesting, Jake. And pretty important," Yolanda said. "I give you credit. The rest of us are just bouncing around, entertaining people and having a good time. But you, you're investigating history and recording it. And writing about the small details of people who lived a thousand years ago. It's amazing to think that. You're all right."

"It's interesting to me," he admitted shyly. "Even today, the Yavapai Indians live in other parts of the canyon. But we think they're from a different group than the Anasazi, who lived around here."

"I'd like to see what these people left behind," Yolanda proposed suddenly. "Could I go see a cliff dwelling?"

"Yeah, me, too," Rudi said. "Could we go with you to see one of them?"

217

Jake hesitated. He thought of Brit slipping on the rock today and knew the dangers for Yolanda and Rudi would be even greater. They weren't as small nor as physically fit as Brit. And, Lord knows, he'd sure hate for Yolanda or Rudi to take a fall. He wasn't sure he could secure Rudi as he did Brit today. "It's risky. The ruins are high up in the rocks. You have to climb up to them."

"Did Brit climb up there?" Yolanda asked.

"Yes . . ." He glanced at Brit with a questioning look. Did she want them to know that she almost fell today?

She put her hand on his arm and squeezed. "I'll tell them."

"Tell us what?" Rudi asked.

"As Jake said, we had to climb up to the ruins. The Indians left little notches in the rocks, like stairs. But it's tricky. You have to keep your balance and it's pretty steep. Today, just when I reached the top, I slipped. Only because Jake insisted that I tie a rope around my waist was I saved from falling twenty feet straight down. Jake caught me and pulled me up. It was pretty scary."

Yolanda stared at her, then at Jake. "You saved her life today? On her birthday?"

"Well, I don't know about her life," he said with a shrug. "But she could have been hurt pretty badly. You people just don't seem to understand. This place, beautiful as

218

it is, can be very dangerous."

"You are one amazing man, Jake Landry." Yolanda placed her hand on his arm in a gesture of appreciation. "Always there when we need you."

"Yes, he is," Brit agreed and gave him a special little smile.

"Please, show us an Indian ruin before we leave, Jake." Yolanda gave him her best, most appealing performance. "It's another thing that Rudi and I have never done. And we might not ever have a chance to again. Ever! Look at what we'll miss."

Brit glanced at Jake. It was obvious that Yolanda was accustomed to getting her way, and no amount of camping in the canyon would change that. Brit remembered when Yolanda had begged Frank to deviate from their scheduled flight path and show her the Grand Canyon. Immediately, Rudi had taken up her cause and practically ordered Frank to please her. Frank had been helpless to resist her whims, and now, much to Brit's aggravation, so was Jake.

"Hmmm, let me think about this." Jake scratched his chin thoughtfully. "Maybe we could go to a different one. There is another ruin that isn't so difficult to reach. It's beyond the waterfall, so it's further away and a longer hike from here. But this one's below ground level. It's relatively easy to see, once you get there. Maybe that one would be best."

"All right!" Yolanda said with enthusiasm. "When?"

"I'll take you in a few days," Jake promised.

Brit was not surprised that Yolanda had gotten her way. Even though she and Rudi had never shown the slightest interest in the Anasazi culture or hiking to their ruins before tonight, Jake was willing to be their guide. She, on the other hand, revered the special places where she and Jake had made love. They had made their own private Shangri-la. Theirs and the Anasazis'. She just didn't want to share the spots with the Romeros. Maybe she wouldn't have to. Jake did say that he would take them to a different ruin.

The festivities continued until late in the night. Jake played another cassette tape, and Rudi and Yolanda danced and cavorted around the campfire. They all joined in until finally, Yolanda admitted she was tired and ready for the party to end.

"Rudi and I got up so early this morning and worked so hard all day getting everything ready, we're bushed. But we had a blast, Brit. Happy birthday!" Yolanda hugged her.

Rudi did the same. "I can't tell you how much we enjoyed just being ourselves tonight. It was nice not to be worried about some kook snapping photos of us in awkward positions or folks leaking to the media about how silly we acted."

"Why, I would never do such a thing." Brit

feigned shock at the idea. "Thank you so much for the party. And for your very unique gifts. This birthday has been one of the best."

The Romeros disappeared in the tent and Brit and Jake linked arms and headed for their little cave boudoir. He helped her climb up to the ledge. They undressed quietly and slipped inside the down-insulated sleeping bag without a word, as if the gaiety of the evening had been snatched into the blackness of the night. The whole event was already a pleasant memory, a part of the past.

Brit smiled privately as Jake's arm curled around her. She settled against him and basked in her happiness. Each of her new friends had performed admirably, giving her a collection of valuable memories that she would keep forever. She kissed his chest, and her lips pressed the Zuni bear fetish. She hoped it would give her good luck, too.

Jake's voice was low and sleepy. "Can you believe this was really Yolanda tonight?"

"She was so generous, making sure everything went well for me." Brit sighed happily. "She was even nice to Rudi."

Jake chuckled. "People change. Maybe she has."

"But will she switch back tomorrow?"

"Who knows? Tonight was certainly special, Brit. It was all for you."

"Funny how it brought out everyone's different personalities."

"Hmmm, you're right," he admitted. "We were all different people tonight. And, it was nice. You know, tonight I had fun, real fun for the first time in ages. I forgot how much pleasure friends can provide."

"You sound like you don't socialize often, Jake."

"I don't. I live a quiet lifestyle."

"But you were great tonight. And when you performed on your flute for us, everyone thought it was wonderful."

"It was special, just for you, my dear. Actually, I never thought I'd play for an audience of non-Indians."

"You mean you've played the flute for Indians?"

"A couple of times they've invited me to play at certain ceremonial events."

"That's quite an honor, isn't it?"

"For an outsider, it is."

"But you aren't an outsider. You're one of them, Jake."

"No. No, I'm not. I didn't grow up with them. And I'm not full-blooded. Only one of my ancestors can be traced to the Zunis. But they want to continue the cultural traditions, like flute-playing; to preserve and encourage them among their youth. And they needed a flute player. I was it."

222

Brit imagined him playing the flute in a gathering of Native Americans. The image of his dark silhouette against the golden blaze of the campfire remained clear and distinct in her mind. "You're a very good musician, Jake. It was truly a birthday I'll never forget."

"Me, too."

Brit's voice was low and choked with emotion. "Jake, I'm very happy tonight."

She waited. She wanted to hear the same from him, to know that he cared for her as she did for him. She wanted to talk about what they would do about *them* when this odyssey in the canyon was over. But there was no response. Then she felt his rhythmic breathing. Curling around her, arms and legs engulfing her, he had fallen asleep.

She kissed his forearm and tried to follow him to sleep. But, even though it was late and she was tired, sleep didn't come as easily for Brit. She thought of all that had happened in the last week and wondered when and how it would end. She feared, deep in her heart of hearts, that she would never be as happy as tonight, on her birthday, lying in Jake's arms.

Brit and Jake spent the next few days working in the ruins. Each day, after their work was finished, they played beside the small waterfall, swimming in the pool, and making love on the pristine white beach. They talked about every-

223

thing, except what to do when their journey was over. There were no easy answers, so they pretended the problem didn't exist.

Jake felt himself growing closer to Brit than anyone since his marriage, closer than he had ever been with his wife. By the time he'd distanced himself from her, he'd pushed away most of his friends, too. He was alone with one thing left. Work.

But Brit seemed to understand him. She cared about his work, even helped him, and didn't pass judgment on his occupation or his lifestyle. It was nice not to have to defend what he was doing. Brit seemed to know its importance.

This day, he was finishing some notes on the portable computer at *Casa Patio*. Brit sat nearby, reading her great-grandmother's book while he worked. He turned to take her into his view, always a refreshing sight that boosted his spirits. Her blond hair fell around her bare shoulders, hiding her face. She was so beautiful, it was almost like a dream, his wildest fantasy, to have her here. Just watching her sometimes drove him crazy, and he wanted to take her in his arms again and make love until they both fell apart, breathless. That was the way they loved, excited and exhausted, and it was a different experience for him. He'd never been so passionate about a woman.

Sensing his gaze, she glanced up and smiled. "What?"

224

"Nothing. Just that you're so beautiful, how can I work?"

"Are you finished?"

"Not quite. I want to take a couple of snapshots of the other ruins before we head back. Want to go along?"

"Sure." She closed the book immediately, and began to hunt for her shoes.

They left most of the equipment near the path that led to *Casa Patio* and hiked around the pool and beyond the small waterfall. About half a mile away, another canyon opened up and in its wide mouth was a large open-pit circle dug into the ground and made sturdily of stone and ancient mortar. There was additional construction inside the large circle that resembled a fire pit and possibly an altar.

"This is a ruin?"

"As old as the others."

"Why is it shaped differently?" Brit climbed down into the round ruin. "Round."

"Different uses. This one is a ceremonial room, so it didn't require the constant protection that a group of families did. It didn't need to be built high on a ledge. They probably only used this on certain occasions for large gatherings and often at night. The circular building identifies it as a *kiva*, which we think was used for ceremonies and dances."

"And sacrifices?" Brit's eyes grew round.

Jake shrugged. "Don't know for sure."

She moved to the center. "You can even see where they had a fire and stairs to the side. Maybe that was where the dancers lined up."

"Could be." Jake took several snapshots from different angles and directions. "We can bring the Romeros here tomorrow if they still want to see a ruin. This one has easy access. I'd be reluctant to let them climb to *Casa Patio*."

"I'm sure they will want to see this one. It's splendid, and quite different from the other one. You can imagine how it once was quite beautiful, especially at night with campfires and participants holding torchlights." Brit walked around, inspecting the intricate construction before noticing that Jake had started to climb up on some rocks. "Where are you going?"

"I want some overhead shots. I think I can get just the angle I need from up here." Without another word, he braced his back against one boulder and his feet on another and thrust himself higher.

Brit watched, fascinated by his agility. He was propped between two huge rocks with only a small space between them. It looked simple. He merely boosted himself up easily, keeping his body balanced as he rose above her head. She tried not to think about the sheer space between the rocks directly beneath him. The laws of physics and the strength of his legs kept him aloft. So it was with admiration and no real alarm that she observed him. He took several snapshots of the ruins from above, then turned the camera toward her. She smiled and waved.

He inched further upward until he was quite high and snapped several more photos. Then he stopped moving for a few minutes.

Brit waited for the whir of the camera. When there was no such sound, she expected him to descend. "Jake? What is it?"

"My foot's caught. Wedged between—"

Brit could see him tugging on his left boot. Suddenly it came loose, and he was free. And stumbling!

Stunned, she watched as he scraped against the rocks, dropped into the space between the boulders and disappeared.

Catching her breath and her wits, Brit ran to the edge of the rocks and peered over. Jake sprawled at the bottom of a chasm, another three feet below where she stood. His arms and legs were outstretched. His eyes were closed. He lay perfectly still. The camera remained clutched in his hand.

"Jake!" she screamed.

He didn't move. No response.

Frantically she sat on the ledge and lowered herself over the edge, clambering over the rocks until she reached his side. He had fallen at least fifteen feet, a plunge that could have killed him.

"Oh God, Jake! Can you hear me?" She touched his cheek, but was afraid to move him, to cradle his head to her breast as she longed to

227

do. He was strangely pale and lifeless. He gave no response to her frightened caress.

KnifeWing had been ill with a high fever for several days before Tuni-Wa came for me. He was delirious with the fever. At first, I thought he had quincy, which had devastated many of his people in recent years. It was another disease given to the Indians by the white man. But when I saw the rash on his chest, I knew that Knife-Wing had the measles. He had caught them from my own little Sara. Many of his people had died from this childhood disease, too. Filled with guilt, I stayed by his bedside for days. The medicine man used drums and chants, while I used cool herbal baths and my own prayers. Together, we worked to keep my love alive . . .

Chapter Ten

Brit took a deep breath to try to quell her growing anxiety. She knew she had to keep her composure in order to help Jake and kept repeating that thought to herself. Stay calm. Don't panic. Keep a cool head. He's going to be all right. He is all right!

Strangely, she began to believe herself and responded rationally, as if subconsciously she knew exactly what to do in an emergency. She felt Jake's pulse. Steady. Good, that's good! See, he's alive. What next? Water, of course, water. She reached for the canteen attached to her waist that Jake insisted they wear whenever they were away from camp. Feverishly she unscrewed the cap, but fumbled it with nervous fingers.

"Oops! Oh—" Before she could get control of the thing, it had dumped some of the contents onto Jake's passive face.

He sputtered and groaned, eyelids fluttering. She sighed with relief. Sloppy, but it did the job.

"You trying to drown me?"

"Jake? Are you all right? Can you hear me? Can you see me?"

"Yes . . ." he mumbled, followed by another, longer groan.

"Then open your eyes. Look at me. Jake, please—"

After a long pause, he obliged, viewing her through darkly fringed, narrowed eyes. She was not sure if he was actually focusing.

"Hey, Jake, talk to me! Oh, thank God, you're awake. Are you okay? How do you feel?"

He mumbled something unintelligible and rubbed his eyes and forehead gingerly. "Ohhh, God . . ."

She hovered over him, anxious to touch him, yet fearful that she would do more damage. "Where do you hurt? Jake, you scared me so much! I thought you'd . . ." she paused and suddenly, anger replaced her fear and anxiety. "I thought you'd killed yourself! That was a stupid thing to do! Why in the world you climbed up there, I'll never know! You could have—" She halted and realized she was losing control now that she could see he wasn't critically injured or worse. She wanted to scream at him because he had taken such a risk, but that wouldn't help. Although he seemed to be okay, she really didn't know if he had internal injuries.

"Where do you hurt?" she repeated. "Tell me."

"All over."

"That helps. Specifically where? Can you move? Maybe you're not okay."

"I'm okay," he mumbled and began to move.

"Maybe you shouldn't move in case something's broken. Any sharp pains anywhere?"

"My pride."

"How do your arms and legs feel? Are they numb?"

Groaning with every breath, he to tried to sit up. But that brought the biggest moan. "Chest, ribs . . ." he mumbled and fell back onto the ground.

"Oh no. Where?"

He motioned to his left side. "Oh, yeah. This is it. Probably cracked a rib or two. Feels like a spear in my side."

"You definitely shouldn't be moving around, then. You might puncture a lung if you have a cracked rib. You'll have to stay here while I get help."

"No, no, I'm okay. Just give me a few minutes to get my breath."

"If I wait too long, it'll be dark soon. Besides, I can't get you out of this crevice without help." She looked around. "Where's your canteen? I couldn't find it."

"With the equipment."

"Back on the path with the backpack? You're impossible! You certainly don't take your own best advice. What was that speech about not go-

231

ing anywhere without water? This is a desert."
She unbuckled her half-full canteen. "Here, keep
this one. It should do until I get back with
Rudi."

"No, Bri—" Jake started to protest. "Don't do
that. I can make it."

She pressed her hand firmly on his shoulder.
"Please, for once, do as I say. You stay put,
right here. You can't climb out of these rocks by
yourself. You're—*we're* going to need help getting out of here and walking back to camp—*if*
you can walk."

"I can walk." His voice grew louder and more
frustrated. "I'm okay. Just give me a hand." He
struggled to get up, but was unable to do so by
himself.

Brit shook her head. "You are one damned
stubborn man. Don't you understand? I'm going
to need Rudi's help getting you back to camp.
So, shut up and lay still. I'll be back ASAP."

Brit stood up and took another deep breath.
It was so hard to talk to Jake like that and even
harder to walk away from him, leaving him lying
there on the ground. He looked so helpless. She
wanted to cry and cuddle him to her breast. But
it would be dark soon and they needed help. She
had to do it. She hoped no wild animals would
cause him trouble. "I'll be back soon, Jake," she
repeated before climbing back to the path.

She sprinted past the waterfall and around the

232

pool, only pausing long enough to grab the other canteen. Knowing she couldn't run all the way back, she did a combination jog and fast walk that enabled her to continue moving rapidly and cover the distance without collapsing. She would have to make the trip again to show Rudi where Jake had fallen.

Yolanda closed her notebook and ambled back into the camp where Rudi hovered over a brewing pot. "Ummm, something smells marvelous. What are you up to?"

He motioned and gave her a sample bite. "What do you think?"

"Well, it's not your very best. But hey, considering the limitations, it's pretty good."

"Chili from a can is very limited," Rudi admitted. "And the spices we have here are few. But, it's chili. It'll satisfy my craving until we get back to L.A."

"Which won't be long, I suppose. Jake said he was almost finished with his work." Yolanda sighed and sat cross-legged on a ground tarp. She studied the towering stone heights around them and the distant blue sky.

Rudi joined her. "What's wrong, babe? You sound as if you aren't anxious to go. A week ago, you'd have given up chocolate for a month to get out of this hole."

233

"I know. But . . . it's strange. This place seems to grow on me. Every day is different. And better. There's a kind of serenity here that we can't get at home. Certainly not in L.A."

"And no pollution here."

"Rudi, I have been so inspired down here. Do you know that I've got the basis for three different stand-up routines written down and a couple of really good ideas for the show? Today I've been making notes on several others. For me, that's amazing!"

He slipped his arm around her shoulders and squeezed. "You haven't written that much since the old days."

She grinned. "You mean the bad old days before the good Big Days? That's because in the old days I had so much incentive to get out of the *barrio*. And I wanted to do my thing."

"But that's where your inspiration came from. That strong desire. And also from your roots."

"Something about being here reminds me of those times, Rudi. I remember so much now, things I haven't thought of in years. Good material for the show."

"Maybe it's the primitive way we're living."

"Maybe it's the lack of diversions. Nothing else to do but think, right?"

"Hey, I ought to bring you back here every year to spark your creativity." Rudi chuckled devilishly at the notion. "As if I could ever get you down here again."

"Not such a bad idea," Yolanda said thoughtfully. "I wouldn't mind it at all."

"You're kidding. You'd want to come back?"

"Maybe with better planning, like the appropriate clothes. I think it would be a better experience if I could wear clean clothes every day and a sweater for the cool nights. Also," she laughed, "I'd bring certain foods I miss, like chocolate."

"Ayee, I can never figure you out, babe." He gestured in the air. "When we first got married, all you wanted to do was make it big in Hollywood. Now that you have, you want to go back to roughing it."

"Well, maybe not too rough." She gazed thoughtfully into the distance. "Or I could bring along some help."

"Yeah, sure!" Rudi slapped his knee. "Sounds like another idea for the show. Yolanda goes to the Grand Canyon to live in the wild for two weeks and interviews hiking companions who like to rough it and cook over a Bunsen burner."

With enthusiasm and their own typical excitement, they verbally created the scene. First, Rudi explained the setup, then Yolanda picked up on the idea. Suddenly, in mid-speech, Yolanda lifted her head and held a finger up for quiet. "I hear something. I'll bet they're coming back. Our little lovers, Brit and Jake. Is supper ready?"

"All but the tortillas. We're out of tortillas," Rudi lamented. "Just chili and crackers." He made a face. "Very Anglo."

Yolanda hopped up and pointed. "Rudi, it's Brit by herself. Running. Hey, she's alone!"

Brit began yelling before she got into camp. "Rudi! Rudi! Hurt . . . bottom of rocks . . . just lying there . . . ribs . . . need you . . ." She halted at the camp clearing, clutching her side and gasping for breath.

Rudi reached her first, gripping her shoulders. "Hold on, Brit, babe. Slow down and tell me what happened." He led her to a log seat.

Brit balked at sitting, even though she was near exhaustion. "But we have to hurry. Before dark."

Yolanda joined them. "Jake's hurt?"

Brit nodded. "He fell into a crevice between two rocks that look like they were made of molded lava. I need help getting him out."

"Okay, let's go!" Rudi responded immediately.

"Now, wait a minute," Yolanda advised coolly. "Do we need any equipment? How badly is he hurt?"

"He was briefly knocked out."

"Unconscious?" Yolanda looked alarmed. "Was he conscious when you left him?"

"Oh, yes. We talked. He thinks he cracked a rib."

"Can he walk?"

236

"I don't know. He said he could."

"But you didn't get him up? Didn't see him walk?"

"I . . . was afraid to try. I told him to stay down until Rudi got there to help him climb out of the rocks."

"Good, good. Now if he'll just do it." Yolanda began filling a canteen with water. "Rudi, get a flashlight. What else do we need?"

"I don't know how he's going to make the trip back, he's in such pain," Brit said. "Jake's not very good at taking advice. But I don't think he's in much condition to help himself right now. I think he'll have to wait on us."

"I'll get the rope, just in case," Rudi said.

"We have it," Brit said. "It's with our equipment on the path. Jake made me wear it when we climbed to *Casa Patio* ruin."

"And now he needs it," Yolanda said wryly. "How far did he fall?"

"About fifteen feet."

"Fifteen feet? What in the world was he doing?"

Brit hesitated. She couldn't fully explain his motivation. At this point the risk of scaling the boulders seemed much greater than the results. "He'd climbed up to take some aerial snapshots of the *kiva* ruin. He was braced between these two huge rocks, when one foot became lodged. He pulled it free and it threw

237

him off balance. That's when he fell."

Yolanda shook her head. "Unbelievable. How stupid." Then she snapped her fingers. "There's a first aid kit in the tent. We'll take that. There may be something in there we need."

"Okay, let's get to him." Rudi took Brit's arm while Yolanda ran to the tent for the kit. "You all right to make the trip again?"

"Absolutely!" Brit led the way down the now-familiar path at a jog.

By the time they arrived, darkness was fast approaching. Jake was, of course, still trapped. Brit held the flashlight while Rudi and Yolanda climbed down to him. She couldn't help smiling as Yolanda began fussing at him the minute she got within earshot. Oh, well, served him right. He needed a good reprimanding from someone besides her.

Yolanda's voice rose with her frustration. "So, you think you're a lizard, Jake, climbing up those rocks like that?"

"If I'd succeeded, you'd think I was a hero, like Spiderman, scaling impossible walls," Jake responded sharply.

But his banter was no match for the queen of comedy. "A hero, huh? But you didn't make it, so I just think you've got the pea brain of a lizard. You've got to respect this place, Jake. It's dangerous." She sat down beside him and opened the first aid kit. "Let's see now. Here is something you can use. An Ace bandage." While Rudi and Brit watched, she raised his shirt and wrapped the stretchy material intended for a sprained ankle around the smooth brown skin of his chest. "Now. Let's see if you can make it."

"Oh, I can make it all right," Jake said stubbornly. With much grunting and groaning and help from Rudi, he got to his feet.

Rudi looped the rope under Jake's arms and tossed the end up to Brit. "Use it to steady him as we come up. Don't pull. And don't try to catch him if he falls. We'll keep him going from this end."

Slowly, steadily, Rudi and Yolanda helped Jake up the rocky climb to the path. Brit kept the rope taut, but knew she couldn't hold his weight if he fell or stumbled. The sight of Jake wincing in agony and moving only with assistance tore at her heart. He'd always been the one to rescue them. He'd always been the strong one. He'd saved them from disaster more than once. Now, in an ironic twist of fate, he needed them to help him.

The most amazing transformation, though, was to see Yolanda and Rudi intent on helping someone, rather than expecting and demanding attention for themselves. Less than a week ago, Yolanda commanded first consideration at everything. Now, she was reprimanding Jake for not respecting nature's dangers. The admonition sounded strange coming from her lips. But good, all the same.

From the moment they had met beside the helicopter, Rudi had been snapping his fingers and demanding attention for Yolanda. Now his primary concern was getting Jake to safety with as little pain as possible. It was so unlike the bossy and commanding Rudi she had known.

When they made it up the rocks to the path, Jake insisted that he would wait while Yolanda and Rudi examined the *kiva* ruin. "Go on, take a look. You might not get another chance to see it."

Brit knew what that meant. They wouldn't be back here. While Rudi and Yolanda walked over to take a quick look at the ancient ruin, she slid her hand into Jake's and pressed their palms together. "Can you make it back to camp?"

"I'll be fine," he muttered through tight lips. "Just slow. It's only a rib. People continue working with cracked ribs. It's no big deal."

"Yes, it is. You're in pain. But it could have been much worse. You gave me quite a scare for a few minutes."

He looked down at her with a curious expression. Then he smiled and winked, shrugging as if it were nothing. She wondered if he really understood how she felt, how terrified she was that he was seriously injured, how her insides tore at the sight of him lying at the bottom of the

240

rocks. She couldn't express her feelings, since she was just coming to grips with them herself. She was just admitting how much she really cared for this man.

Instead of saying anything, she bent her head and lifted his hand to her lips. She kissed the back of it, letting her lips linger on the smooth brown vein trails. His hand felt strong and sinewy, and she knew that he possessed a greater strength than she had ever known. He had a special inner strength that transcended physical pain. Suddenly she wanted to cry, to exclaim, *What is going to happen to us?* But Rudi and Yolanda were approaching, asking Jake questions about the curious building patterns of the primitive ruin, and she quelled her feelings.

Rudi led the way back to camp with the flashlight. He acted as a brace for Jake, staying close by his side for the entire long trip. They stopped at the spot where the equipment was piled. Yolanda slipped the heavy backpack onto her back without a complaint, as if she did this sort of thing daily. Brit lifted the strap of the portable computer to her shoulder.

Realistically, she knew that this would be their last trip to the beautiful turquoise pool with its sparkling waterfall. There would be no more lazy afternoons lying in Jake's arms on the white beach. She gazed longingly at the water, which seemed dark and ominous in the growing twilight. Even the crystalline sand was shadowed. Brit remembered their lovemaking there and their speculation that the Anasazi had been here before them, perhaps making love on that same spot. She thought of their laughter, of their shared moments of quiet pleasure. It was over, she knew.

Sighing, she fell into line behind Yolanda. They moved slowly and methodically toward camp. Jake couldn't make it any other way. By her second trip back to camp, Brit was exhausted.

It was dark when they arrived. They quickly agreed that Jake should sleep in the tent since climbing up the rock wall to their little cave was out of the question. Brit switched the sleeping bags and tried to make the bed comfortable for him.

He joined her inside the tent. "I hate to move Rudi and Yolanda to that cave."

Brit glanced up. "What? You mean it's okay for me, but not good enough for them?"

"No." He scoffed. "Of course, that's not what I mean. It's just—"

"I know what you mean, Jake. But button it up. They don't mind. You're injured and you need to be here. And I . . ." she paused and grinned, "need to be with you. Actually, a hard-surfaced mattress is what you need. It'll keep you flat and more comfortable."

242

"Would you help me with this thing, Brit?"

"Sure, Jake. What?"

He raised his arms slightly. "Make it tight, Brit. Tight as you can."

She tried to ignore his obvious pain as she pulled the Ace bandage taut around his smooth dark-skinned chest. "How's that? Does it hurt? Too tight?"

"Ahhh, no. It's good. Now I know how a corset feels. Awful. I can't believe women wore these torture devices willingly."

"All to attract our men," Brit commented wryly, helping him put his shirt back on. "But it wasn't usually worn with a broken rib."

"Feels like . . . hell."

She watched him kneel with effort and pack away his camera. Was it worth it? she wanted to yell at him. Was it worth risking your life for a couple of photos? But she didn't because she was afraid his answer would be yes.

When they returned outside to eat, there was no campfire because Jake always started it. But supper was ready. Rudi handed Jake a bowl of chili. "It's not exactly homemade, but it's the best I can do down here."

"It smells great, Rudi. Thanks."

Yolanda brought him hot chocolate and a couple of aspirin. "Here you go, Spiderman. I wish I had something stronger for the pain, Jake, like a little whiskey."

Jake smiled, but it looked more like a grimace. "Thanks, Yolanda. This'll be fine. You've all been great. I could never have made it out of there without you."

She grinned and winked at him. "Hey, I think we owed you a couple, Spiderman. At least, I did."

"Naw, you owe me nothing," Jake objected modestly. "You sure you'll be okay sleeping up in the cave? I'm sorry to—"

She held up one hand to stop him. "It's no big deal, Jake. If you and Brit can sleep up there, so can Rudi and I. It'll be something to tell our grandkids about." She gave Brit a generous smile. "Someday I may even write a book about our experiences, like Bonnie did. Wouldn't that be a hoot?"

Brit chuckled. She couldn't believe this was the same Yolanda who screamed about the loss of her valuables and objected so strongly to sleeping on the ground their first night here.

Before long, Brit and Jake decided to turn in for the night. Brit went with him into the tent, ostensibly to help. Jake removed his shirt, then stretched out on the sleeping bag. Brit removed his boots and socks and tugged the legs of his jeans. He was a spectacular man, so masculine with long lean legs, a slender waist and broad muscular chest. The sight of him, his coffee-colored skin glowing in the lantern light, took her

244

breath.

How could she sleep with him and not make love? Then, the Ace bandage binding his ribs reminded her that it was painful for him to move. And she knew they would do nothing except sleep.

Brit removed her clothes, Jake's shirt and jeans, and folded them. She looked up and saw him watching her.

"You're beautiful, Brit. Sometimes I forget what a fabulous woman you are under my sloppy clothes."

"You're beautiful, too, Jake." She turned off the lantern and slid into the sleeping bag beside him. "But you're injured. And you need rest."

He sighed heavily. "Just because I can't love you tonight, doesn't mean I don't want to. But I can imagine, and dream."

She moved alongside his warm body and wrapped her leg around his. "Me, too." Reaching out, she rested her head on his arm and nestled her hand in his. Touching him was the only way she could communicate the depth of her feelings tonight.

Everyone in camp spent the next day helping Jake in every way they could. They fixed his meals and brought them to him. They helped him up and down. They played cards with him.

245

Finally, at dinner around the campfire, Jake said, "This is it. I'm ready to head out tomorrow."

Brit froze. Did she hear him right? They'd be leaving? So soon? She felt frantic, slightly nauseated. It was crazy, having such physical reactions to something she'd wanted for so long. Or had she?

Rudi and Yolanda exchanged quick glances. "You sure you can make it, Jake?" Yolanda asked anxiously.

"With your help, I can. Aren't you ready to go?"

She smiled shyly. "Jake, I know you aren't going to believe this, but I'm actually enjoying it here."

"You're right. I don't believe it. I know you've been out of your element and it's been extremely difficult for you and the others. Now that this has happened, I'm ready to go. My work is basically done, except for more photos I had hoped to take. I thought a rescue chopper would be here by now, but Frank must have had problems getting out."

"What do you think happened?"

"I'm afraid he got lost somewhere along the way. Perhaps he took a wrong turn. He could be injured, too. Who knows? The best we can do is get ourselves out and send help for him. Tomorrow we hike. It'll take two to three days to reach

Phantom Ranch, the only place to stay in the base of the canyon. Then we can get help."

Later that night, in the darkness, Brit whispered, "Jake, you asleep?"

"No. Thinking about tomorrow. Anxious, I guess."

"Me, too. I'm like Yolanda. Reluctant." She propped up on her elbows and tried to see him in the darkness. She could only make out his form. "Kinda hate to leave."

"You women are amazing. First, you hate it here, hate everything about it. Then you don't want to leave. I don't understand."

"It's been a learning experience, as they say. So beautiful, so quiet. I'll miss this . . . miss everything here." *Miss you,* she thought, near tears.

"Me, too."

"You?" She forced a laugh. "What could you possibly miss?"

He pulled her head down to rest on his chest and stroked her hair. "You. Everything here. Everything we've done. My social life has been more active here than at home."

"You must be a hermit."

"Well, Flagstaff is a small town. And lately, I've been so focused."

"On what?"

"Work, mostly."

"Don't you have a girl?" She grinned at him in

the dark and wished she could see his face. "I mean, don't you have a woman friend? Don't you go to movies? Play cards? Dance?"

"No."

"Jake, I don't believe that."

"It's true. I'm a loner. I wanted to establish myself at NAU as a full professor. I'm on a tenured track. And you know how it is. They expect publication and research development. I went there fresh from my divorce. I was pretty angry. And bitter. I didn't trust people . . . women, especially. Donna embodied all my mistrust."

"Donna?"

"My former wife."

"Are you still bitter? Is that why you're a loner?"

"You've changed that, Brit. Changed my life and my mind. You give me a chance to laugh, to have fun. I've loved having you here, Brit. I can't imagine what it would have been like without you."

"Quiet."

"Lonely."

"I've loved being here, Jake. I hate the thought of going back. I don't want to leave you."

"Then stay awhile. Stay with me in Flag and . . ." His hand came under her hair, and he gently stroked her neck. "We'll have our own private party every night." He rubbed her back.

"We'll eat in a real restaurant." His hand slid lower and caressed her rounded rear. "We'll make love in a real bed."

"Sounds wonderful. Just being with you would be enough for me. I've realized since we've been down here, that people and relationships and love are more important than anything. Especially money or the things it buys. And you are the most important of all, Jake."

She turned into the curve of his body, her spine to his chest. His hand moved over her, gentle fingers tracing her feminine curves, her breasts, her waist. He touched her lower, deeper.

"I like a man who chooses something and goes after it. But Jake . . ."

"You, Brit," he said in a low breath. "I want you."

"Tonight?"

"Now."

"But, how—"

"I'll show you . . ."

While he recuperated, KnifeWing told me stories of his people. They were ancient tales, related from one generation to the next, from the beginning of time. The stories were strange to my ears, yet somehow familiar. They reminded me of Bible stories my grandmother used to tell me when I was a child. Some were tales about the beginning of the Zuni people; others had lessons for good behavior, like how to treat each other and how to respect the earth. Those stories helped me to understand KnifeWing, and we grew closer after that.

He wanted to know if my people had stories, and I told him about how my grandparents came West in a covered wagon and lived in a sod house. My grandmother was a teacher and Mother traveled for the county extension service, teaching farmers first aid and how to cook and can and preserve vegetables. Our worlds weren't so different, after all. It was a beautiful time for KnifeWing and me.

Chapter Eleven

Brit woke early the next morning. All was quiet except for a confused dove coo-cooing at the last stars. She knew that the nocturnal creatures would be making their last journey across the rocks before daylight and heat drove them into hiding. In some ways, she envied the animals who could stay here in this exotic paradise with their mates.

Lying very still beside Jake, even without touching him, she could feel the heat from his body. She loved that feeling. *This is the beginning of the end of my great adventure,* she thought sadly. *And of my great love.*

Brit tried to evaluate this strange sense of loss she felt. Her loss was not of something actually attained, for her relationship with Jake was just beginning. But the potential of what they could have was monumental in her heart. It was a love she felt, but could not understand or even express. Her feelings for him started with admiration, with respect for what he did and how he thought and behaved. She smiled to herself. *Yes, I love his mind.*

But their physical attraction could not be ignored, either. Yes, she found him irresistibly handsome. Dark and somewhat exotic. Sexy. When he touched her, she became his. Even before he touched her, she was his in her own imagination. Her thoughts of him, of them together, were privately exciting. But the reality was something quite different. She wasn't sure that he was hers at all. He had never made any commitment to her.

Suddenly, a lump that felt as big as her fist filled her throat and Brit wanted to cry, to lament along with the lonely-sounding dove about her soon-to-be-lost love. She slid out of the sleeping bag and dressed quietly to avoid waking Jake. While she made coffee for their last morning in camp, she recalled a brief passage that Bonnie wrote in what was now getting to be a well-worn book.

Leaving KnifeWing's camp was a mixed blessing. I was glad to get back to Sara and the comforts of home. But I missed KnifeWing terribly. I missed the ordinary things—seeing him every morning, sharing the day's activities, hearing his ancient stories at night, and more.

Brit felt that she understood what Bonnie meant. There was the unwritten speculation that Bonnie and KnifeWing were already lovers, and undoubtedly Bonnie missed his loving along with the "ordinary things." Brit was full of those same mixed emotions now, too. She wanted to get back to civilization and the comforts of home, yet did not want to leave Jake. Unfortunately, both were inevitable.

When everyone finally awoke, they all worked together to break camp. Brit marveled at how Yolanda and Rudi eagerly pitched in, packing exactly as Jake instructed since he was not able to bend or carry much weight. Adequate water, a minimal amount of food, and sleeping bags would be carried along in backpacks. The remainder of Jake's equipment would be piled at the edge of the clearing where supplies were dropped and covered with the tarp where a helicopter would pick it up later. By noon, they were ready to hike.

"Wait!" Yolanda balked. She wore a strange, almost timid, expression. "We have to say goodbye to this beautiful camp."

"Oh, good Lord!" Rudi exclaimed. "Haven't you had enough of this place?"

"There are memories here, Rudi," Yolanda explained. "Good ones as well as the not so good."

"Especially the not to good," he responded quickly. "I almost lost you here, so you'll excuse me if I don't get sentimental. Come on, babe."

Still, Yolanda stood there. She looked up at the trees, around the camp, and down at the pool and stream where she'd nearly been washed away. As if called into some mystic ritual, a large golden eagle circled overhead, bidding them farewell from its wild, remote domain. "Yes," Yolanda yelled with a wave to the grand bird. "It's time for us to go, but we'll be back."

Jake led the way down the trail with Rudi right behind him. Brit fell into step with Yolanda. "I understand what you're feeling."

"I'm glad you do, 'cause I sure don't."

"I sort of hate to leave, too. It's funny, isn't it. Weird that we want to leave and yet . . ." Brit paused and gazed at the towering red cliffs where the eagle was making one last circle.

"Yeah, it's crazy, but I feel sad right now. I know I want to return someday." Yolanda spoke with conviction. "Definitely want to return here. Not exactly the way we came, but I'd sure like to come back here. It's a special place."

"Yes," Brit agreed in a low voice. "Yes, it is." And they walked the vague path in silence.

Occasionally along the way, Jake pointed out wild animals. From a lofty ledge, a couple of bighorn sheep watched them solemnly. They rounded a curve and scared a lone coyote drinking from the nearby stream. At one point in the heat of the afternoon, a hawk suddenly appeared, swooped down and, amid a cacophony of screeching, caught a small bird in midair. Just as suddenly, it disappeared with its prey.

"How awful!" Brit exclaimed, voicing the

254

horror they all felt.

"It's a perfectly natural act," Jake explained, shading his eyes to view the distant spot where the hawk vanished. "He's gone. Probably feeding his family. Or *her* family. You've got to remember that hawks are predators. This is how they live. We just witnessed a rare sight in nature."

"I can do without that kind of rare sight." Brit shook her head and stumbled along. "Can we rest now?"

During the course of the afternoon, they stopped frequently for water and rest. None of them was in top physical shape for such a hike. Jake was still in considerable pain with his cracked rib. After a couple of grueling hours, Rudi was redfaced and panting. Yolanda and Brit had no stamina in the heat. Their pace was slow and agonizing.

By late afternoon, the heat took its toll, and Jake called for a rest stop that would last several hours. They ate peanut butter and crackers for supper and watched a small herd of deer grazing across the stream from them. Then they continued walking after dark when it was much cooler.

The next day was much the same. Slow. Hot. Agonizing. Hiking out of the canyon was turning out to be a laborious trip. Several times during the two days of hiking, they heard tour planes flying over the canyon. No one said anything, but they were reminders that civilization was not far away.

The second night, they camped close to the stream. Everyone had willingly taken to the icy water, wading to soothe weary feet and splashing water over their dusty bodies with no regard to the chill. Supper was, again, cold and dry since they hadn't brought the stove along, and no fires were allowed in this part of the canyon.

"I'm ready to go home," Yolanda admitted as she cuddled next to Rudi. "It's hard to believe this place is so cool at night when it's hot as blazes in the daytime."

"I'm tired," Rudi said, and everyone agreed with silent nods. "Bone tired. And this backpack seems to get heavier by the hour."

"At least we don't have to pack our garbage out like Jake threatened in the beginning," Yolanda said with a scowl.

"I thought you'd appreciate having it airlifted with the equipment," Jake said, patting Yolanda's knee.

"Thank you, Jake." She gave him a perfunctory smile, then added, "I'm hungry. What a lousy way to lose weight."

Jake leaned back and propped his ankle on his knee. "This will be our last night camping. By tomorrow we'll reach Phantom Ranch. You can eat all you want there. And connections with the outside can be made."

"You mean, we could call for a rescue?" Rudi

asked. "All right! We could get a helicopter out, babe."

"No helicopters, no planes," Yolanda repeated adamantly. "We're still in the bottom of the canyon. I told you, I'm not flying out of here."

"Ohhh," Rudi groaned. "I don't think I can make it out on foot."

Brit massaged her feet. "At least you have shoes. All I have are these thin moccasins."

"There is another way," Jake suggested. "We could get the park service to bring down some mules for us. We can ride the mules out of the canyon from the ranch."

"Ride mules?" Rudi asked incredulously. "You must be kidding!"

Jake shrugged. "Beats walking. I'm sure we'll be ready for something other than walking by tomorrow."

"I think it sounds like a good idea." Brit reclined into the curve of Jake's outstretched arm. His body warmed her, thrilled her, and filled her with desire, even though she knew they could have no privacy tonight.

"Sounds like agony to another part of my anatomy," Rudi grumbled.

"Aw, honey. Riding a mule could be fun," Yolanda encouraged.

"It could be a lot of things, but 'fun' isn't one of them," he retorted.

She chuckled devilishly. "It could provide

more material for the show. Yolanda rides a mule in the Grand Canyon."

"At my expense!" Rudi grumbled.

"We'll all suffer through it, believe me," Jake warned with a rueful laugh.

Brit sighed wearily. "I can't believe this is our last night in the wild. It's been quite an experience."

"And we owe it all to you, Jake," Rudi said. "You've saved us. And when we get back, buddy, we're going to repay you for your generosity."

"No, no—" Jake began.

"Of course, we will," Yolanda insisted. "You took us into your camp. You saved my life. I owe you everything, Jake. Trouble is, I don't know how to repay someone who saved my life. Maybe I should simply support you the rest of your life."

Jake just shook his head at them. "Thanks, but I have a job. I don't want any payment. Just remember the things you learned about the canyon and the life down here. That's all."

"Well, you've certainly opened up another world for us," Brit said. "Not only is it totally unlike our hustle-bustle cities, but it's been a nice quiet change. We all probably needed a little break from the rat race to make us appreciate the finer aspects of life."

"I wonder why we haven't come across any trace of Frank." Yolanda sat up and looked around. "Isn't this the route he followed?"

"Should have," Jake agreed.

"No traces of fires or anything."

"Well, he knows campfires aren't allowed in this part of the canyon. I figure he took a wrong turn somewhere, or crossed to the other side of the river for some reason."

"I'm worried about him," she said with an uncharacteristic sympathetic tone. "Down here with all the dangers and wild animals."

"We'll find him," Jake assured her. "He's probably out by now, even if he did wander off the beaten path."

"Maybe he found another of those Indian ruins and has decided to abandon society and live down here," Yolanda suggested in a teasing tone.

"It's possible," Jake admitted. "I'm sure there are more places, maybe even civilizations that we haven't discovered."

"It's like a secret cosmos down here," Yolanda said. "And it's a rough one. I can't imagine what we would have done without you to help us after the crash, Jake. I'm sure we couldn't have survived."

"Sure you would," Jake said. "You would've learned how by trial and error."

"Hey," Yolanda said, laughing. "I think that's what we did!"

"I learned about flash floods," Rudi mumbled unenthusiastically.

"But mostly, we learned a lot about ourselves," Brit said quietly. I never imagined that I could go two weeks without all the material stuff I take for granted. Like chewing gum. And shampoo with conditioner."

"And chocolate!" Yolanda chuckled. "When it comes right down to survival, you can't eat diamonds."

"We lost a lot of money in that crash," Rudi grumbled.

"But we lived," Brit said quietly. "Somehow, Italian shoes don't equate."

"When I found the crash and you guys were fighting, I wondered if we'd make it together for long," Jake said. "But all of you have come through okay."

"Tomorrow, civilization," Yolanda said dreamily. "And chocolate! Creamy, rich chocolate!"

"A cold beer," Rudi added, with relish. "And a huge platter of *nachos!*"

"Black walnut chocolate chip cookies. And my own clothes," Brit said, joining the wish campaign. "A warm bath instead of an icy one. A hair dryer and curling iron."

"Getting my nails fixed," Yolanda added with a laugh. "And makeup!"

"A mirror," Brit said.

"You look fine," Jake assured her in a low voice as he stroked her hair.

"I want to see for myself. What about you,

Jake?" she asked. "Don't you miss anything?"

"Sure, all those things, except the curling iron. And getting my nails done. But I came here knowing what to expect, how rugged it is, so I was prepared."

"No one said they'd miss TV," Yolanda pouted.

"I miss it," Rudi said with a wink and hug for his wife. "I miss our livelihood."

"Now that I've met you, I'll watch the tube, just to look for your show," Jake promised. "Actually, I'm going to miss you all, too."

Brit stiffened. She knew, in that earnest, dreadful moment, that they would part soon. Jake was already anticipating it, and so should she.

The next day, as Jake had predicted, they arrived at Phantom Ranch before one o'clock. There was great excitement among the staff of the only lodge on the floor of the Grand Canyon when they realized that these were the long-lost survivors of the helicopter crash they'd heard about more than two weeks ago. Everyone was especially thrilled to meet the TV star, Yolanda, and gave her first-class attention.

The four hikers were treated to a hot meal, rooms with real beds, and the use of the pool and a telephone. At Jake's request, arrangements were made for mules to be sent down for tomorrow's final leg of the long journey to the

261

canyon's rim. Several female employees even found fresh clothes to fit Yolanda and Brit.

After a meal and a warm shower, Brit felt better, although she was still sore and tired. Jake stood at the window, legs apart, hands loose by his sides, when she entered the room with his folded jeans and shirt in her arms. "Thanks for these. I'd like to keep the moccasins if you don't mind."

"Are you going back?" he asked roughly.

She hesitated, not sure exactly what he was talking about. She placed the clothes on the chest of drawers and asked for more explanation. "Back?"

"To L.A.?"

"Of course. I have to oversee Bonnie's movie. I'm sure they've already started on it. They don't really care if I'm there, but it's important to me. For Bonnie. I plan to stay with it until they're finished."

"Where are you staying?"

"I'm not sure, exactly. I have an address. One of the producers rented an apartment for me. He was to meet me when I arrived. I suppose I'll call him when I get to town."

"How long will the movie take?"

"I don't know exactly, since I've never done anything like this before. Probably about three or four months." She felt encouraged by his questions. "Are you sure you won't consider being our Native American consultant on Zuni ways?"

"I—" He halted and turned around and looked at her. "Brit, I don't want to lose you."

"Are you just now realizing that this is almost over?" She knew she sounded angry, but dammit, he hadn't made any effort before now to face this.

"I haven't wanted to think of it. I've been too concerned about getting everyone out safely."

"That's the most shortsighted view, and lame excuse, I've ever heard of!" She felt so frustrated with him that she could scream. "So everyone is almost out safely. What about us, now?"

"You don't have to go back, Brit. You can live anywhere. Come live with me."

She looked at him steadily, one part of her wanting to fall into his arms and submit to his generous offer. Another part of her, though, wanted to stand her ground. "I have the movie, Jake. In L.A. Come with me—"

"But I have my work."

She propped her hands on her hips. "Let's talk about my work." Pointing her thumb to her chest, she repeated. "Yes, *my* work, Jake. You know how you feel about the importance of learning and teaching the truth about the Anasazi? Well, I feel that way about my grandmother's story. Here is a faithful record of the way Bonnie lived in rugged country working with the Indians fifty years ago; she even wrote it down for us. It's real, honest-to-God history, and it's a beautiful love story of two very dissimilar people, from vastly separate backgrounds. This is a story that says a lot about people in general, about equality of sexes, about life. I intend to see that Bonnie's story is portrayed on screen accurately."

"Nice speech. You make it sound . . . worthwhile."

"It is worthwhile!"

"I have no interest in doing—"

"So? No one asked you to direct it. Just consult."

"You know what they do in Hollywood, Brit. They rewrite history. They distort everything. Look at what they did with westerns all those years. Everyone has input and powers to change things. All for entertainment. And for profit."

"That's why I have some contractual controls over this one. It's why I care what happens in the portrayal. That's why I want you involved with me. You know what's right and true for that era."

"I have my work, Brit. I can't just leave."

"You could arrange something if you wanted to."

"I . . . I can't imagine me doing something like that, Brit." He shook his head and a pained expression came over his face. "Movies . . ."

"One movie. My movie, Jake. You know, two

264

weeks ago, I couldn't imagine me living in a camp on the floor of the Grand Canyon. But I did. I couldn't imagine falling in love with a man that I met down there who was so very different from me. But I did."

"Brit . . ." He reached for her, but she stepped back.

"This is ridiculous, Jake. Here we are, the night before parting, trying to figure out what we're going to do with us. I'm begging. And you're resisting. You've got to have it your way or nothing."

"Not true." His dark eyes narrowed. "I want you. But . . ." He paused and gazed out the window. His dark straight hair was long and shaggier than ever, giving him a rugged appearance. He looked more like she imagined Bonnie's lover, KnifeWing, than ever. It was uncanny.

When he turned back to her, his expression was filled with turmoil. "Brit, I don't really know what I feel right now."

"You're afraid of love."

"No! I'm afraid you're my fantasy. A beautiful blond from California, who happens to be making a movie, for Pete's sake! I mean, what better fantasy could a lonely professor create?"

She walked to him and placed both hands on his chest, careful not to press too hard on his injured rib. She felt his heartbeat beneath her fingers and knew her own was pounding just as hard. "I am no fantasy, Jake. I'm me. Real, flesh and blood, a person with feelings, desires, and my own life. I just want it to include you. If you can't handle that—"

She got no further before his hands grasped her shoulders, hauling her lightly against him. His lips covered hers, forcing them open. The kiss was all-encompassing, overwhelming, exciting. Brit forgot her argument. She forgot their disagreement. She only knew she wanted him.

There was no question that Jake wanted her. Within moments, her fresh, clean clothes were discarded on the floor and she helped him shed his. Then they were together on the narrow bed, needing only space for one body, one bare, nude body pressed to the other.

Flattening his shoulders, she made him lie back so he wouldn't be in pain from the rib. "I'll be gentle," she murmured teasingly, kissing his chest and the black Zuni bear pendant that always adorned his nude body. She touched his hair, running her fingers through every morsel of it, memorizing the shape of his head and the feel of his coarse dark hair between her fingers and against her whole hands. She rotated his face to her and kissed him roughly, passionately, then embraced him with a special sensitivity to his injury.

Jake responded by gathering her tight against his aroused body. He tried to repay the caress by jamming his fingers through her hair, which was still wet from her shower. His fingers struggled in her knotted hair, combing and untangling it.

"Come to me," he murmured, pulling her down to him so he could kiss her forehead, her cheeks, her chin. "You look like an angel tonight. An angel who spreads her golden wings to dry in the sun. So beautiful." He kissed her palms and the insides of her wrists.

Brit writhed and moved against him, then placed a kiss on his bare, smooth chest. Her tongue circled one nipple, then the other, and he made a soft urging noise. Her lips grazed his navel and her tongue dipped inside.

"Yes—oh, yes," he muttered.

She stretched with him, her legs spreading his, her body lightly on his. Her tongue laved each tightly beaded nipple and the surrounding framework of muscles of his chest. A low moan escaped his lips, but he had no desire to escape. And she had no intention of letting him get away. It was a game of loving that they played as she hovered over his outstretched body, teasing and enticing.

She wanted him everywhere, touching all her private places, pressing himself to all her secret spots. She moaned and wanted to tell him something about love, but he kissed her again, hard and open-mouthed, and she forgot everything except that kiss.

She received his tongue as it enticed her,

reaching deeper and deeper until she formed an O with her lips and created a wildness of rhythm. Then, just when she thought she would burst, he moved to another area. His hands molded her body, touching her form as if to memorize her shape, and suddenly she wanted him to ache for her as she ached for him. She wanted him to love her as she loved him.

He slid his hands down her smooth legs, caressing from her thighs to knees to calves, then back up the length of her long legs, up to the most feminine part of her. His moist kisses drove her crazy and she cried out for him . . . softly, she hoped.

He was kissing her again, closing her mouth with his. Strong brown hands firmly grasped hers, clasping and lacing fingers as he pulled her over him, kissing her ear, her neck. His muscular arms paralleled hers, pulsing wrist to pulsing wrist. The motion was symbolic. They would soon be as one, throbbing together. She gasped for air and begged him to "Hurry! Now, Jake . . ."

Brit pressed her soft breasts to his solid chest, and they lay nipple to nipple. She could feel the pounding of his heart match hers, sharing the quiescent energy. His brown body seemed to reach for her pale one, tempting and promising fulfillment. His long sinewy legs aligned with hers, rubbing, bare feet and toes clawing at each other. Her knees opened to surround him, to make their union complete.

She embraced him, taking his hot maleness into her warm shelter. He moved in her, hard and piercing, seeking, ever seeking the ecstasy growing within them both. He slowed, driving upward with deliberate skill. He would not be satisfied to make this sensuous journey alone, and she knew it. He waited, silently insisting that she go along.

She arched, taking all he offered, rising with him, the wanting as strong in her as in him. The rhythm and strength of their love rocked them into oblivion, taking them beyond fantasy, beyond dreams to more. And more.

Then, no more. She slumped over his spent body.

The tight coil deep inside her unwound slowly, leisurely. All was quiet except for their labored breathing. Eventually, reality returned. They were no longer on a fantasy flight, soaring above reality. They were back to being two bare bodies, entwined as one, on a small bed in Phantom Ranch, at the floor of the Grand Canyon. That much was real and apparent. What was not visible, but just as real, was that tomorrow they would part.

Even as Jake still lay with her, tears stung Brit's eyes. Tonight would be their last. How could she bear it?

Early next morning, the park service sent

four mules and a trail boss to escort them to the canyon's rim. The junket took more than four hours of rough riding, with a promise of sore bottoms tomorrow. But everyone, even Yolanda, agreed it was the best and fastest way out.

For some unexplainable reason, none of them was in good spirits. Jake was unusually quiet. Yolanda and Rudi snapped at each other for the first time in days. Brit felt like a time bomb, ready to explode, on the verge of collapsing in tears.

She had given her all to solving their problem and could think of nothing else left. She, too, was quiet on the journey and couldn't even admire the spectacular views they encountered from the backs of the plodding mules. Nothing could be grander than what they had experienced at the camp and Indian ruins on the canyon floor. Nothing could be more beautiful than the white beach where she and Jake had made love.

None of them expected the confusion and cacophony at the rim when they arrived, least of all, Brit. Tourists, fans, and the generally curious lined the rails. Hundreds of them. They cheered and yelled as the small wretched caravan rode their mules into sight. But the most amazing, and most aggressive, were the news photographers.

Dozens of them flashed cameras and stuck

microphones into the riders' faces shouting urgent questions. "What was it like? Were you scared? Did you get hurt? What did you eat?" And then a familiar face stepped, or hobbled, out from the bank of reporters. Frank came forward, and he was on crutches. In spite of the former ill feelings, they all hugged him and listened to his tales of spraining his ankle and practically dragging himself to a clearing and waiting until he was spotted by a touring plane. He was rescued and flown immediately to the rim.

They left the mules and mingled with Yolanda's eager fans and the reporters. Someone led them to a circle of microphones where they were all questioned. "Are you hurt? Do you need to see a doctor? Where have you been? Are you ready to go home?"

Somehow in the melee, Brit and Jake managed to slip away, leaving Yolanda and Rudi surrounded by flashing bulbs and screaming journalists.

"Brit, I will never forget you . . ."

She blinked. They were alone, against a wall, hiding between two buildings. The clamoring world was a thousand miles away. She and Jake were alone in the world, just the two of them. What was he saying? . . . *never forget you* . . . That wasn't what she wanted to hear. She wanted—"Jake, now is not the time—"

He kissed her roughly, quickly. "We'll stay in

touch. This is for luck." He pressed something into her hand and was gone.

She wandered out to the front of El Torvar Hotel and was again surrounded. Police officers, an official of the park service, someone from the company that owned the downed helicopter were all talking at once, ushering her into a waiting limousine.

Brit leaned her head back and closed her eyes. The seat was unbelievably comfortable. The air conditioner blew cool, refreshing air over her. The radio played low, relaxing music in the far distant background. She was lulled into a half-sleep.

Finally, a voice broke into her conscious. "Brit, are you all right? Do you need anything? A drink?"

Brit opened her eyes. She looked around. She was alone with a strange woman and man who spoke in cool, soothing tones. They were very nice, very concerned about her welfare, and obviously wanted to meet her every need. Airline reps, no doubt. She wanted to assure them that she had no intention of suing, but lacked the energy.

Brit was disappointed beyond belief. Jake was gone. She had expected—hoped—that he would regain his senses at the last minute and go with her. But he had not.

She looked down at her hands. One had been clinched in a sweaty fist since they left. Painfully, she opened her hand. In the grimy palm lay Jake's black bear fetish, a small jet figure with a single turquoise eye. "For luck," he had said.

For months there had been significant pressure for KnifeWing to marry a Hopi girl. It was an arrangement that would be good for both families and both tribes. He had resisted until he was asked by the tribal leaders to consider her. So, he went to the Intertribal Ceremonial at Gallup, New Mexico, to meet her and her family. I was quite upset at the prospect and informed him that if he should marry her, or anyone, that he could forget about me. I would not tolerate the Zuni custom of having more than one wife.

KnifeWing was very stubborn, and declared that he would do what he thought was best. He visited me the day before he left for Gallup and gave me a Zuni bear fetish for good luck. The black bear was made of jet with an inlay of turquoise leading to its heart. So, he went on his way, and I was sick for three days. I kept the fetish under my pillow for luck, and felt there was no luck in it.

But I was wrong. He returned, after eight days, without a Hopi wife.

Chapter Twelve

Los Angeles was a cultural shock to Brit. The problem was that she had discovered another world, a serene world which held beauty at every turn and allowed the individual time and space. It was a world in which she found a place for herself and felt peace. But there was no peace here. This place was too big, too busy, too noisy, and Jake was gone from it. Brit felt all alone. But she wasn't. Michael was there.

He had called her immediately on hearing of her rescue and driven to Los Angeles from San Diego the very next day. She had been less than happy to see him, and it was obvious that everything was wrong between them. Brit wanted to give herself time to be sure, but the more they were together, she knew she had to do something about it. When they parted in Las Vegas, before she laid eyes on Jake Landry, she realized she didn't love Michael. And now, after Jake, she couldn't love anyone else. She had hoped to salvage something of their relationship, perhaps a

274

friendship, and wondered if that were possible.

Brit stood at the window of her apartment, staring at her view. Oh, it wasn't a bad apartment. It was rather nice. Comfortable furniture. Heart of the city. Ten minutes from the movie studio. What more could she want?

Only Jake.

The towering red cliffs, glistening turquoise pool, and crystal waterfall of her imagination melted into her actual view . . . a half-acre parking lot rimmed with palm trees. The dark lean figure with black straight hair to his collar and piercing jet eyes of her memory faded to the reality of . . . Michael.

Blond, good-looking with muscular arms from lifting weights, Michael followed her around the room. "So where were you, Brit? Where did you sleep? You actually expect me to believe you were camping outside all this time?" He hooted with laughter. "You? Who has to have her nails perfect and every hair in place?"

"It's true. Slept under a canopy of stars." She grinned with the admission. It did sound preposterous for her, and Michael still didn't believe her, she could tell.

"What were you doing down there every day?"

She shrugged and brushed at her immaculate, sharply-creased jeans. Michael wouldn't believe that she'd worn a man's sloppy clothes and bathed in a stream. "We did nothing much. Relaxing mostly, since we couldn't get out right away. It was absolutely beautiful and so peaceful, Michael." She sat cross-legged on a flower-cushioned window seat and watched two cars rush to beat a yellow light at the intersection. A jet thundered overhead, low, coming in for a landing. The sound vibrated the room for a couple of seconds.

Michael paced before her. He was so accustomed to noises, he hadn't even heard the jet. "How did you live? What did you eat? Nuts and berries?"

Brit smiled tolerantly. "Canned stuff, mostly. We cooked over an open fire and a one-burner stove. Did you know the bottom of the Grand Canyon is a desert?"

"I do now because you've told me enough. How did you manage in that heat? And I can't imagine Yolanda being content to stay there, too."

"Well, Michael, no one was content to stay. We had no alternative. We all went down together. We all came out together. Except Frank, the pilot. He left early to get help, but got lost. And injured his ankle. Finally he was rescued and met us at the rim. He was lucky twice." She laced and unlaced her fingers. God, she was jittery, and she hated this feeling.

"Then, the three of you—no, there were four, right?"

Brit slammed her hand down on the cushion beside her. "Dammit, Michael, is this a quiz?"

"I'm just curious. Don't you know that I was worried sick about you all that time? I thought you were—" He halted and walked across the room to her. "I didn't know how you were or if you were injured, and I was scared. Now, I just want to know exactly what happened, that's all."

"I'm sorry, Michael. I know it must have been bad for you, just waiting to hear something. And not knowing." She felt terrible. Of course, he'd been worried and she wasn't handling this well. She should just come to the point and tell him how she felt. But the timing was bad.

He came closer. "Actually, honey, you don't look worse for the wear, all things considered." He picked up a strand of her hair and rubbed it between his finger and thumb. "Better, in fact. Your hair's lovely, maybe even a little softer."

"It's that clear, pure water I had to wash it in. No chemicals." Inadvertently, she shook her head free of Michael's touch, remembering the time Jake had shampooed her hair. His hands worked magic . . .

"Your skin's always been gorgeous, but now it has a little glow. I guess it's from being free of air pollutants."

"Yep. All that fresh air and sunshine." Brit looked away as he brushed her cheek with his forefinger.

277

"Well, you definitely are slimmer. More fit."

"It's all that walking and climbing on rocks. But riding those mules out yesterday nearly killed us." She laughed and rubbed her rear. "We were all complaining by the time we reached the top."

"I'll bet." His finger slid beneath her chin and lifted it slightly. "How about a kiss?"

Brit hesitated just long enough to take in a quick breath. "Sure."

He touched her lips with his. When she gave no response, no further encouragement, he backed away. "Okay, obviously you need to acclimate, get used to everything . . . to me."

She hopped up and walked around the strange room, stuffing her hands into her back pockets, the way Jake used to do. "You know, I probably need a brisk five-mile hike to make me feel better." She laughed nervously. "Yeah, it would help me stretch, loosen up."

Michael stood across the room where she had left him. "You hiked five miles every day? What about Yolanda? Did she walk like that?"

"Well, she and Rudi certainly hiked out of the canyon. And that's more than five miles."

"I can't imagine her doing any of this."

"Hiking out was her idea," Brit explained. "We probably could have gotten out sooner, but Yolanda refused to fly after the crash. Dreamed

278

of crashing again and simply would not fly out of the canyon."

"So you all stayed with her? Because she wanted to?"

Brit nodded. Michael wouldn't understand, so she gave up trying to explain. "That's right."

"Strange. This whole thing is so strange, Brit. And, I must admit, you seem . . . different. Almost like you're sorry to be here."

"I know it's kind of hard to believe. You can't understand what it was like there. I think you just had to be there, Michael. I suppose I do need some time to adjust. Everything has happened so fast."

"Um-hum. I guess." He waited a moment, then asked, "So, who was the man?"

Brit frowned at him. "What?"

"Don't play coy, Brit. It isn't like you at all. You know exactly who I'm talking about. The man who came out with the three of you. The tall one. Dark hair. Indian look."

"Oh, you mean Jake Landry." She tried to say his name casually, tried not to show the deep emotion she felt in merely uttering his name. "The man who saved our lives," she finished succinctly.

"Right. Tell me about him."

She folded her arms. "What do you want to know?" What could she say to Michael about Jake? That he was the smartest, most interesting

279

man she'd ever known? That he was the best
lover she had ever had? That he had completely
captured her heart, then sent her away?

"What was he doing down there right where
you crashed? Quite a coincidence, wasn't it?"

"Well, he wasn't exactly where we crashed. We
had to hike to his camp." She paused, remembering. It seemed like eons ago that they'd first
followed Jake to his encampment and begun
their odyssey.

"Why was he there?"

Brit propped her fists on her hips and took a
deep breath. "Look, Michael, I'm sure we've hit
twenty questions by now, and I'm tired of it.
The man's an archeologist and professor from
Northern Arizona University. He was working on
a special project to chart and document ancient
Indian ruins in the canyon. Did you know that
there were people living in that area when Columbus discovered America? We had to wait
until Jake finished his project so he could lead
us out. Now, enough about him."

Michael eyed her suspiciously, then gave a
shrugging motion with his hands out. "Okay,
okay. Don't come unglued. I was just making
conversation."

Brit turned away from him and stared again
out the window at her limited view. Yes, she was
touchy about Jake. She couldn't talk about him
casually, that much was obvious.

"So what was Yolanda like? What did you say to her?" Then he asked rhetorically, "What does one say to Yolanda."

Brit turned around. Maybe Michael was just curious about her experiences, after all. His questions made her realize that he was impressed with Yolanda's status. She was, indeed, a TV star, something Brit had lost sight of during their canyon journey. Most people didn't think of Yolanda's routines as a performance and her writing as a job. They, including Michael, thought of her as being just glamorous and automatically funny.

"Yolanda was . . . okay. In the beginning, she expected certain things. Especially Rudi, her husband. He hovered over her like a nanny making demands for his spoiled brat. But there were no conveniences for anyone; we were all the same down there. When they realized that, they came around. Yolanda was great." Brit smiled to herself, remembering their fun.

"I can't imagine her sleeping on the ground and eating from a can."

"She volunteered to help the cook and got pretty creative with dried and canned stuff. She even made a special meal for my birthday. There were *nopalitos* from the local cacti." Brit chuckled warmly. "And Rudi made a big pancake with a candle. It was . . . great."

"You had a party down there?"

281

"It was a creative endeavor. We had to make the best of what was available to us. Yolanda and Rudi like to party. Actually, they're caring, congenial people." Brit paused. "But when we reached the top yesterday, the media besieged us. Yolanda was the only one who felt at ease, so we let her have them."

"I noticed you didn't have much to say."

Brit shook her head. "And then things happened so fast, we never even got to say good-bye."

"You came together as strangers. Maybe it's just as well that you parted the same way."

"But we weren't strangers when we parted. Far from it. We'd lived together and—" Brit gritted her teeth and a knot formed quickly in her stomach at Michael's glibness. Had she and Jake parted as strangers? She certainly didn't think so. Did they mean nothing more to each other than that? It hurt her to consider it. But sitting here, talking with Michael about it wouldn't do a thing except make her more miserable. This was between her and Jake. And apparently, he was satisfied with them going their separate ways.

"And what?" Michael waited for her to finish her sentence.

But Brit changed the subject. She had to get out of here; had to get busy, before Michael wanted more from her, wanted what she was not capable of giving. "Say, Michael, according to the shooting schedule, they're filming some scenes this afternoon on *Long Ago and Far Away*. Why don't we go over to the studio and watch?"

"You want me to go along?"

"Sure, why not?"

"Okay," he agreed as he considered the prospects. "It'd be fun. We might even see some stars."

The producer was a short, busy man. Shorter than Brit, Isaac Holtzbach was so energetic, he could hardly sit still. His desk was overrun with a mountain of papers and the phone rang incessantly, interrupting their conversation at least a dozen times.

Holtzbach sprang from sitting to standing while talking to her and Michael, anxiously pacing the tiny space behind his desk when he was on the phone. Each conversation bounded strangely from one subject to another with no coherence or transition, so that most of the time, it made absolutely no sense to listen to him. He used the same technique when talking to them until Brit's mind was a blur trying to keep up with him.

He was animated and spoke with his hands as well. "Avalon is perfect for this role. Why she's

Bonnie, herself, reincarnate. You're going to love her, just love her, Brit. And Julio Riva *is* her Indian lover—eh, eh, whatsisname."

"KnifeWing," Brit answered, aggravated that the man couldn't remember the hero's name. He made her nervous.

"Yeah-yeah-yeah. Knifewnggg." His voice dwindled away and he held up one finger to them while he answered the phone again and began jabbering into the speaker.

Brit squirmed and gave Michael a weary glance while Holtzbach paced and jumped subjects. She had never felt so out of place in her life. Was this the man who held *Long Ago and Far Away* in the palm of his hand? She shuddered to think it was true.

Holtzbach halted his telephone diatribe, hung up as abruptly as he had begun and continued his conversation with Brit as if there had been no interruption. "Riva's Mexican, but he looks Indian. So, you want to meet him? He's one handsome hunk. He's doing the scene this afternoon where he plays the flute. And Bonnie gives him the first kiss. Come on and we'll watch."

Brit perked up. This was what she needed, to watch the action of the actual movie. The flute scene was one of her favorites. Right away, she thought of Jake and the night he played for her by the campfire.

Before they could leave the office, the door

swung open and a man with a baseball cap on backwards and wearing a black tank top with a skull and crossbones on the front burst into the room. He looked beyond, or through, Brit and addressed Holtzbach with a pointing finger that punctuated each loud, angry exposition.

"Avalon cannot act! She cannot kiss! She cannot walk across the street with a natural motion, much less climb onto a horse without falling off the other side! Either she goes or I do!"

Holtzbach smiled hugely. "Come on, Laird-baby. Take it ea-sy, ea-sy. You'll stir your blood pressure up again. I'll talk to her."

"I've talked to her and it's useless. She's a brick wall. Maybe you want to delay production while someone gives her acting lessons."

"Now, now, now, that won't be necessary. I'm sure that she—"

The man called Laird interrupted. "I'm not waiting around for her to get the hang of this. Dump her by tomorrow, Isaac. I mean it!" And he wheeled around and left.

Brit blinked. Had she seen what she thought she had? It was crazy.

"The director, Laird Sutcliff," Holtzbach said in a low voice, ushering them out of his office. "My wife's cousin. Trouble with a capital T. But don't you worry about this movie. I won't let him interfere with the production. I'll calm him down, and he'll do a great job. Everything de-

285

pends on Avalon, and of course, Julio. But they're great."

"Isn't the director the most important?" Brit asked, alarmed by the bizarre behavior and explosive display of the director of *her* movie. "Doesn't he steer everything in the movie, make it work or not?"

"Well, yes, of course. But Laird's a wee temperamental. This project means so much to him. He wants to get everything just right, and of course, so do I. But he's a perfectionist, and you know how impossible they can be. Don't you worry your pretty head about a thing."

Brit worried. Tension between brothers-in-law who worked on her movie sounded like potential havoc to her. And neither seemed to have the integrity of the story at heart. It was obvious to her that they both wanted to control, and that was a frightening prospect.

Wide-eyed and curious, Michael and Brit followed Holtzbach to the set. They came from a polite world where people's opinions mattered. They had entered a world of rudeness and ruthless power struggles. The way Brit saw it, all of this hassle was so each one could make an individual contribution to the movie. But this was Bonnie's story, and Brit was here to see that it remained so. She couldn't let herself lose sight of that.

Holtzbach pointed a spot where they could

286

stand and watch the performances, yet remain out of the way. Brit was quickly taken with the handsome Julio who held the lovely Avalon in a passionate embrace.

"Cut! Cut!" yelled the director.

Just like in the movies, Brit thought, delighted.

But this director was like none she had ever imagined. "Do you call that a kiss? Let me show you!" And he lunged between the couple, grabbed Avalon and bent her backward in a long, involved kiss.

"Hey!" Julio grabbed the director's shoulder and hauled him away from the struggling actress.

Brit feared, for a moment, that there would be a fight between them. She had, after all, experienced the quick explosion between Frank and Rudi after the crash in the canyon.

"You're impossible!" Avalon shrieked, running from the set, sobbing.

"No, honey, you've got that backward," Laird called after her. *"You're* impossible!"

Julio stalked away sullenly.

"Damn! He's screwing up everything," Holtzbach mumbled, adding something about "back later." He disappeared with Laird, leaving Brit and Michael alone to poke around the set for the next hour.

When filming resumed, Laird seemed more subdued. Avalon was not in sight, and Julio brought out the flute.

"Great," Brit whispered to Michael. "This part's going to be good." She was disappointed that she hadn't had the chance to meet everyone yet, but things had been disorderly today. There would be other times, she reassured herself. As soon as the flute music began, Brit knew it was wrong. All wrong. She could not stand by and let it continue. She had an obligation to the truth.

Slipping to the director's side, she said, "Excuse me, Mr. Sutcliff, but this isn't the way it would be. It's all wrong."

Laird glared at her for a long second, then turned his horse-face back to the set, ignoring her.

Brit frowned. After a confused pause, she insinuated herself in front of his view of the set. "Excuse me, but I don't think this is the way it would be."

"And who are you?" he muttered between clenched teeth.

"I'm Brit Bailey. Bonnie was my great-grandmother and I—"

"I don't care if you're Bonnie, herself. Get out of my face."

Brit was not intimidated. "I'm an advisor for this movie and—"

"Who says?"

"Pardon me?"

"Who says you're an advisor?"

Brit was astonished. No one had informed the director of her role around here? She had been gone and completely forgotten. Well, she wouldn't stand for this. "Mr. Holtzbach hired me," she said, confident that his name would clear the way for her.

"Holtzbach can go to hell," Laird said.

Brit swallowed, momentarily stunned. She quickly decided to abandon the producer and simply state the facts. "In the first place, Knife-Wing wouldn't be sitting on the trading post roof, playing his flute like that. This isn't *Fiddler on the Roof*. He wouldn't have been performing. He would play it in tribute to the world around him."

Laird folded his arms. "You're nuts. A real nut cake. Get out of my way."

"No!" Brit stood her ground. "I'm here to advise. I have to make sure Bonnie's story is right."

"Preposterous! It's as right as it'll ever get! Get out!"

Michael took her arm, but Brit jerked away and continued to face Laird. "And another thing. Native American flute music doesn't sound like a jazz clarinet jamboree. It sounds like . . ." her voice softened, "like the wind and the coyotes and the ancient spirits."

Laird stared at her. Silence blanketed the set. Everyone stared at her. Brit looked around and

289

spotted Holtzbach. "Have you ever heard Native American flute music?" she called. "It doesn't sound like this. Tell him. Get it right."

Laird turned to Holtzbach. "Would you get this nut cake out of here?"

"I'm afraid she stays," Holtzbach said, approaching. "It's in the contract. But we'll work it out. Maybe she's right, Laird. This is a little too commercial. Seems to me, it should have more of an eerie sound, like . . ."

"Like nature," Brit added enthusiastically. "Like the animals. And the birds. It's a beautiful, rather exotic sound, like none other."

"We can do that," Holtzbach said. "Give us twenty-four hours, and it'll be done."

Laird balked. "You have flipped, Isaac. You let everyone tell you how to make this movie. Everyone but me."

"Okay, Laird, what do *you* think?"

"I think it doesn't matter how it sounds. He plays the flute to entice her. And it works. Embrace. Kiss—if we can find an actress who can do that." He clapped his hands together. "Cut. End of scene. Fade to black."

"No!" Brit gritted her teeth. "He has no intention of enticing her with the flute. He plays for himself and his relationship to his world. Bonnie must prove that she deserves to join his world, that she cares as much about his different world as she cares about him." Brit stopped. Both the director and producer were staring at her. So was Michael. And what was she saying, anyway? Who was she talking about? Bonnie? Or herself?

"She's got a minor point," Holtzbach said after a moment. "We'll study it, Brit."

"Study, hell!" Laird exclaimed. Defeat was apparent in his face and he hated it. His day had not gone well, and he was furious. Furious at everything and everyone.

"I want . . . I want this to be right," Brit tried to explain. "It's important that Bonnie's story be accurate. There have been enough misconceptions about Native Americans out of Hollywood. I want her story to be truthful, which means different from the others."

Michael took her elbow. "Come on, honey. Let's go. Let them handle it. They know how."

"No, they don't." Brit ignored him and stood her ground.

"Look, Brit, darling," Holtzbach said. "We endorse your wishes for this movie. We want it right, too. We'll get a consultant, someone who knows the Indian culture."

"Zuni," she blurted with exasperation. "He has to know the Zuni Pueblo Indians. KnifeWing was Zuni, and it's different. Every tribe's customs are different in some ways, similar in others. It's important to know—"

"Okay, okay," Holtzbach said, patting her shoulder to pacify her.

"I know someone who can do it," she said without thinking.

"Oh? You do? Who?"

"Jake Landry. He's an archeology professor at Northern Arizona University in Flagstaff, Arizona. He's part Zuni and he knows."

"Sure, sure. Tell my secretary. We'll be in touch."

"Thank you."

Michael led her away, and she could hear Laird exclaiming, "You'll get nothing! I don't need a damned consultant!"

They were quiet in the car driving back to Brit's apartment. Too quiet. She knew that Michael was furious with her. And when she had given Jake's name as the consultant—it just slipped out, she didn't know how—Michael had tightened up all over. She could feel the tension between them in the tiny car and it accompanied them into her apartment.

"You really lost it, Brit."

She pressed her lips together stubbornly. Maybe he was right. But she would not give in to Hollywood's demands on *her* movie. "They are impossible."

"I don't understand why you had to intrude with your two cents' worth," he continued. "It didn't matter that much."

"What do you mean?"

"In the total concept of the movie, this is a minor element."

"It is not a minor element. Anything to do with the Indian culture and the relationship between Bonnie and KnifeWing is major to the movie."

"This is not a documentary. It's a movie, for God's sake!"

"These people were real. They'll live again on the screen. Their story is real. I want it right when it's shown in theaters across the country."

"Today you could see that these men were already having major conflicts. Why couldn't you leave them alone just today?"

Brit glared at Michael, unbelieving. "The fact that they're not agreeing with each other, or have personality conflicts with the actors, has nothing to do with me. But when their power fight affects this movie, it matters to me. A lot."

"Why can't you let them do it their way?"

"Because they're wrong. Don't you understand?"

"No. I'm afraid I don't. You've already made your money when they purchased the rights for this movie. You'll get paid as an advisor whether you open your mouth about a single item or not. Why can't you be satisfied with what you already have? Keep your mouth shut, collect your paycheck, and enjoy."

She turned away, more angry than she had ever been. This attitude was typical of Michael and at the heart of why she could not love him. Once she had seen this side of him, she could not ignore it. And the love—whatever love there had been between them—had perished.

"I just can't," she said simply. She was tired of defending herself. If he didn't understand by now, she could proceed no further with him. "I think you'd better go, Michael. I believe . . . it's over between us."

"Yeah, you want to get rid of me," he muttered bitterly, "so you can call in your Indian to do the job. Consultant, ha! Pretty good, Brit. Quick. Gotta hand it to you."

"No, you're wrong." She lifted her head proudly. "Jake isn't why we're through. It's been over for a long time. We just didn't have the sense, or the guts, to call it an end."

"Let's do that now." Michael strode to the door and slammed it behind him.

The apartment was quiet, dead quiet. Then the whole place shook as another jet zoomed in close for touchdown at the nearby landing strip. Brit figured she had just about ruined her life, certainly her emotional stability, in the last twenty-four hours.

She had parted with Jake. She had ended a dwindling relationship with Michael. She had made enemies and doubters on the movie set.

Nobody really trusted her, even Holtzbach. She knew no one here, for her real friends were back in San Diego. She was all alone. All alone in L.A., city of angels.

it down for us. It's real, honest-to-God history.

Chapter Thirteen

The weeks stretched into a month, and she hadn't heard from any of her Grand Canyon companions. Her days were busy and fuzzy. Her nights unbearable and hazy. Her only salvation was talking on the phone with her friends in San Diego. But even they couldn't really understand her unhappiness. They only knew that she was.

One night, the phone rang. Brit jumped for it, expecting to hear Ana's or Kelly's voice on the other end. She had no idea how long she had been sitting there on the floor, holding the Zuni bear fetish in her palm "for luck." But it was dark outside, so she must have been there for hours.

"Hello."

"Brit? Brit—"

Her heart pounded, for the voice was vaguely familiar. Wonderfully familiar. "Yes?"

"Brit! Hiya, babe. This is Rudi."

"Rudi!" Brit felt such a sweep of happiness

296

that she almost cried. "I'm so glad to hear from you. How are you and Yolanda?"

"It's a helluva adjustment, huh?"

She laughed, feeling close immediately. He knew what she was going through. "Only you two would understand that."

"Never better! It's like we're in love all over again. And get this—we weren't home twenty-four hours, she hadn't even had her nails patched, and she was begging me to take her back down there! Can you believe it?"

"Yes, matter of fact, I can." Brit smiled sympathetically as she gazed around her clean, comfortable apartment. "Sounds crazy, but I know exactly how she feels."

"We do want to make a trip back down in the canyon, but it'll have to be later. Probably next year. Right now, we're behind schedule on filming the show and working our butts off on that. And we're doing something else. For that, Yolanda and I would like you to meet us for dinner. She's working up a new routine and needs a trustworthy audience. Remember the night around the campfire when she gave a rough draft?"

"Yes, of course."

"Well, she's refined it and wants to try it out before taking it to the public. You're one of the ones she wants to be there. It'll just be close friends and family. Can you make it next Wednesday night?"

"Sure, Rudi. I'd love to. Where?"

"La Luna. Great Mexican food. Are you familiar with it?"

"I've heard of it," Brit said. She had heard that La Luna was the best, and most expensive, Mexican restaurant in L.A.

"Seven o'clock, Wednesday. We have a room reserved in the back, so ask at the desk. Okay?"

"Got it. And Rudi, thanks."

"Hey, we're like family, no?"

"Yes," she murmured. "Like family. I'm looking forward to it." Brit hung up with a smile on her face.

She missed them all, couldn't help it. They had experienced a lot together in those weeks in the canyon and had grown close, perhaps closer than any of them realized until now. It was difficult to shut the door on such a relationship. Initially, she had feared that the Romeros had done that. She understood that they were busy and had their friends and work. But this proved that they hadn't forgotten what they all shared and, most of all, hadn't forgotten her. Only Jake had, it seemed.

On the next Wednesday night, Brit stood beside the buffet table, nibbling. She didn't know any of the twenty-five or so people gathered, so she stood near the food and tried to act like she belonged. It was a feast fit for a king. Crab, shrimp, beef, chicken, and caviar shared the table with corn and flour tortillas, tamales, and refried beans.

When Rudi arrived, though, he grabbed Brit in a huge bear hug, then tucked her into the curve of his arm and introduced her to everyone as an "old" friend. It was all she needed to be completely and wholeheartedly accepted. By the time Yolanda appeared, she felt at ease.

Yolanda was met with applause as she stood at one end of the room and greeted the group. "Hey, applaud yourselves for always being there for me," she said with an uncharacteristic seriousness. "You are the people dearest to me and I want you to know how much I appreciate you. Tonight, I'm going back. Back to the good parts of the good ol' days. This is something I used to do many years ago when I was trying out my acts. My sisters know how it was." She pointed to several women in the audience who giggled at the attention she brought to them.

"And my brothers . . ." Yolanda waved them away with one shiny-nailed hand. "They made my life miserable with their teasing, but I invited them, anyway. They married nice girls."

She paused while everyone laughed.

"Still, it was such a good idea, I'm renewing the practice. So, expect more invitations in the future. But you have to work for your dinner by giving me your honest opinions of the show. That's why you're here."

Everyone cheered happily. Obviously, no one minded this kind of work.

"Tonight we're celebrating. We just signed to do a special that Rudi and I designed after our little excursion to the deep pit of the Grand Canyon. It'll be called *Come Join Our Grand Comedy,* and it'll air in a few months."

Again, everyone applauded.

"Now, if you recognize yourself in any of these routines, just remember that I'll change your name, and no one will ever know, unless *The Inquirer* offers me big bucks!" She paused for more laughter, then proceeded with her act.

Brit was surprised to notice that Yolanda, who had always been cool in the spotlight, was nervous at first. But as each punchline drew more and more laughter and occasional applause, she calmed down.

After each act, Yolanda halted and discussed the comic qualities with the group. At first they were reluctant to criticize. But she insisted that they be honest, and soon they were telling her what they liked and disliked about the piece. Her secretary was nearby making notes. When she finished the complete program, waiters brought in dessert. Pies, ice cream, cake—everything was chocolate, except the flaming baked Alaska.

Finally Yolanda approached Brit with a hug. "How are you, honey? Ready to descend into the canyon again?"

"Whenever you are," Brit answered gamely.

"I would love to go back, but *this time,* Rudi's right. Next year will have to be soon enough. We have too much to do now. And it's great, huh?"

"Yeah, we have to get back to our real lives."

"You aren't dieting, are you, Brit? There should be black walnut chocolate chip ice cream. I ordered it just for you."

"I've got my eye on it," Brit said with a grin. "Thanks so much for inviting me here tonight, Yolanda. It's fabulous. And your show is going to be fantastic. I laughed until I cried tonight."

"You get the credit, y'know."

"Me?" Brit shook her head. "How? I didn't write a word."

"You didn't recognize yourself?"

"The whiner? That wasn't me. It was you!"

"Me? Never!" Yolanda grinned devilishly. "Besides, it was your suggestion while we were still in the canyon that we look at the funny side of things. And that was before the mule ride!"

"Notice I wasn't laughing at that part." Brit shook her finger as if she were scolding. "Whoever said riding mules was funny?"

"I notice one of us is missing tonight," Yolanda said with a solemn smile. "Jake. Have you heard from him? Oh, forget I said that. It's none of my business." She clamped her hand over her mouth.

Suddenly, the atmosphere turned somber for Brit. "It's all right. I haven't heard from him, and I don't expect to. We . . . uh, said goodbye at the rim."

"Oh." Yolanda looked disappointed. "I always

liked a good love story and had great hopes for you two. Like Bonnie's story. How's the movie coming along?"

Brit rolled her eyes. "I'm fighting an uphill battle. Those people have no idea how folks lived in the early West. They've seen too many fake western movies."

"Well, if you need any help, maybe Rudi can help. He knows a lot of people."

"Thanks. I'll remember that."

"Uh, Brit, I thought you should know we're flying Jake out next month for the show."

Brit looked surprised. "He agreed?"

"What could he say? I owe the man my life and I want him there. The least I can do is make fun of him!"

"Serves him right," Brit mumbled, dry-mouthed. "I can't think of a better compliment." In spite of her pain on learning that even Yolanda had talked to Jake, Brit managed to pretend it didn't matter. She wondered how she would react to seeing him, and if she could avoid him altogether.

"Hey, I've gotta talk to one of my sisters. She's pregnant again. I hope this one's a girl. Try that ice cream." Yolanda hugged Brit. "You're too skinny," she said, and disappeared in the crowd.

Brit heaped black walnut chocolate chip ice cream on her plate. She licked her spoon, grateful that the Romeros were still her friends. The ice cream was good, but better was the fact that Yolanda remembered what she liked. Remembered her. What they had developed in the canyon remained. A good friendship. It was too bad the love she thought she and Jake had developed didn't last.

"So, how can you tell?"

Cole Washburn looked hard at his friend. "Jake, buddy, if you think I'm going to comment on that one, you're crazy."

"Look, you've been married for a long time. You know how this stuff works." Jake ran his hand through his dark disheveled hair and walked the length of the room, then paced back. He stopped, momentarily, and stared out the window.

"You were married," Cole shot back.

"It wasn't love. It was lust."

"Isn't it the same? Who the hell knows about love?" Cole got up from the laptop computer and went over to the stereo.

"You, of all people, know it isn't the same." Jake watched curiously as his friend started sorting through Jake's CDs. For the last month, the two of them had been trying to organize Jake's notes and compile the information into a cohesive report on the Grand Canyon explorations. Jake had been quiet and contemplative. But today, he was totally distracted. He hadn't been sleeping well. He couldn't concentrate. He was miserable. And he saw to it that Cole was, too. Jake wanted some instant solutions and hoped that Cole would help. But Cole was too shrewd for that.

"Without sex, where would we all be? Nowhere, that's where." Cole grinned. "Is that a line from a song? Well, it should be."

"Look," Jake said earnestly. "I'll admit, the woman turns me on. She's damn good-looking, blond, and has the sexiest green eyes, not to mention, a good bod. But, that's not enough to mess up your whole life, is it? *Is it?*"

"Mess up your life?"

Jake gestured. "Change it. You know what I mean."

"She would change it, all right." Cole began making a pile of certain CDs.

Jake figured he was looking for something specific and ignored him. "I screwed up the last time so badly, both Donna and I came away bitter and angry at the opposite sex for years. She's still . . . not married. I'm sure I'm to blame."

Cole looked up. "Funny, most divorces aren't the fault of only one person. Why do you insist on taking the full blame?"

"I was at least seventy percent of the fault. Maybe more."

"How do you figure that?"

"I made too many demands. I expected too much. I refused to give in to anything. I—"

"All right! Enough! I guess you were a jerk, after all." Cole pointed to the stack of plastic-encased CDs, then swept his hand over them to spread them like a fan on the floor. "There you go. All these are about love, from Paul Simon to U2, from Natalie Cole to Sting. Then there's the Beatles, Elvis, and Frank Sinatra. And more than half the country music ever recorded agonizes over pure love, lost love, true love, and wronged love."

Jake propped his fists on his waist and demanded, "Have you researched this?"

"Yeah, I've done my share of agonizing. Everyone has something to say on the subject. Everyone in the world—*the world,* Jake—agonizes over love. Listen to them, all of them, and see what they have to say. Maybe one of them will strike a chord with you. Then you'll know."

Jake shook his head. "You're nuts. No song can tell me what I need to know about this situation. What the hell am I supposed to do? Give up everything I've worked for?"

Cole wagged his finger. "Maybe. Maybe not. My point is, these songs can come as close as I could."

"But you know me, personally. You know—"

"I'm not getting between you and your feelings. You have to figure them out for yourself." Cole moved back to the computer that Jake and Brit had hauled around at the bottom of the canyon and started tapping the keys.

305

Jake stood at the window and silently studied the San Francisco Peaks that towered on the outskirts of Flagstaff. He could not get her image out of his head, that hurt expression in her green eyes when he said goodbye.

Methodically, Cole packed up the computer and all the scattered papers. "I don't know the answers. If I did, I'd be rich." Cole stood at the door for a second. "I only know one thing, Jake. You are one miserable SOB, and I can't get any work done with you brooding like this. I'm taking everything to my house to finish."

Jake turned around and started to say something. But, in mid-thought and with his mouth open, he forgot what he'd intended to say before it could escape his lips.

"I understand." Cole smiled wryly. "Just remember that women are romantic creatures. They like the little things that show you care, *if* you care. That part's up to you."

Jake barely noticed when Cole shut the door. He pondered the craggy San Francisco Peaks which were snow-capped most of the year. Only now, they were bare, down to the rocky earth. Jake had hiked to the top once and was surprised to find exquisite, delicate wildflowers in a place where he assumed would be too rocky and barren for the existence of any beauty. The twelve-thousand-foot mountaintop was like the mile-deep bottom of the canyon, which looked sterile and empty. Once there, however, you could find a wealth of beauty hidden from public view.

Suddenly, Jake knew what he had to do. Right now. Immediately. It would help him think. He stripped down, put on running shoes and shorts, slid a pair of Walkman earphones over his head, and took off running. Running as fast and as far as he could. Running to think . . . running away from his thoughts . . .

When he returned home, hours later, a feminine voice that he would never forget was on his phone message machine. He sat in the dark and played it over and over.

"Jake, they're making a mockery of Bonnie's story. I know it isn't important to you, but it is to . . . Bonnie. To her memory. And to the truth. I . . . really need . . . your help on this movie."

She didn't say her name on the recording. But he knew. Her name and her image had echoed in his brain since the day he left her at the canyon's rim. Now, he said her name aloud until it filled the rooms of his empty house and reverberated in his soul. "Brit . . . Brit . . ."

Jake walked through the rooms. "Brit . . . Brit . . ."

Her name conjured her image—the green eyes and blond hair and sassy smile . . . did he want to ruin both their lives as he had once before with Donna? He didn't think he could stand another foul-up with his life.

* * *

KnifeWing was a runner in the Zuni tradition. Stripped down to a loincloth, black hair bound with a headband and flying loosely around his shoulders, he looked magnificent. KnifeWing was one of a rare breed who could run great distances and even catch a deer. He told me stories of the ancient Zuni men who would chase a deer for miles until they caught it. He said the secret was not in speed, for the deer was faster, but in having the stamina to outlast the creature, for the deer had poor endurance over distances.

KnifeWing had wonderful stamina and would often say, after a run, that he caught a deer, but let it go because no one needed the meat. I never knew for sure if he caught a deer. But neither we, nor anyone in the tribe, ever went hungry. He took very good care of us all.

Chapter Fourteen

"That didn't take long." Brit tried to grip her emotions as she gripped the doorknob. The sight of Jake was both electrifying and devastating at the same time.

His voice was steady and velvet. "I'm not here just because you said you needed me for the movie. I'm here because I need you."

Brit's hands grew sweaty as she opened the door wider to admit him. He looked leaner than she remembered. But he was still dark-skinned and handsome. Her heart raced and she clutched involuntarily at her chest. "Wh . . . what?" For a moment, she felt dizzy, then giddy. Oh God, she had to seize her emotions and the situation. After all, she had called him for help on the movie. That was why he was here.

He handed her a single perfectly-shaped long-stemmed pink rosebud.

Without moving or taking her eyes off his face, she accepted the flower.

Jake smiled tightly. "I never had a chance to

romance you, to show you how much you mean to me. Let's take our time and enjoy, get to know each other."

She backed into the room. "Love takes time, Jake. More than we've given it."

"Right. I want to know for sure," he continued as he stepped inside and shoved the door closed with his foot, "that I really do love you . . . as much as I think I do right now at this minute." He took one hand and pulled her close. "You're beautiful, and I've missed you like hell."

His arms swept around to frame her back, forcing her against the hard length of him.

"Oh, Jake, I've dreamed of this. Am I dreaming now?"

"You weren't a two-week stand in the Grand Canyon. You have remained with me every waking moment since we parted. And I can't even escape you when I sleep. You're in my dreams, too, Brit. In my conscious and subconscious. In my blood . . ." His lips found hers then, and he kissed her long and hard until they both came up panting for air.

He touched her face, her cheeks, her arms. "I've missed this, missed you . . ."

"Nothing like I've missed you." She stood on tiptoe and kissed him again. "I thought we were through. I thought it was over—"

His finger pressed her lips. "Don't think. Just love me."

She leaned her head back and laughed. "I love

it, love to hear you say that. I'd love to love you, Jake, because I do."

He kissed her neck and scooped her up in his arms. "Where's the bed. I want to make love to you in a real bed. Let's not waste any more time."

She laughed and tried to wriggle down. "Careful! Don't hurt your cracked ribs."

But he held her. "All healed," he vowed and looked for a likely doorway.

She pointed with the rose and clung to his broad, strong shoulders as he carried her to the bedroom. There, with feverish motions, they peeled off shirts and jeans and underwear, leaving them in a hurried heap, laughing as they came together, bare body to bare body, to love. And how they did love. Hot. Passionate. Sweet. Hungry. Both of them sharing the same desires. And exchanging the same love.

He stroked and kissed all her secret places, rubbing his cheek to her belly and thighs. He told her of her beauty, then admired her with his caresses. She felt his soft, thick hair and the gentle brush of his lips over her body. That same wild stirring from within encompassed her, reminding her how much she loved him and longed for him with her every day, every night.

With both hands, she traveled the length of his aroused body, thrilling to his responses, teasing him with her touch. He was smooth and firm with muscles taut and ready. He still had an athlete's body in form and perfection, and she reveled in each kiss she applied to it.

When he came to her, urgent and insistent, his body seeking her, she drew him closer. He quivered with anticipation, then they were one, loving with intensity and splendor, building, growing, piercing, exploding together. Loving. Her wild little cries overwhelmed his low moans and created a glow of satisfaction over them both.

After a while, he stirred. "That was too fast. Next time, we'll take it slow."

"Will there be a next time?"

"Of course. I'm here to stay. To help you with the movie. To love you slowly and thoroughly." He brushed her hair back.

Brit looked at him, loving his darkness, his words. "What about your job? What about teaching and your project?"

"My colleague, Cole, is finishing the Grand Ruins project. And I have taken a sabbatical leave from NAU until the movie's done and we decide what we're going to do and where we're going to do it."

She propped up on one elbow and looked at him. "Am I hearing this right? You are going to be a consultant on this movie?"

"I want to make sure the Zunis aren't portrayed incorrectly. They are specific; and there are certain elements about them that should be accurate, don't you think? Anyway,

I want Bonnie's story right. Don't you agree?"

"You know how I feel about that. I can't believe I'm hearing you right."

"Why? It's logical."

"It's a part of my dream, hearing you say this."

"Being with you is my dream, Brit."

"But, here?"

"I don't know anything about the movie business, but I'm willing to learn."

Brit flopped back down beside him. "Well, we'll learn together. It's a crazy business. The original director for the movie has been fired and we have a new one."

"When did that happen?"

"Just this week. The new one seems to have a better angle and more understanding of the story. She's agreeable to hiring a Zuni consultant."

"She? A woman director?"

"Of course. Rudi says she's a terrific director making her mark in Hollywood's good ol' boys' club. She has already decided that we're going on location for some of the shots. Won't that be great?"

Jake caressed her tenderly. "Anything with you will be great."

"Jake . . ." She took his hand and kissed it on the back and then turned it and kissed the palm. "You've made me the happiest woman in the world."

"And I'm the happiest man." He placed his still-moist palm on one breast, rotating it against one alert nipple and kissed her again. And again . . .

After the taping of Yolanda's show, friends and family gathered for a late-night party hosted by the Romeros. Brit and Jake were invited as honored guests. Again, the feast was fit for kings. This time, a band played lively music and the crowd was exuberant and boisterous.

Rudi was ebullient and went around embracing everyone, even Jake. "Hey, buddy! Glad you could come. Isn't that woman fantastic?"

"Which one? Yolanda or Brit?"

"Hey, that's good! Both, of course!"

"The show was great," Brit added. "The public is going to love it!"

Yolanda joined them. "You two weren't offended, were you? I didn't mean to make fun of you—"

"Yes, you did," Brit said with a shrewd smile. "And we loved every minute of it."

"So, how's the movie going?" Rudi asked.

"Not bad. We go on location next week."

"And what about when it's over?"

There was a moment's pause when no one spoke. Then Jake said casually, "Oh, we'll probably move to Flagstaff, get married, settle down and have one-point-four kids."

314

Yolanda leaned forward. "Run that by me again. Did you say you two were going to get married?"

Brit beamed. "Yes, but I'll probably finish college before the kids. I've always liked history, but I think that, in light of what Jake does, anthropology would be best for me. That way, we can complement a project from both angles."

"Congratulations, bud," Rudi said shaking Jake's hand and hugging Brit.

Yolanda hugged them both. Then she walked on stage and interrupted the band in her unabashed manner. "Attention, everyone! I have an announcement. There's going to be a grand wedding to go with my *Grand Comedy,* and all this came out of one little accidental trip to the grandest place down in the earth. Break out the champagne for a celebration!"

Jake pulled Brit closer and kissed her. "Grand is right."

"As right as it'll ever get," she murmured. In her heart, she knew that Jake would be her everlasting love. He was truly a wonderful and rare breed.

KnifeWing and I married in the Zuni tradition. We loved each other deeply. He cared for Sara, as much as any father could, even though she was not his blood child. When our son was born, KnifeWing was very proud. All the days of his life, KnifeWing loved me genuinely and beautifully. He was truly a rare and wonderful man to love.